Universal Tele...

The ultimate journey...

...: a voyage to a wondrous new planet where humanity has a second chance. Where the sickness that has afflicted our children does not exist. Where the shattered dreams of humanity's youth are once again as fresh and clear as the new sky above...

The ultimate danger...

...a voyage to an unknown, primitive land. Where every misstep means life or death. Where the native fauna is as mysterious as it is diverse. And where someone— far below them—is watching...

The ultimate adventure...

EARTH 2

A NOVEL BY

MELISSA CRANDALL

Based on the teleplay written by:
Michael Duggan, Carol Flint, Mark Levin

WARNER BOOKS

A *Warner* Book

Earth 2, a novel by Melissa Crandall, based on the teleplay
written by Michael Duggan, Carol Flint, Mark Levin

First published in the USA in 1994 by Ace Books.
First published in Great Britain in 1996 by Warner Books.
Published by arrangement with MCA Publishing Rights,
a Division of MCA, Inc.

Copyright © 1994 by MCA Publishing Rights,
a Division of MCA, Inc.

The moral right of the author has been asserted.

A CIP catalogue record for this book
is available from the British Library.

ISBN 0 7515 1743 7

Printed in England by Clays Ltd, St Ives plc

UK companies, institutions and other organisations wishing
to make bulk purchases of this or any other book
published by Little, Brown should contact their local
bookshop or the special sales department at the address below.
Tel 0171 911 8000. Fax 0171 911 8100.

Warner Books
A Division of
Little, Brown and Company (UK)
Brettenham House
Lancaster Place
London WC2E 7EN

This book is for

my husband, Edward, who, with his quiet support,
makes mine the best of all possible worlds;

my editor, Ginjer Buchanan, who thought of me at
the right time;

Tony and Luke Perkins, and Anthony, Theresa, and
Sharri Everett—for whom I wish a better world;

Gil, in memoriam, the very best of cats;

and Amanda and Duncan, with sorrow and regret.
This in no way atones, but it's yours nonetheless.

I saw a new heaven and a new earth: for the first heaven and the first earth were passed away; and there was no more sea.
— REVELATION 21:1

I called the New World into existence to redress the balance of the Old.
— GEORGE CANNING
THE KING'S MESSAGE
DECEMBER 12, 1826

We must build a new world, a far better world—one in which the eternal dignity of man is respected.
— HARRY S. TRUMAN
APRIL 23, 1945

For there is a new world to be won.
— JOHN FITZGERALD KENNEDY
JULY 15, 1960

Prologue

· · · • • • • ●

Year 2184

Patience had never been one of Devon Adair's strong suits.

Its lack in her personal makeup had served to mold her into one of the most single-minded, career-driven women in the history of the Earth, not to mention one of the wealthiest and most famous. She was recognized everywhere she went as the foremost designer and developer of the various space stations that graced the solar system from Venus to Neptune, and there wasn't a closed door on or off Earth that her name wouldn't immediately open.

None of that meant a tinker's damn to her right now. In fact, if things went as she feared they might, her life was about to change forever. There would be no going back to any befores.

Wound tight as a spring, she paced the length of the waiting room in solitude or sat and shifted restlessly in one of the chairs until nervous energy drove her once again to her feet and the noticeable path she was wearing in the nap of the deep green carpeting. Every nerve felt charged and twitchy. She couldn't seem to hold still for more than a few seconds at a time.

Her eyes rarely strayed from the set of wide, white double doors at one end of the waiting room. Beyond that secure barrier lay a world of examining rooms, patients' quarters, and diagnostic laboratories which Devon Adair could not pierce, a sanctum into which she could not pry no matter how many times her name was invoked. Those doors were the only blockade she had ever encountered that would not yield to her name . . . her position in life . . . her *power*. All of her beseeching and pleading, all of her arguing and demanding, fell on Dr. Vasquez's purposely, infuriatingly deaf ears. Until further notice, she was not welcome beyond this point, and that was that. He didn't care who she was, or how powerful, and had, in fact, given her such a withering look when she tried that tactic, that she retreated from her demands like a spoiled child beaten at her own game. Who she was in the outside world mattered little within the sterile confines of this station hospital.

Other people came and went through that portal with a facility that grated on Devon's nerves. Some hurried by, their faces pinched with worry, irritation, or frustration. Others strolled past, seemingly bored and disinterested in anything but the closing hour of their shift. All moved with an unconscious air of carte blanche that set Devon's teeth on edge. Not one of them met her eyes for more than an instant's curious glance that darted away with a hint of guilt coloring its edges. The looks came not in response to her notoriety; she was certain of that. The looks were for another reason, a reason that screamed silently along the building's quiet corridors and shouted voicelessly within the recesses of Devon's own mind. There was only one reason for her, for *any* parent, to be in this particular hospital, and the knowledge blazed forth, making her a pariah. On this day, there were no other parents present to share her fears, and that suited her just fine. She wasn't in the habit of opening up and spilling her guts to strangers.

Devon's son Ulysses was somewhere beyond those closed doors, secreted away into an examining room to be poked and prodded while seemingly everyone but his mother could reach him. The sharp realization of an impotence she had never before experienced ate at her vitals with an intensity that made her want to scream in frustration. What was the point of amassing power if you couldn't use it when you needed it the most?

It was slowly dawning on young Devon Adair that all the power in the universe was worth diddly-squat in the face of reality.

Her fingers curled against her palms, making tight fists, and she pounded the tops of her thighs hard enough to hurt. "Not *my* child, dammit," she intoned under her breath. She repeated it over and over again, chanting it like a protective mantra or a beseeching prayer. Unfortunately, there was no protection under which she could hide from this threat, and there were those who said God had packed his bags and vacated the premises a long time ago, leaving the tenants to take care of things themselves. If this all turned out poorly, she'd be inclined to agree with that hypothesis and curse the absentee landlord for breach of contract.

Ulysses had started life as a hale and robust infant, the delight and ultimate achievement of his mother's twenty-five years. His birth brought a supremely rosy glow to Devon Adair's idyllic life. Unfortunately, the joy was short-lived. Within a matter of days, Uly began to sicken and fail. Unwilling to believe what her gut instincts told her

3

was true, Devon deluded herself into thinking that he was just suffering from the usual childhood maladies modern science hadn't yet pinned down and gotten around to curing. If she spent a few sleepless nights in worry over her child, she was no different from any other parent, right?

Except the illness lingered and worsened until Uly was a shadow of his former self, wasted and tiny in the confines of the immuno-suit she forced him to wear despite the tears and tantrums. Finally, Devon knew she couldn't afford to delude herself any longer. "Just to make sure," she brought Uly to Dr. Vasquez at the station hospital where he endeavored to treat children (it was always just children) afflicted with this strange new disease which, so far, had eluded their research and become colloquially known as The Syndrome.

Not that Uly had it, of course. He was just a little sick, that's all.

"Ms. Adair."

The quiet summons came from a voice modulated by countless exhausting hours inside these walls. It caught Devon unaware and startled her, for she hadn't heard a door open or the sound of approaching footsteps. Her head jerked up from her silent ruminations as her eyes flashed open and fastened on Dr. Vasquez standing just a few feet away. Her cheeks burned with regret that a stranger had momentarily caught her with every defensive barrier down. That didn't happen very often, and she hated when it did. The only ones allowed behind her public facade were her closest friends, and there was only one of them.

If the older man noticed her discomfort and embarrassment, he didn't react to it. He merely smiled with the strained and practiced ease of one who is forced by circumstances to smile when least inclined to do so. Devon noticed that the false emotion never reached his eyes, and those eyes were what she now watched so intently from her

4

seat. Let him bestow smiles upon those who fell for their balm. Despite her years, she felt herself to be an old hand with smiles. She knew about the many ways in which they could be used. Eyes were the key. Eyes told the truth. He wasn't fooling her for an instant.

She wished for a moment that she wasn't so damned smart. Right now, it might be kind of nice to be a little bit stupid.

"Beating yourself isn't going to change things, Ms. Adair," he said quietly, and paused to rub his eyes. The slow motion spoke of his exhaustion more eloquently than any words might have.

Devon shot to her feet with her hands to her face, covering her mouth as horror bloomed deep in her guts like a bloody rose. "Oh, please, no—"

"Don't lose control!" Dr. Vasquez snapped in a tone that tolerated no argument, killing the words in her throat and leaving her gasping on empty air. His brow furrowed in either anger or strain, but Devon couldn't tell which it was. "I'm sorry, Ms. Adair, but I don't have the time or energy to deal out platitudes right now. I can send for a therapist if you think you need to talk to someone right away; otherwise, we don't have the luxury." He waited, watching her, and Devon found herself shaking her head without any clear idea why. He nodded and held out an arm in open invitation. "Come with me."

Come with me. That was it. Three words as simple as abracadabra, and *now* she could go beyond the imposing barricade. If she was not an altogether welcome visitor, she was at least tolerated because of having been invited by Vasquez, who played some sort of erstwhile Moses as he parted the doors with the open palms of his hands and led her into the corridor beyond. The doors swung closed, snicking quietly, a soft sound that was explosion-loud,

5

fateful and dark inside Devon's mind. A part of her instantly regretted wanting any part of this hidden world.

"This is Admissions."

Vasquez's voice startled her again, making her realize just how far off stride she really was. She focused on him with effort, catching the tail end of an arm wave that took in the work station and offices to her left. Behind a chest-high counter done in eye-soothing colors, employees worked with an intensity evocative of a hive complex or an ant's nest (neither of which Devon had ever seen in reality). Not a single person smiled as they labored, though one or two glanced up and bestowed upon Dr. Vasquez a brief head nod or some sort of face-stretching rictus that might have been intended as a smile as they passed by.

"On our right is Counseling." The doctor gestured briefly at a closed door inset with a window. In the reception area beyond, a person in a hospital uniform (a therapist?) sat beside a man whose back was bowed, his face in his hands as he rocked back and forth in silent anguish, while a woman, seated on his other side, stared angrily at the wall.

"Physical Therapy is down this hallway," Vasquez continued in the same neutral tone and pointed down a corridor that crossed theirs. "After a certain point in Syndrome degeneration, the children can't do much for themselves. We don't want their muscles to completely atrophy, so manual and machine manipulation are introduced to hinder the process. The exercise helps them retain a small amount of muscle control and elasticity, and appears to improve their mental outlook as well.

"The laboratories and our medical library take up this next corridor and the two running parallel to this one we're presently in," he went on. His voice never deviated from its trained litany, and Devon was suddenly reminded of the trip to Earth her parents took her on when she was seven years old. ("On your left, ladies and gentlemen, is the Statue of Liberty," the guide had enthused. "Sadly, due to acid rain, only the feet and the hem of the gown remain.")

"The bulk of our research is done in this complex," Vasquez continued. "And our findings are compiled for analytic integration with the stations-wide medical computer system."

No mention of Uly. Nothing was being said about his condition beyond the inference she'd assumed at the doctor's first words. Devon didn't know if this was a good sign or a bad one, and she was suddenly, and ashamedly, too frightened to ask Vasquez directly. She would, of course, but not yet. She wasn't quite ready to hear that her entire world was about to fall apart.

"Now, if you'll come this way, Ms. Adair, we'll—"

"May I see the children?" she interrupted, not even knowing what she was going to ask until the words were already out.

Ahead of her, Vasquez stopped and turned around. His eyes narrowed quizzically, and he studied her face for what felt like a long time before replying. "Why?" he finally asked quietly. In that one word was suddenly encompassed all the love, despair, and protection he felt toward these dying children under his useless, fighting care.

She hadn't a clue. She didn't want her reason to sound trite, or meaningless, or freakish. She knew that if it did, Vasquez would march her through the hospital with nary a glimpse of the patients. Why *did* she want to see the children?

"I don't know," she answered honestly. "I'm curious. I just want—" She shook her head, angry at her inability to express herself, to find the correct words that would sound truthful in her own ears, let alone his. Her hands came together, the fingers twining around one another and tight-

7

ening. "No, it's more than that. I just want to *know*," she said in a small voice and shrugged, hating the way she suddenly felt like a small child caught by her Teacher in the midst of doing something wrong. "I *have* to know . . . because of Uly."

Some undefined emotion flicked through Vasquez's eyes, and he nodded. "Thank you for being honest, Ms. Adair. Too many people make that request because they want a peep show, to get a glimpse of the freaks and go away secure in the knowledge of how lucky they and their children are to be untouched by The Syndrome. Concern for the children afflicted with it is the farthest thing from their minds." He smiled suddenly, a slight uplifting of his lips that did wonderful things to his face. "I like your attitude, Ms. Adair. I'd be glad to introduce you to the kids. This way, please." He turned and led her along a spiderweb of interconnected corridors.

She found that she believed him when he said he was glad to introduce her to his patients, and it wasn't just because she'd given him the "right" answer to his question. Pride had joined the pain he carried like a heavy weight across his shoulders, and Devon found herself intrigued by the realization. "You genuinely like these kids, don't you, Dr. Vasquez? I mean, beyond caring for them as their physician. You like them as people, too."

"Ms. Adair, I genuinely *love* my patients and am proud to say so. Their grace and dignity in the face of insurmountable odds constantly astounds me. They've taught me everything I'll ever need to know about life and death. I stand in awe of their wisdom and humbled by their bravery." He stopped before one door and lay a hand against it as he turned toward her. "The children are not in private rooms, but stay together in a ward due to their immense need for one another's company."

"I'm not sure I understand . . ."

"You will," he assured her with quiet confidence and pushed open the door. "Please come in and meet my friends."

The room was not what Devon had anticipated. She had expected a sterile atmosphere and ranks of silent beds occupied by still forms. Instead, there was color, color pervading, *invading*, a rainbow array that assaulted her eyes and was as obtrusive as a noisy toddler in a library.

The display chafed Devon's raw nerves. The decor was a blatant attempt at cheerfulness in a place where it could not possibly live long. It left a bad taste in her mouth.

There were twelve, maybe fifteen, beds in the room, spaced in uneven rows. In each lay a gaunt and sickly child, a few of them infants like Uly and the rest somewhat older, cocooned in the sterile immuno-suits they were forced to wear to prolong their short lives, until death claimed them.

Devon's stomach rolled over at the thought. For a moment, she thought she might be embarrassingly sick right here in front of these kids, but the moment passed and she kept her control. She'd read the infrequent news accounts and seen the vids and *thought* she knew everything there was to know about The Syndrome. But reading about it and comprehending the reality of it, particularly in sudden regard to her own family, were two vastly different things.

She had expected it to be quiet in here, filled with nothing but the whisper of respirators forcing air into laboring lungs and the sound of strained breathing as the children fought for each precious drop of oxygen. That wasn't the case. While the sounds of the respirators and the children's breathing were evident as background noises, overlaying it all was the sound of their voices, pitched low due to weakness and lack of breath, but voices nonetheless— talking, laughing, singing, and reaching out to one another

9

with the golden buoyancy of a determination to live as much life as was offered them, and then to demand more. Suddenly she fully understood what the doctor meant by their need for one another's company.

"Hi, Dr. Vasquez." A weak but happy-sounding voice hailed the doctor. A dark-haired girl of seven or so with huge brown eyes in a square-jawed, hollow-cheeked face smiled sweetly at them and struggled with the bed controls that would help her sit up.

A full, genuine smile graced the doctor's features as he crossed the room to greet the child. "Hi, Leslie. Can I help you with that?"

"Are you . . . joking?" Her voice rasped through her respirator. She gasped between words, fighting to get enough breath into her lungs to form the next one. It took an extreme effort, but she was obviously as bound and determined to carry on the conversation as she was to do things on her own. "I'll get out . . . and kick the silly thing if . . . it doesn't work . . . soon." That option didn't seem likely, given her condition, but she kept poking at a series of buttons inset into the armrest, until the bed suddenly responded with a busy whir and the upper end lifted her into a comfortable sitting position. "There! I told you . . . I could . . . do it!"

"I never doubted you for a second, Les," he responded honestly. "You've got more determination in your little finger than most people have in their whole bodies, you know that? How are you feeling today?" While he bantered, Vasquez gave her a going-over with his eyes that would have made an intern shuffle with unease, but it didn't seem to affect her in the least.

"Like usual. Coughing . . . and stuff." She shrugged, obviously unwilling to talk about it in front of a stranger. She offered him her hand as he sat down on the edge of the bed, turning it so he couldn't see the vital signs readout on the suit's wrist monitor. "Are you going . . . to take . . . my pulse the . . . old-fashioned . . . way again? That was really . . . neat!"

"You liked that, huh? Then whatever the lady wants." His fingers closed gently around her wrist, and he glanced at his watch.

Devon had never seen this done before. She stepped closer, to see better, and instantly fell victim to Leslie's steady scrutiny. The child's stare was, without a doubt, the most thorough, and the most disconcerting, eyeballing she'd ever received.

"Are you Dr. Vasquez's . . . girlfriend?" Leslie asked bluntly, her eyes darting between them in a way that spoke volumes.

The doctor sputtered with fake indignity. "Hey! I thought *you* were my girlfriend!"

She laughed, her pale cheeks coloring a faint pink at the suggestion. "You're too *old* . . . Dr. Vasquez."

He winced. "Ouch. That's a cut to the quick. Thanks a bundle, kiddo. See if I take you to the prom."

Devon smiled at the girl and held out her hand. "I'm Devon Adair."

If she expected the response she was used to getting when her name was mentioned, she was sadly disappointed. Leslie glanced mildly from her face to the outstretched hand, but didn't move to shake it. "Hi," she returned lightly, almost dismissively. Her gaze alighted briefly on Devon's face again and then returned to Vasquez. "Have you . . . heard . . . anything from my . . . parents?" she asked with a seriousness directly at odds with her former brightness. The skin around her eyes and at the corners of her mouth had gone pinched and tight-looking.

Bitterness fueled the emotion behind Vasquez's eyes. "Not yet, kiddo. Maybe in a day or so."

"Yeah. Maybe in a day or so," she agreed listlessly. The light his visit had brought into her eyes vanished completely. She settled more deeply into her pillows and pushed a button to lower the bed again. "I think . . . I'll get some . . . rest and—"

A tone sounded at the far end of the room, cutting her off in mid-sentence. Immediately all conversation ceased, as several nurses and doctors rushed in from different doorways, racing the length of the room almost silently on their soft-soled shoes.

Leslie raised a sardonic eyebrow. "Looks . . . like Evan . . . finally made . . . it," she whispered. "Lucky guy." For a moment, she watched the press of bodies around a bed at the far end of the room, then she rolled over and closed her eyes, feigning sleep.

Devon shook her head, confused. "I don't understand. What's going—"

Vasquez's slicing hand motion gestured her to silence. One hand under her elbow, he steered her out of the room and back into the corridor. Only when the door had swung closed behind them did he release her. She was startled to see how faded and gray he looked all of a sudden, and that tears stood out in his eyes. "Dr. Vasquez!" she exclaimed. "Are you—"

"One of the children in there just died, Ms. Adair," he said bluntly, wiping unashamedly at his eyes. "His name was Evan Cortero. He turned eight just last week. He always said that if the animals ever came back, he wanted to be a butterfly."

The enormity of it, and the profound sadness of the boy's wish, took a long and terrible moment to sink in. On the heels of it came horror at Leslie's mild acceptance of Evan's death and the obvious envy in her voice. Devon didn't know what to say. "I'm sorry. I didn't realize—"

Anger darkened Vasquez's eyes, so stark and harsh with pain that she took an involuntary step backward, certain for a moment that he meant to strike her. "No one realizes, Ms. Adair," he snarled angrily. "That's half the problem. No one but the kids and their parents and my staff. If I had my way, the world would have to eat, think, and sleep these kids like *I* do."

"I've seen the vids, but I didn't—"

"The vids aren't reality, Ms. Adair. Reality is in *there*." He stabbed a finger back at the ward room. "*That's* reality. If I had the power, there wouldn't be a moment when the universe could forget The Syndrome exists. I'd have it plastered on walkway billboards and vidded in place of those stupid commercials. I'd wipe people's noses with it and shove it down their throats until they couldn't eat. I'd ram it in their faces until they couldn't go to sleep at night without seeing it printed on the insides of their eyelids like a never-ending movie. I'd make it impossible to forget about, impossible to lay aside and ignore the possible causes and the all-too-likely ramifications. Maybe then it would get some attention at the level it needs to!"

The blaze in his eyes suddenly dampened, and he cleared his throat, embarrassed at being caught soapboxing for his pet project. Except it obviously went deeper than that. He was no mere advocate, jumping on a new fad or party line as the whim moved him. He believed in what he'd just said, and his frustrations were clearly profound. "Excuse me. I didn't mean to preach."

She nodded, sincerely liking him for the first time since she'd met with him regarding Uly's condition. "I'm glad you did. Maybe more people need to. It's gratifying to know you're serious about this."

13

"It's something to be serious about, Ms. Adair. It directly impacts on the continued existence of the human race."

There was no arguing with that tone, not that Devon had any desire to. "It sounds as though you have some interesting theories," she said speculatively, her curiosity aroused despite the chill his words caused.

He waved a hand. "Another time, perhaps." He turned, leading her away from the ward and back to the corridor they had been in before.

"If it's not prying, Dr. Vasquez," Devon said as they walked, "why did Leslie ask about her parents?"

He didn't look at her when he replied. "It *is* prying, but I think you may as well know about that side of things, too. Leslie's parents brought her to me six years ago, admitted her to the hospital under my care, and then dropped out of sight."

She frowned in confusion. "What happened to them?"

He favored her with a look usually reserved for congenital idiots. "Who knows? They just vanished and they've done a good job of covering their tracks." When she just blinked at him, he sighed. "It's called abandonment, Ms. Adair."

She stopped, her heart suddenly pounding in her chest. All of her mother love, awakened in her with Uly's birth, warred with the concept, unable to comprehend how a parent, any parent, could do such a thing, particularly to such an obviously bright, loving, and intelligent child as Leslie.

What about your own folks, Devon? She caught herself wondering. *They kept you, but they ignored you. Abandonment has a lot of different faces.* Maybe that was so, but at least she'd had Yale. To her mind, the Teacher was worth any number of parents.

14

She licked her lips, fear turning her stomach to ice, and decided that it was time to face the future with open eyes. "Dr. Vasquez, does my son have The Syndrome?" There. It was finally out, said and done.

His face and eyes never changed expression. "Yes, Ms. Adair. He does."

Devon's mind reeled, and she caught herself with one hand against the wall. Breath jammed in her throat and tears stung deep inside her eyes. *There you have it, Devon. It's out in the open for all the world to see. There's no turning back now.* Even so, she closed her eyes against the sight. From somewhere deep inside came a wail of mortal pain which never escaped her lips. Her heart still pumped, her organs still functioned, but something in her had just died, as quietly as Evan Cortero passing from this life. Vertigo threatened, assailing her mind with a whirling maelstrom of emotion. Eyes still closed, she clamped down on it hard, damned if it would control her, and doubly damned if she would faint like some two-penny heroine in one of the ancient novels.

"Ms. Adair? Devon?" It was the first time Dr. Vasquez had called her by her given name, and she thought that was about right. They should be on a first-name basis now. She wondered idly what his was, but it didn't really matter at the moment. It seemed they were going to have plenty of opportunity to get to know each other better.

She opened her eyes and shook her head at his silent offer of a steadying hand. "May I see my son now?" she whispered.

"Are you sure you don't want—"

"I'd like to see my son, please." *Hang on, hang on, hang on, hangonhangonhangon . . .*

He nodded, understanding. "Of course."

It wasn't much farther down the hall to the examining

room where Uly waited. Decked out in his immuno-suit, he lay on his back in the depressed cup of a soft-cushioned table, with his eyes vacantly tracking the motion of some program tuned on the vid to keep his infant mind amused. The sound of the door opening drew his attention away from the play of color overhead, and he gifted his mother with the wide, joyous, toothless smile of a typical baby.

A typical baby with The Syndrome, that is. Gone were the hoped-for days when he would shout his exuberance to the stars as he ran. "Hi, sweetheart," she said, hating how watery her voice sounded. She tickled his tummy and bent to give him a hug. "How's my big boy? Were you good for Dr. Vasquez?"

Uly gape-grinned at her and drooled down his chin. His fingers fluttered, practicing hi-bye, and grabbed for his toes. There was a faint bubbling sound to his breathing that Devon tried as hard as she could to ignore, losing herself instead in the wide expanse of her child's eyes.

"Hi, Champ." Vasquez offered his finger to one of Uly's questing hands and smiled slightly when the baby's fingers curled around it. "Sorry we took so long. I was showing your mom around the hospital and lost track of time. Can you forgive me?" He shook the finger and smiled broadly at Uly's gabbled reply.

Watching them together, it suddenly occurred to Devon with gut-freezing clarity exactly why Vasquez had given her the hospital tour. Shoving him abruptly aside, she bent and swiftly gathered Uly into her arms, glaring over his head at the very surprised physician. "You're not keeping him here," she declared stoutly.

Vasquez's expression melted. "You're not serious."

"I'm very serious." She straightened and started toward the door.

He moved to intercept her. "Ms. Adair, you can't possibly care for Uly at home. Perhaps initially, yes, but what about as the disease progresses? He'll need round the clock attendance and there aren't enough hours in the day—"

"Then I'll find the hours, I'll *make* the hours! But no one is taking my child away from me, do you understand that? No one! My child is not going to d—" She cut herself off, unwilling to voice the word, afraid of tempting fate. "Good-bye, Dr. Vasquez."

"Ms. Adair, please—"

The closing door cut him off in mid-sentence. To his credit, he didn't try to follow her out. Devon didn't know what she would have done if he had. Faint? Fight? Get hysterical? Relinquish Uly? She looked down at the child in her arms as she paced hurriedly through the hospital and down a level to the exit, and her arms tightened around him. *Never.*

"Uly?" she asked, trying hard to sound cheerful when everything in her wanted to break apart at the seams. "Honey? How'd you like to go to the zoo, pal? We could see the Tyrannosaurus Rex and the beagle." It wasn't a live zoo, of course. Both of those animals had long been dead, but the virtual reality figures were very, very lifelike, done in a manner perfected a long time ago in Earth's now-defunct amusement parks.

He couldn't really reply, of course. He murmured slightly with a baby's nonsense noises that would one day be words, then nestled his head into the hollow between her arm and breast and fell asleep even as she watched.

The ease with which he slipped away from her into sleep chilled Devon to the bone. If he could leave her this easily just by closing his eyes, what was to prevent him from leaving her forever?

17

She went to the zoo anyway, carrying her sleeping child from display to display, looking at everything but too busy thinking—thinking long and deep and hard—to really notice much. She watched the T. Rex and the beagle, the horses and the whales, the lemmings and the aardvarks, until it suddenly occurred to her that she stood in a theater of death. Not a single one of these species survived today in living form anywhere on Earth or off it. They were gone forever, as gone as real grass, or snowfall, or Evan Cortero, or Leslie's parents, or—

"Quoth the Raven, 'Nevermore,'" Devon murmured, and fled.

She let others take her place aboard taxis, trundles, or tube jets. Still carrying her child, who was much lighter than he had any right to be at his age, she strode like a woman possessed through the afternoon shoppers, going-home crowds, early diners, and change-of-shifters, pacing off the hours in the rapid cadence of her feet. If anyone noticed her, it was only to get out of the way of a woman with a face of such sheer determination that it built a nearly tangible wall around her, plowing a way clear through the throng. A few of the people cast pitying looks at Uly in his immuno-suit, and she all but snarled at them. Who were they to gawk and stare? Better that they go home and hug their children and thank their lucky stars their offspring were whole and healthy. Only when she had completely made up her mind did she turn her steps toward home.

The Adair quarters were as palatial as any to be found aboard the space station. Money and standing and status and clout had a way of achieving so many niceties. She despised them now. What good were they to her when her child lay dying in her arms?

She shifted Uly higher onto her shoulder to free a hand

only long enough to punch in her code. The door opened before she could reach for the fingerpad, revealing Yale, as tall and imposing as the very first time she'd ever seen the Teacher. She didn't know if he'd been watching for her, or sensed her approach, or been worried because of the lateness of the hour. There was something of all three in the expression on his face, and much more besides.

"Devon!" the old cyborg admonished. "I've been worried sick! Do you have any idea how late it is? Where have you—" He saw the look on her face then, made stark by the bright lights of the room behind him, and instantly reached out to take Uly onto his stronger, mechanical arm. Only now, only to Yale, could she relinquish her child. "Don't say a word. I'll put him to bed. Dinner's still warm. I'll be right back." He strode quickly out of the room and down the hall to Uly's toy-festooned bedroom.

He'd prepared one of her favorite meals, but never in her life had Devon felt less inclined to eat it. She poked at the food for a few minutes in a useless attempt, then pushed it aside and moved across the room to an ornate cabinet. She did not often indulge in drinking alcohol, as the synthetic stuff made her sinuses ache, but one of the privileges she'd incurred through her meteoric career was the availability of the real thing. Right now, she felt as though she wanted it, *needed* it, and maybe even a lot of it. She poured herself a tumbler of whiskey and sat back down at the dining room table.

Yale found her there a few minutes later. He paused momentarily in the doorway, clearly sizing up the situation, then approached and took the chair opposite hers, lowering himself into it slowly and sitting back with a sigh. "You know, someone once said that there's no such thing as smooth whiskey," he remarked conversationally. "Only rough whiskey and rougher whiskey."

Devon nodded, only half-listening, and suddenly began to cry. Despair cut her like a knife in the vitals, but she did not wail or scream her fears and terror as she had thought she might. Perhaps it was due to Uly being just down the hall and her not wanting to frighten him. Whatever the reason, the tears rolled silently down her face in a steady stream, catching in her throat and chest and nearly choking her. She began to shake so hard she had to put down her glass for fear of breaking it against the table's edge. The next thing she knew, she was somehow in Yale's lap, as if she were still a tiny child and he her brand new Teacher (and the first adult who ever really paid her any attention).

He held her until she quieted, stroking her hair the entire time as she soaked the front of his shirt with her tears. Head against his chest, she listened to the comforting thump of his oft-repaired heart. "Uly has The Syndrome, Yale," she said quietly. "They wanted to keep him."

"Presumably over your dead body?" he asked dryly. He rubbed his cheek against her hair. "I can hear you thinking, Devon Adair. I smell the insulation burning. What is it you're up to now?"

She raised her head to look at him and wiped the tears from her face with the backs of her hands. "I've gone through it all today, Yale. I've gone through denial and I've gone through anger, but I'll be damned if I'm going to accept a verdict of death when it comes to my son."

"And so?" he inquired easily, not challenging, not testing, but merely asking.

She took a deep, shuddering breath, knowing at once and without question that he would be with her no matter what she decided, and finding all the confidence she needed in the simple knowledge of his faith and support. "And so I've been giving the whole matter a lot of thought since I left that hospital." Her eyes grew steely and she felt something very

20

much like resolution harden down deep in her guts. "I don't care if it costs me everything I have, Yale, or if I have to travel to the ends of the universe to do it, but I'm going to find a way to save my son."

Chapter 1

. . . . . ● ● ●

Eight Years Later

The past played across Devon's brain in a brief, vivid reminder. In the course of her association with Dr. Vasquez (for, of course, she'd returned to him for help with Uly), she'd thought about his theory on The Syndrome's origins several times: how the escape of the majority of the Earth's population to the space stations six generations ago, leaving them unencumbered by the hardship of terrestrial existence, might be proving to be more of a detriment than a boon.

As a designer of those stations, she'd naturally fought the idea at first, but she couldn't deny the proof of her own eyes. Life aboard the stations was sterile, ordered, efficient, and pleasant enough for people who dreamed of nothing else. Until the coming of The Syndrome, that is, and its catastrophic effects on the stations' children.

23

Few were affected in the beginning, but a marked increase had been clearly charted in the ensuing years, and it looked to only get worse as time went on. Dr. Vasquez postulated that, rather than being caused by the presence of a virus as so many physicians seemed to think, The Syndrome was caused by an *absence*—an absence of all that Nature once provided, before the mining and logging communities pillaged every resource. There was an utter lack of such things as naturally fresh air and water aboard the stations. What Vasquez felt these children needed, what he felt *all* of humanity needed, particularly if there were to be future generations, was *Earth* itself. But Earth was dead, lost to them in the pursuit of riches other than those of the soul.

The theory was radical, wildly inconclusive, based mostly on guesswork and hunches, with a huge dollop of gut instinct thrown in, but the more Devon had talked with the doctor, and the more she read his research, the more she believed that what he said was true. Until one day, she had thrown her cards in with his in a bid to find another Earth for her son and all of the other afflicted children. And the result was this.

She broke out of her reverie and paused in the doorway of the cramped, darkened stateroom aboard the Eden Project Advance ship. Yale and Ulysses were in the middle of what looked like a geography lesson. If either of them noticed her arrival, they gave no indication. A floating, glowing holographic globe spun between them, projected into the air from the end of the Teacher's mechanical hand, and painted their faces—Yale's wizened by age and knowledge, and Uly's pale and pinched by disease—with a wash of gentle light.

The slowly turning white, green, and blue orb looked

suspiciously like Earth at first glance. Only upon closer examination did one realize that the enormous land masses were shaped differently from those of Earth, and were separated from one another by vast tracts of blue-green ocean that looked nothing like the grayish sludge of Earth's seas.

The globe held Devon's eyes with an intensity bordering on fascination. Pride swelled her heart, making her chest ache and tears threaten. Eight years ago, this had all been just a dream, a wild scheme concocted by the equally wild brain of a woman determined not to watch her son die a slow death by degrees and a doctor who felt the same way. For eight years there were only outlandish plans and outrageous hopes as gossamer as a spider's web.

But a spider's web is surprisingly strong, and now an image of the new reality, the reality crafted largely by the force of Devon's dreams and the will to get what she wanted, floated before her eyes not two feet away. That planet—G889 on the navigational charts—was going to be their new home and, God willing, the cure The Syndrome children and their families had been praying for.

Yale paused in his narration and studied the child before him. Sheathed in the immuno-suit he was forced to wear continually like a second skin, Uly sat with his head canted over onto one hand. His eyes were on the hovering globe, the very picture of attentiveness, but they were unfocused and his mind was obviously elsewhere.

Yale cleared his throat and made his deep voice even deeper in, Devon supposed, an attempt at intimidation. She wished the Teacher lots of luck. He was twined around Uly's pinky just about as securely as she was . . . and the boy knew it. "Ulysses—are you listening to me?"

Uly jerked slightly, blinking the world back into focus,

but seemingly unperturbed by the faint note of disapproval in his tutor's voice. If he felt any guilt for having zoned out during the lecture, he didn't show it. "Hey, Yale?" he asked, the sound of his respirator overlaying the harsh drag of his breathing. "D'you think when we get to the planet I'll be able to run? You know, like, just run right out of the ship?"

Yale sighed, and Devon's heart went out to the kindly cyborg. He didn't want to dash Uly's enthusiasm outright, nor did he want the child building too intricate a dream until they learned the reality of this world they were betting so much upon. "No," he said cautiously. "Not right out of the ship. But . . . in time, I'm sure. Now . . . may we please continue your geography?"

Uly's mouth curled with frustration, and he slumped farther down in his chair with a sigh, clearly bored out of his mind. It was hard for a child with such an active imagination to be physically confined within the strict parameters of an immuno-suit. His brain and heart longed to run and jump like any other eight-year-old, but his traitor body had other ideas.

"To continue, we believe New Pacifica to be bordered on the west by the Sea of Antius." Yale traced the area with his free hand, his remaining human hand. "And it's on this coastline that we'll be landing."

Uly shifted restlessly and caught sight of his mother standing in the doorway. His eyes brightened with an animation that his frail, gaunt, and sickly body could not share. "Are there going to be beasts on the planet, Mom?" he asked eagerly.

Devon's eyes met Yale's over the top of the child's head in a communion of shared tolerance and slightly sad amusement, each of them biting back a smile the boy might

26

take offense at, thinking they poked fun when that wasn't really the case at all. As Uly grew and his physical condition continued to deteriorate, his mental capabilities broadened exponentially, ostensibly in compensation for his weakened body. His imagination was particularly vivid. By now, both adults were used to the child's fanciful stories, but sometimes it took other people a little while to realize the boy was just giving his brain a good workout and meant no harm by anything he said. Occasionally, it was even hard for his mother to remember.

Devon stepped the rest of the way into the stateroom, and the door slid shut behind her, cutting off a brief glimpse of the corridor beyond. Three steps was all it took for her to cross their cramped quarters, and then she bent down to brush back her son's hair and kiss his forehead in greeting. "What kind of beasts, Uly?" she asked, turning the collar monitor on his suit toward the light of the globe so she could better make out the digital reading. She was pleased to see everything seemed normal, or what passed for normal in a child with progressive Syndrome. Turning the monitor back to its original position, she glanced at Yale and nodded, motioning for him to pick up the boy while she turned away to pull back the covers on his bed.

Uly shrugged, having suffered his mother's attentive ministrations with good grace, and raised a hand to comb the hair back down over his eyes. "I dunno. Big," he determined with a decisive nod, clasping his arms around Yale's neck as the Teacher stooped to lift him from the chair, then turned and, in two strides, deposited him on the bottommost of three bunks set against one wall. "Bigger than this whole ship even!" His eyes glowed with the force of this imagined creature, and a faint, rosy hue touched both pale cheeks with illusory color which hinted at health that just was not there. "With skin like . . . like . . . y'know that elephant from my virtual reality? Yeah, but with *teeth* . . . !"

He coughed, a single expulsion that momentarily broke off his recitation. In anyone else, in anyone not afflicted with The Syndrome, it would hardly have been noticed or remarked upon. But for Devon and Yale, the not-so-simple cough was a harbinger of fear and an advance man for Death. They both froze, their eyes locked on the boy as he struggled for breath.

"And tusks!" Uly continued enthusiastically, apparently completely unaware of the inner turmoil currently besetting his mother and his instructor. "Tusks that shoot out from his face like, like tentacles! And, and . . ." More coughing patterned his speech like drops of rain and bent him double, with his face, now slightly bluish, nearly against his drawn-up knees. Stricken with panic, Devon landed beside him on the bed. She reached for a water tube snugged into a wall socket by the head of the bed and offered him a drink while Yale checked the oxygen flow on the suit and made a minor adjustment to the mechanism.

Uly drank obediently (he had little choice with his mother practically shoving the tube down his throat), coughing around the plastic mouthpiece and patently determined to finish the description of his creature. "And . . . and on the end of each tentacle there'll be a *hand* with *nine* fingers!" Whether it was having finally gotten it all out, or the drink of water, or the changed oxygen flow, or just the passing of this most recent coughing jag, the spasms abated as suddenly as they had begun. Uly leaned back against his pillows with a grin of utter triumph. "Do you think there'll be any monsters like that on the new planet, Mom?" he asked, his voice and his eyes full of wistful hope.

Shaken as she was by every single one of these unnerving episodes, worried as she was that each one would be the last in all the wrong ways, Devon took a deep breath and released it slowly, silently willing her heart to ease its frenetic beat against her rib cage. Every time Uly coughed, every time he so much as cleared his throat, her heart kicked into fearful overdrive and the image of her son lying dead in his bed floated before her eyes with a frightening clarity.

She ran a hand back through her hair, careful not to foul the delicate headset she wore to keep her in touch with all the administrative goings-on aboard the ship, and returned the water tube to its holder before answering her son's question. "I certainly hope not," she said with more calm than she actually felt. She pulled up the covers, tucked them under his chin, and gave his chest a gentle pat. "Now, rest. Big day tomorrow."

Reminder of what the next day would bring apparently polished away the child's worries over not having a monster to slay anytime in the immediate future. "Can I sit by the pilot when we launch?" he asked eagerly.

The thought of hotshot space ace Alonzo Solace being forced to tolerate her inquisitive child's never-ending questions while trying to launch the ship made Devon smile. "Sure," she replied lightly, thanking God for small favors. At least Uly hadn't asked to pilot the ship himself . . . yet. Then she added as a grave afterthought, "*If* you're quiet."

Yale snorted through his nose. "Alonzo has nothing to worry about, then, does he?"

Uly's eyes popped wide. "Hey! That's not true! I can be qui—"

Devon's headset beeped loudly enough for all to hear. She waved a hand, shushing them to silence. "Now's your chance to prove it," Yale whispered, teasing the boy, who stuck his tongue out in reply.

Devon frowned at the joking disrespect more out of habit than anything else and hinged the microphone into its On position. Two optic feeders curved around in front of her eyes. She blinked twice to adjust her sight to their closeness, then focused on the face of Commander Broderick O'Neill as it appeared bifocal-style in her field of vision.

The big, blustery man's broad, florid features and bulking shoulders always reminded her of the grizzly bears in one of Uly's virtual reality programs. Except this grizzly was a former military man (with all that implied) and in possession of more savvy about the red-taped corridors of bureaucracy than almost anyone else she knew. She was grateful he'd found their project worthwhile enough to join. God knows he'd proven his worth a dozen times over in the years since she first approached him with this desperate, harebrained scheme. If it weren't for his help and support, she wondered if they would have ever made it this far.

She greeted him with a brisk nod. "Good evening, Commander. What can I do for you?"

No amenities were forthcoming, which was nothing new with O'Neill. "Big fire, Dev. Cockpit."

He wasn't talking about a real conflagration, with flames. She knew that at once and was intrigued, but still his timing wasn't the greatest. "Please, Commander, I'm putting my son to bed."

He shook his head. "Can't wait. I need you now." Without further ado, his image vanished, his blatant assumption being that she would bring herself front and center immediately and on the double, as well trained as one of his recruits.

Devon chewed on the inside of her bottom lip and contemplated the empty space where his visage had been. The assumption rankled her, as well it might given the vein

30

of independence running deeply through her bones. For a moment, she considered ignoring the order, but scotched that idea almost immediately. She had no desire to alienate the Commander by taking offense where none was meant. Short and to the point just happened to be O'Neill's way, and she wasn't about to quibble over semantics. He *was* the commanding officer on this journey and due all the respect that post implied. She'd learned from experience to trust his judgment, just as he had learned the depth of her feelings for her ailing son. O'Neill wouldn't be calling for her if her presence wasn't absolutely necessary.

Sighing, she hinged back the microphone. The optic feeders swung back into position, leaving her pinned under Uly and Yale's curious stares. Her shoulders lifted in a shrug. "Who knows?" She smiled apologetically at her son and reached out to ruffle his hair. "Sorry about this, Champ. I've gotta go."

"What's wrong, Mom?" Worry lines creased Uly's forehead. He held the top edge of his sheet so tightly that his knuckles were white. "Are we going to have to stay here?"

"There's a problem. I'll go check it out. I'm sure it's nothing for you to worry about." She massaged his fingers, loosening their grip, and tucked them back under the sheet. "We're making that launch window tomorrow on schedule. I promise. Nothing's going to keep us from our new home." She poked him gently in the chest with one forefinger. "Now get some sleep."

"Okay." He inched down deeper into the bed and blinked tiredly at her, already more than half-gone, any residual energy leaving him in one swift "whoosh" she could almost hear. "Mom?"

"Sleep," she ordered.

"I will. But, Mom—"

31

"*Now*." Sparing a gentle squeeze on the shoulder and a silently mouthed *Thank you* for Yale, she let herself out of the stateroom and hurried away through the throng clogging the corridor at even this late hour. Unlike most crowds, this group was relatively quiet, going about their business in a briskly controlled and efficient manner, every mind set on the loose ends that needed tying before the departure time less than twelve hours in the future.

The future. It was all she'd thought about since Uly was diagnosed with The Syndrome. Now it was here, within reach, and she intended to grab on to it with both hands and never let go.

A few minutes of brisk walking brought Devon to the cramped catwalk overlooking the containment area for the cold sleep capsules. From this height, the bunks looked like a bunch of lozenge-shaped suppositories, but they were the only way the travelers could be kept safe, protected and unaging in suspended animation, until their ship arrived at New Pacifica, twenty-two light-years ahead.

Far below her, crew members, wearing the multi-hued Eden Project logo over their left breasts and on the front of their billed caps, bustled here and there across the deck, attending to the final prep and last-minute check of each capsule before anyone took up temporary residence.

She gave the capsules no more than a cursory glance as she crossed the spiderweb of walkway. She knew the height of the capsules' efficiency and safety rankings, but they still made her uneasy. They reminded her too much of coffins. Considering the precious cargo they would soon carry, she found that thought ill-timed.

At the end of the catwalk, she stepped into the empty cage of an elevator and pressed a button. Within moments, she was let out on the cockpit level. A door on the opposite wall opened obediently upon her pressing the handpad, and she stepped inside.

One hand on his holster at his hip, Commander O'Neill stood over a computer console and stared down at it as though contemplating chewing off its face, if it had one to chew. Beside him, a technician named Baines worked over one of the comm panels with an expression of sheer determination, fingers deft and sure on the controls. Beyond them sat the pilot, presumably working out some diagnostics of his own, and the navigator.

Alonzo glanced over his shoulder when Devon arrived. His tense expression made her stomach knot deep inside. His hand flicked up in a brief wave of acknowledgment before he returned all his attention to his screens. Beyond his left shoulder, Devon spied the picture of some girl taped to the console in front of him and wondered who that was in a probably long line of wives, girlfriends, and/or mistresses.

O'Neill grinned at her with a grave irony Devon wasn't certain she liked. "What's going on?" she asked apprehensively.

"Something you should see." He jerked his head down at Baines's console.

Devon frowned quizzically and stepped up beside him to get a look. A digitally scrambled video news transmission was coming across the console, becoming more intelligible as Baines worked to clear away the bugs. Suddenly the picture bloomed crystal clear, showing a well-known news team seated behind their desks, their expressions solemn. "The expedition had been in planning stages for six years despite virulent opposition from both medical and scientific fields," one reported.

Devon glanced curiously at O'Neill. "What is it? InterNet Satellites?"

33

The Commander shook his head, waiting silently as Baines pulled up more digitized images. "To repeat," the newscaster continued, "the Eden Project, bound to set up the first colony in the G-8 system, met with disaster this morning, exploding upon departure. There were no survivors."

Every ounce of blood drained out of Devon's face. She flung a hand at the console. "What is this?" she demanded harshly. "Some kind of sick joke? We haven't even taken off yet."

One grizzled eyebrow lifted slowly as O'Neill eyed her. "That's government released, Adair," he said pointedly, making it clear this was not just some farce. "Preapproved by three panels nine hours before broadcast. No jokes."

Baines nodded in confirmation, glancing up first at O'Neill and then at Devon. "Coded for oh-nine-hundred tomorrow morning," he added seriously.

Devon stared at him, hardly daring to believe what she'd been told. "That's an hour after we launch," she murmured wonderingly. Suddenly she laughed. This was ludicrous, but her laughter had a bitter, metallic quality even to her own ears. "So what are you saying, O'Neill? They've given up trying to stall us, so they're just going to *kill* us?"

He shrugged. "We find a better world out there than these sanitized cans, they lose control," he said, making the politics clear as day. His steady gaze never wavered. "I'm running a resonance scan of the entire ship right now."

Devon knew when someone was being serious with her, especially when that someone was O'Neill. Still, it was so hard to believe . . . "You really think there might be explosives on board?"

He blinked slowly, like a snake, and his expression said he knew better. "You don't?"

34

She swallowed hard. "We can't risk another delay," she stressed, her anger kindling at the mere thought of postponing their trip, let alone canceling it altogether. They'd fought too hard and too long to give up now. "There are over two hundred Syndrome families on the Colony ship prepping for cold sleep right now. They might not live through another delay." A chill ran the length of her body. She stared at the console, which was replaying the message again, and then looked back at O'Neill.

"No delays," he promised. "We'll launch on schedule."

Devon stared him straight in the eye. "We need to go now."

The Commander gave her a long, speculative look, then a subtly cocky smile crept across his face. He turned and raised his voice slightly to be heard over the churn of conversations in the cockpit. "Solace, what's our status?"

"We're at zero minus eight-and-a-half hours," the pilot shot back promptly over his shoulder.

"You weren't hired to tell me the time, Solace," O'Neill chided.

The space jockey turned then, irritation bright in his dark eyes. He stared at the Commander for a moment, clearly weighing what he had heard against what he had not. In a moment, an insolent, million-dollar smile bloomed across his handsome features. He glanced at the vid screen. "Portal's yawning wide open," he remarked offhandedly, as if it were of no importance. "I'd say they're expecting a freighter."

O'Neill grinned hugely, snapped an about-face, and barked across the cockpit to the crew. "Advise Colony we're moving. And someone get the Operations crew together—*now*." His eyes sought Devon's once more. "This is it, Dev," he said, offering her a way out. "It's now or never."

Devon tapped her fingernails against the console screen still running the death announcement, and her lips tightened into a thin line. "Now."

Chapter 2

"Dad? Dad?"

Danziger heard his ten-year-old daughter coming along the passageway before he actually saw her. Upside down high among the ceiling panels here in the guts of the Advance ship, he looked down and watched True peer into the room. Coming to some decision, she entered and started down the narrow corridor beneath him at the swift, ground-eating trot that had been her standard mode of transportation ever since she'd taken her first toddling steps.

This was a rare opportunity to watch her unobserved, and he gratefully grabbed for the few seconds offered. She'd grown a lot in the last year, shooting up like a weed and outgrowing most of her stuff until he was hard-pressed to keep her in decent clothing. The increase in height hadn't changed her stubborn attitude one bit. (*And who'd she inherit that from, John?* he asked himself with a grin.) The additional inches made her seem skinnier than ever, not that he'd ever been able to keep much meat on her bones anyway with the way her metabolism functioned. The girl had one speed, and one speed only, and slow wasn't it.

It was damned disconcerting for Danziger to watch his little girl grow up, and not just because it made him feel older than the hills (which it did). His discomfort was mainly because she was beginning to show the first hints of developing, well, *curves*. Maybe even some time in the near future. Were ten-year-old kids supposed to do that? Last year she'd been nothing but a rod, a stick, built like a boy from head to toe, three times tougher than any other kid he knew and with a brain like lightning. Now . . .

Well, now she was still sharp as a tack, not to mention his boon companion, star pupil, and the best partner he'd ever had, but she was starting to do things with her hair and watch herself in the mirror when she didn't think he was looking. And pretty soon, if nature ran true to course, there would be *boys* noticing the things he was trying so hard to ignore.

She reached the end of the passageway without finding him and now turned around with her hands on her hips, evidently annoyed, but it was hard to say if it was at him or herself for being unable to find him. "Dad?" she called again. "I know you're in—" The room shifted gently and True instinctively grabbed the wall. Suddenly, her voice lost its former exasperated tone. Now she sounded concerned and anxious, and once again she was just a ten-year-old kid after all. What a relief. "Dad? We've moving."

Danziger shifted in his harness, swinging around until he was head-up instead of head-down. It took just a second to secure the open ceiling panel he'd been working in, and then he spider-skimmed his way to the floor, landing with an

38

easy grace born of good knees and many years of working in ships' Operations. "Feels like it to me," he said to her by way of greeting. "What's up?"

True jerked her head back the way she'd come. "They're looking for you." She crossed her arms and gave him the maternal look he'd had to tolerate from her since she was about four. "They tried to raise you. You're not wearing your headset." The word "again" was clearly implied by her tone.

Danziger didn't rise to the bait. It was an old argument between them. He hated the headset and was always purposely forgetting to put the damned thing on, though he always carried it wadded up in his pocket like an old handkerchief. He hated people being able to find him no matter where he was.

He shrugged away her look. "I'll take care of it." Taking her by the bicep, he swung her around and gave her fanny a gentle pat. "Go make yourself useful," he suggested with a paternal smile and started down the passageway without once looking behind to catch the vengeful glare he just *knew* was being volleyed at his back.

The closest video connection was in the cold sleep area, just a short jaunt from where he'd been working. Several other members of the Operations crew were already there, crowded around an available screen. Danziger elbowed in beside them, nodding hello as he wiped his hands clean on his pants, and glanced at the vid. He was instantly sorry he'd let True find him. If he'd known it was O'Neill wanting to pontificate, he might never have come out of the ceiling.

Danziger sighed irritably. He had work to do, certainly something more constructive than listening to O'Neill's latest message of encouragement to the working masses. He had nothing against the Commander personally. He just didn't care for the man's style. There was too much military still left in that big sack of meat.

"We have good reason to suspect there's an explosive on board," O'Neill reported, his expression grim over their exclamations of surprise. "The resonance scan came up with ninety-seven nonregistered items. We need a physical scan of all specific areas immediately."

A murmuring groan went through the assembled crew. Explosive or no explosive, that was a load of additional work they hadn't counted on doing. Not that they were about to quibble, of course. One little boom and there wouldn't be enough left of anyone to send home to Mom in a bag.

The work was beans. Something else entirely had grabbed hold of Danziger. Something having to do with O'Neill's request and the ship at present. He leaned toward one of the guys beside him. "Explosive check and *launching* at the same time?" he queried softly, needing to see if it was just him, or if the idea really was as ludicrous as he thought.

The other man gaped, blinking in astonishment as the import of Danziger's words sank home. O'Neill glared from the screen, having overheard the quiet remark, and tried to stare down Danziger with eyes that had turned into hard little rocks.

Danziger blinked placidly at him, unimpressed. He'd had bigger fish try to intimidate him before.

"Hey," the Commander said quietly, his voice clipped and brittle enough to break. "Just find it." The screen went blank.

"Just find it," the mechanic repeated wonderingly in disgust. "I wonder how much time we have to 'just' find it?" Growling in contempt, he turned and stalked away.

The controls moved under his hands with practiced ease as Alonzo slowly rotated the Advance ship into position behind the more massive bulk of the Colony vessel in which The Syndrome children, their families, the medical and security crews, and the rest of the colonists would ride, wrapped in cold sleep, all the way to G889. He smiled with satisfaction, liking the way the ship handled.

"Hospital ward reports all two hundred forty-eight Syndrome children are secured." The Colony ship's pilot, Shelia Willis, was an old friend. She briefly flicked her eyes toward Alonzo over the vid monitor to his left, as her hands danced over her controls. "Ready and waiting, Advance."

Alonzo nodded, as relaxed and comfortable with this routine procedure as if he and Shelia were having drinks in a dockside bar and negotiating a tryst. The usual cockpit commotion going on around him barely infringed upon his awareness as he lined up Advance's push bars behind Colony. "Brace yourself, Shelia. We're just about to kiss you here."

A second vid screen, situated above the one currently showing the other pilot sticking out her tongue, flared to sudden life with the screen-flattened features of a launch controller.

"Eden Advance, this is Port Control One-Nine," said the controller, her voice monotone in the depths of her noninterest. "Please advise. We're showing a No-Go here."

Alonzo leaned back, taking his eyes from the screens for only the barest fraction of a second as he sought O'Neill. "Commander? You want to handle this?"

Leaning against a weapons' locker in the back of the cockpit, O'Neill and Devon raised their heads from the screen monitoring the Ops crews' continued search of the ship. The Commander sauntered forward with Devon at his heels and stopped just behind the pilot, leaning in over the screen and smiling with the easy, disarming charm of an old-time matinee idol. Watching him, Alonzo would have

41

bet that the Commander had been something of a ladies' man in his heyday.

"This is Commander Broderick O'Neill with Eden Advance," he said pleasantly, just passing the time of day. "Just stretching our legs, One-Nine. Getting in position for mañana."

"We show a No-Go, Eden Advance," the launch controller repeated blandly, as if she thought O'Neill was some sort of moron unable to comprehend a simple sentence. "Please remain in your berthing until otherwise notified. Unauthorized movement is an endangerment—"

O'Neill pressed a button, cutting off the audio portion of the transmission. The controller, unaware of it at her end, continued mouthing her routine speech on station safety.

Alonzo grinned approvingly. "I never could find a way to shut her up. I like your style, Commander," he said in a complimentary tone.

O'Neill chuckled. "Thanks, Solace. I'm rather proud of it myself. Besides, I thought we could use the break." He glanced past Devon's nervous look and back toward the rear of the cockpit. "Any word from Operations?" he called.

"All negative so far, Commander," Baines responded.

"Keep monitoring and keep me posted," he ordered and faced front again, resting both big hands on the back of Alonzo's chair and leaning his weight forward. "I think I'll hang out here for a while and see what happens," he said easily, and grinned.

Danziger moved systematically along a stretch of corridor, removing various panels as he went and sticking his head deep inside the wall for a thorough look around with a flashlight and a handheld scanner. Operations had split into teams, the locations of O'Neill's "ninety-seven nonregistered items" divided among them for quicker examination.

Even so, they still had to thoroughly check each area as they moved through it, just in case they came across something the resonance scan hadn't picked up the first go around. The slow work made Danziger want to grind his teeth down to stubs. If there were explosives on board, what sort of detonator was being used? More importantly, what kind of timetable were they on? Did Operations have all the time in the world, or almost none at all?

The thought of someone attempting to sabotage their trip, and in the process blow to pieces a couple hundred Syndrome-afflicted children (not to mention all the rest of them), was not a surprising one to Danziger. As low-key and unobtrusive as he strove to be, he was not unaware of all the hoopla and controversy Devon Adair had stirred up with her plan to single-handedly find a cure for the diseased and dying children. There was a lot of name-calling and mud-slinging in the higher echelons in a direct counterpoint to the upswell of public support in response to her pleas. Just another one of the worker bees, Danziger discovered he couldn't help but be cognizant of a lot of what went on, not that he fancied he knew the entire story. Not by a long shot. But he knew enough not to be surprised by this turn of events, which wasn't to say it didn't make him angry as hell.

One of the crew came into view ahead at a corridor juncture and waved at him to catch his attention. "Danziger!" she yelled. "Put on your damn gear!"

Abashed as well as irritated, he put down his equipment long enough to pull the wadded-up headset from his pocket and shove it down over his head. It wasn't his daughter who burned into his vision as the optic feeders curved into place, but one of the crew, a short, lanky kid by the name of Weigman. "Nothing on seven deck, Chief," he reported, reminding Danziger that someone had named him one of the team leaders. He wanted to remember who it was so he could do something nasty to them one day soon. "You?"

"Trust me," Danziger replied. "I'll let you know. Keep to your grid pattern and report in as needed." A ready-light at the extreme edge of his vision strobed red, letting him know he had another call coming in. "Talk to you later, Bill," he said by way of sign-off and flicked in the second call. "Yeah?"

Larry Stidd's round face and bald, bullet-shaped head bloomed into view. Behind him, a woman with long, curly, dark-brown hair wrung her hands in distress. Danziger recognized her from the massive orientation/cocktail party O'Neill had held before they all came aboard the ships, but it took him a moment to place her face with her name. Martin. Bess Martin. If he remembered correctly, she was married to some government official sent along on this shindig as a liaison. She didn't look very happy and he could hardly blame her. There was nothing like having your privacy invaded by some stranger, particularly Stidd. Gentle as a lamb, he looked like he chewed on the bulkhead for recreation.

"If you could just tell me what you're looking for," Bess said earnestly. "Maybe I could help—"

Another member of the Ops crew, this one a fellow named Vergos, came into view beside her with a black valise in one hand. "Ma'am, what is this?" he asked, his voice crackling over the transmission.

Bess swallowed hard, eyes wide and innocent. "It . . . it's my husband's."

Vergos ran his scanner over the box, got no reaction, and nodded. "No triggers." Flipping the latch, he popped it open. A wealth of frilly, fluffy lingerie cascaded out of the suitcase and over his hands. Danziger grinned hugely as

Vergos blushed beet red and Stidd brayed laughter. "Your *husband's,* ma'am?" he asked.

"The case is his," she replied primly, cheeks aflame, and she reached over swiftly to shut it. "The contents are mine."

Still laughing, Stidd met Danziger's eyes through the link of their headgear and smiled easily at his boss. "Like I was about to say, Chief, Government Quarter Sector Three clear. You got anything?"

"Negative," Danziger replied, still chuckling, and wondered who was more discomfited, Vergos or Bess. "I'm up to comm deck. Out." He cut the transmission, letting the feeders fall away from his eyes, but kept the headset on so his team could reach him. As he waited for the elevator to arrive, the voice of one of the other team leaders came over the line. The message wasn't directed at Danziger, so he guessed the other mechanic's mike had been accidentally knocked into its On position.

"I'm sorry to inconvenience you, Dr. Heller," the voice said politely. "But—"

There was a noise that sounded like things either being thrown into or out of a locker, and a woman's strident voice cut him off. "Somebody's got to tell us what the hell's going on around here! We are *moving* and there are people who have not boarded the ship! What are you looking for?!"

"Explosives, ma'am" was the calm reply, and the other end went suddenly silent. Danziger checked his mike just to be sure, but, no, he hadn't inadvertently turned it off. The line was still open, but things in Medical were suddenly very, very quiet. Ha. Let the good doctor chew on that one for a while.

The elevator arrived and the doors parted. Danziger stepped inside, nodded a brisk greeting to the other man occupying the cage, and leaned against the wall to think of life's strange parallels. This was Bess Martin's husband,

45

Morgan. He was dressed in a business suit that looked as if it were pretending to be expensive, and the words "Government Employee" could practically be read across his forehead, as though they'd been stamped there. He paid no attention to Danziger, and paced back and forth in the narrow confines, all but shoving the mechanic up against the door as he passed behind him. "What the hell's going on?!"

"What?" Danziger asked, startled to be addressed directly.

More softly, Morgan asked again, "What the hell's going on?" and stared into space. Danziger suddenly realized he wasn't the one being spoken to.

"What the *hell's* going on?" Morgan asked a third time, addressing the floor this time as he practiced his line.

Great. Bad enough he was shut up in an elevator with someone who worked for the government, but Morgan was obviously a lunatic as well. Danziger wondered if he was going to become violent.

The elevator doors opened at the cockpit level, and Morgan brushed past Danziger as though he didn't exist, hurrying toward the cockpit entrance with his coattails flying. Danziger let him go, glad he didn't have to keep him company any longer, and proceeded in his wake at a slightly slower pace with the silent scanner held outstretched in one hand.

"What the, ah—" The authoritative voice stuttered and abruptly changed tactics. "What's going on?" someone asked with mild curiosity.

Devon turned, rankled by a voice that at first was so demanding and then suddenly so meek, and eyed the newcomer with disapproval. Needing and having government backing for the Eden Project had guaranteed the "necessary" presence of a mediator aboard her ship, but that didn't mean she had to like it. She prided herself on being able to work with almost anyone, but after getting to know Morgan Martin's intrusive, yes-man personality, she liked his presence here even less.

"You're our government liaison, Martin," O'Neill rumbled, sounding like an upset stomach. "Why don't you tell us?"

"What are you talking about?" Morgan asked, stepping up between them. His arm swung, taking in the cockpit, the Colony ship, and everything else beyond their screens. "Who authorized our departure? We don't have level six clearance."

Vid audio was back on, having been reinstated by O'Neill, though no one on the ship was doing much talking back and forth with the control tower. The formerly quiet, persuasive voice of the launch controller had risen to a buzz of irritation. "Eden ships, you are in violation of Port Ordinance. Acknowledge."

"Will someone with some weight talk to these nice folks, please?" Alonzo asked, leaning back in his chair to fix them with a beseeching eye. "I've kinda got my hands full here."

Devon speared Morgan with a look that had him retreating fast even before she grabbed his lapels and pressed him into a corner with his back thrust uncomfortably against a jut of machinery. Her eyes bore into his in a way that had made stronger men wince. When she spoke, her voice was low and toned in such a way that he could not question her seriousness. "Since you're still on board, Mr. Martin, I assume you don't know what your friends on level six have planned for us tomorrow."

He blinked at her in simple confusion. "They're releasing us to Planet G889."

She smiled without humor. "Guess again."

A monitor directly in front of Alonzo flared with light,

drawing Devon's attention as it resolved into the features of another controller. "Solace?" he asked, trying to exude charm and calm, talking to the pilot as if they were old bar-crawling buddies, which they may have been for all Devon knew. "Are you out of your mind? You're not one of these lunatics. Orient and redock before they take your charter bars."

Alonzo chuckled. "You wanna pay my freight, One-Nine? I doubt you can match these people's credit weight. I just may retire after this run." He popped his knuckles.

"Eden Advance." The first controller was back and trying her best, but her edges had worn thin. All the time they jabbered, the ships were still moving forward, the nose of the Advance ship thrusting Colony along. "We still show No-Go," she reported needlessly. They all knew that. "Return to dock facility. Repeat. Return to dock facility. If you do not return to dock facility immediately, we will contact Port Authority."

O'Neill leaned closer to the vid monitor to ensure that his next words, and the expression on his face, would not be misunderstood. "Feel free to contact whoever you damn well please. We're making a run for it."

Chapter 3

· · · ● ● ● ● ● ●

Pandemonium broke out at O'Neill's words. The control tower was thrown into riot, the babble of voices rising momentarily to drown out everything in the cockpit but Morgan's outraged *"What?!"* as he pushed past Devon and was drawn up short by the Commander's enormous hand planted firmly in the center of his chest. In the confluence of sound, Devon heard the doors open again. At once both weary and resigned, she turned to deal with whichever disgruntled person had just butted in uninvited.

It was one of the Ops people, his headset canted slightly askew over one ear and the name "Danziger" printed over the left breast of his uniform. His flat, speculative gaze slid over and past her as he hefted his scanner in a self-explanatory motion in case it was needed, and then all but ignored her as he turned away and began a circuit of the cockpit.

The launch controller's voice cut through the cacophony in the tower, stilling the clamor behind her with her no-nonsense tone. "Eden, we have initiated portal closure. You will not clear portal. Reverse thrust immediately."

One step brought Devon directly behind Alonzo's right shoulder. She leaned forward with O'Neill on the pilot's left, and stared at the portal doors. They were, indeed, beginning to close with an infinitely sweet, tantalizing slowness.

"Those doors won't reverse, Solace," came the voice of the other controller. "And we're shutting down Apex Guidance."

Devon watched with growing horror as the tunnel's guidance system lights shut down one after another, leaving their way blank and dark, with only the two ships' running lights and the meager lights around the distant, *closing* portal doors to serve as a beacon.

"Now, when's the last time you piloted manual, Lonz?" the first controller asked. Her expression was supremely confident, her voice toned to the utmost patience. She *clearly* had nothing but Alonzo's very best interest at heart. Right. And pigs (if there were any left) would pilot shuttles.

The woman's ingratiating tone both rankled and worried Devon. Did she think Alonzo an idiot, to fall for something so blatant? Worse yet . . . would he? And if he did, what would happen to them then?

"You breach that hull, we'll have a hell of a mess on our hands," the woman warned in the friendliest, I'm-only-doing-this-for-your-own-good manner.

Alonzo leaned forward and ran his hands almost caressingly over his control console, depressing keys here and there in a seemingly random pattern. Devon didn't have a clue what he was doing, but he looked supremely capable of doing just about anything he put his mind to. "Thanks for the vote of confidence, One-Nine," he shot back lazily, totally unaffected by the hoped-for persuasiveness of the woman's argument. "I'll keep that in mind."

O'Neill leaned down and put his mouth so close to the pilot's head that his breath stirred the little hairs near Alonzo's ear when he spoke. "Now's the time, kid," he said quietly. "If you're as good as you say you are." His eyes narrowed. "Reach down and get it . . ."

Alonzo nodded slightly and a grin teased the corners of his mouth. Devon suddenly knew what was about to happen, what she had sanctioned to happen with her desperate need to leave this place *at once*. Her fingers tightened on the back of Alonzo's chair in response.

"Nav," Alonzo said, all teasing and banter gone as he knuckled down to business. "I'll need verbal marker positioning."

The ship's navigator turned and fixed him with wide, incredulous eyes. "*Inside* the launch tube?" she asked, staring at the back of his head as if she expected to see brain matter dripping out of his ears. "Without Apex?"

His eyes were stern and hard when he looked at her. "Just follow my marks," he instructed firmly, leaving no room for argument. O'Neill's prowess notwithstanding, there was clearly only *one* pilot aboard this ship.

Devon swallowed hard, her eyes fixed on the space between the portal doors, which was narrowing too rapidly to suit her. Forward to the future. Forward to a child without illness. "Come on . . ." she whispered, nearly dancing in place with agitation. "Come on . . ."

"Where are you going, Devon?" a tightly controlled, extremely seductive voice asked behind her. She stiffened in surprise, not having expected it, and then slowly turned around. Beside her, O'Neill swore under his breath and did the same.

A monitor at the rear of the cockpit had flared to sudden life, startling Baines, who sat beside it. The sleep-rumpled countenance of Dison Blalock, the Port Authority commissioner, filled the screen. He did not look happy at having been woken in the middle of the night, but you could only tell that if you knew Dison well, as Devon did, and if you knew how deeply to look into his persuasive eyes.

Devon took a deep breath, ready to counter him with any argument she could devise, but Morgan cut in front of her and leaned into view of the monitor. "Mr. Blalock, sir, Morgan Martin, level four. I just wanted you to know that I in no way sanctioned—" He squealed sharply as O'Neill roughly shoved him aside.

"Go back to sleep, Blalock," the Commander recommended, his voice as silky-smooth as the PAC's. "You're just having a bad dream."

Blalock ignored him, and ignored Martin as well. He fixed his gaze on Devon with an intensity she found both unnerving and annoyingly intrusive. "You have a scheduled departure in eight hours, Devon," he said soothingly. "Movement like this could put your clearance at risk."

Devon could glimpse the front screen out of the extreme corner of her eye. The ships were almost upon the closing portals, with the star-studded egress a fine sliver to her eye and already narrower than she thought they could safely make it through. Still Alonzo pushed them forward. O'Neill was back behind the pilot, leaving her to deal with Blalock alone. She didn't know whether to feel bolstered by his confidence or abandoned.

"Devon," Blalock continued, drawing her eyes back to his face. "All these years of planning, Devon. All those obstacles . . ."

"Eleven north, four degrees," Alonzo murmured behind her. The portal doors loomed like the walls of a canyon. Devon's armpits grew suddenly wet.

"Mark," the navigator responded softly, staring intently at her board. Sweat dotted her upper lip.

"I know we've been difficult," Blalock admitted, trying his best to look contrite. His tone suddenly changed, chiding her as though she were his reluctant child. "But now, eight hours to go, and this final insubordinate act?"

Being patronized was one of the things Devon hated above all others. She realized with sudden clarity that Dison Blalock had always patronized her and she'd always let him, without even realizing it, so skilled was he in hiding it behind a facade of parental concern. Understanding that gave her a boost of confidence she desperately needed. "Let's just say after years of clearance stalls, I'm a tad antsy," she replied with a shrug, hands out with the palms up.

Frustration shimmered through Blalock's eyes and was gone, dampened by professional aplomb, but she'd seen it and that was enough. "Devon, everything we've done has been for your benefit—to protect you from the unknown."

"Blalock," she said, and let a drop of irritation creep into her voice. "You've seen the probe info. The planet has a habitability rating of eighty-three."

"I know," he agreed readily, putting her even further on her guard. "But nobody's ever been as far as G889, Devon. I don't think you're going to like what you find there."

At the edge of her vision, Danziger slid into view, systematically moving from console to console with his scanner. Out of sight of Blalock, he waved it over a bank of smaller wireless monitors near the PAC's vid, three of which carried smaller duplicates of Blalock's image. Suddenly every light on the scanner's face blipped with mechanical excitement.

Devon's heart skipped a beat just as O'Neill's unexpected voice spoke quietly in her ear from the headset gear she still wore. "Keep him on the hook, Adair. We've got a live one here."

She swallowed hard, trying not to look nervous, trying not to look angry, trying to look like anything but what she was actually feeling and mostly trying not to let Blalock know they were on to him. Sweat beaded across her upper lip, and she wondered how much he could see, how much she was giving away without meaning to. "Think I like staying on the stations, Dison?" she asked. "These Syndrome children are dying. In two generations, we may all be extinct."

Blalock nodded with all of the paternal compassion and understanding of a favorite parish priest, though she knew from experience that he didn't really believe those facts and figures. "Devon, no one is more sorry than I am that your little boy is sick. It is sad when children die. People have always died. That doesn't mean we have to run away from all we know."

Beyond Blalock's line of sight, O'Neill bent to help Danziger wrench the suspicious monitor from the wall and turn it around. Fused to the back was a small, squat object.

"Oh, my God," Morgan whispered somewhere behind her. "They're gonna kill us."

O'Neill shot him a silencing look that withered Morgan on the spot. Danziger stuck the monitor under his arm as if it were nothing more important than his lunch sack, and carried it out of the cockpit with a swift nonchalance Devon admired. O'Neill spared her a telling glance, and then he was gone as well, accompanying Danziger as they rushed to dispose of the thing before it detonated and made all of

54

them—the ships, the children, everything—a piece of tragic history.

"What's the point here, Dison?" Devon asked, determined to hold his attention as O'Neill had asked. She couldn't believe he hadn't heard Morgan and she winged a silent prayer for that luck to whichever god might be listening. "I thought we *had* clearance . . . ?"

"Everything but level six, Devon," he oozed placatingly. "You know that. I'm doing all I can to make that happen."

And without level six, we go nowhere. She hazarded a look over her shoulder. Morgan whipped around and stared through the cockpit window as their ship, pushing the Colony Advance vessel before it, entered the space between the closing portals, scarcely wide enough to let them through. He clutched the back of Alonzo's chair, knuckles white with pressure. "Oh, my God . . . Oh, my God . . ."

"You know as well as I do, Devon, there are people who don't want you to succeed."

Devon turned back, determined not to look at those doors again until she was doing it from the other side. Silently, she prayed that Alonzo had shoulders wide enough and strong enough to hold her confidence. O'Neill's voice was a sudden thready whisper in her ear. "Adair, keep him cool. Need some time here."

Time? How much time? Where were they and what were they going to do with the bomb? Behind her, Morgan was in a full froth, terrified of being clipped by the portals. "Two little ships, Dison. A handful of unwanted, whispered-about families. Most people think of this as a cleansing."

He held his hands wide and shrugged his shoulders ingratiatingly. "Hey, were it up to me, I'd've let you leave long ago." His voice grew a little heavier, a parent being forced to explain to his child some of the more unlovely aspects of life. "This is a difficult situation, Devon, rife with internal politics."

She folded her arms across her chest and widened her stance stubbornly. "No Syndrome child has ever lived beyond the age of nine. My son is eight. I won't watch him die." How many times had she said those words? How much longer would she have to keep this up?

A faint, whiny cry echoed faintly through the cockpit as the rear of the Advance ship squeezed through the portals and the doors closed behind both ships. The sound drove Morgan to the floor, hands thrust between his knees. "Oh, my God . . . Oh, my God . . ."

"We're through," Alonzo murmured softly for Devon's benefit. "Now, if the rest do their job right . . ."

"Devon, I'm *imploring* you." Expression intent, Blalock leaned forward, filling the screen with the force of his personality. "Do not leave station sub-space zero. *Stay in proximity* for your own good."

She cocked an eyebrow. "Why, Dison? Are you trying to tell me something? Are you saying we're at risk?" Where the hell were O'Neill and Danziger?! Taking the damned monitor for a stroll? Panic welled in her, making her feel shaky and foolish. She was going to botch this if something didn't happen soon.

There was a sudden exhalation from Alonzo and a quiet, satisfied grunt. "Into the chute," she heard him mutter. "And out with the rest of the trash." Devon suddenly realized he'd been monitoring O'Neill and Danziger's progress all this time. It made her want to kiss him, except she figured he'd enjoy that way too much.

"Devon, you're at risk any time you're out there without us." Blalock's voice had once again taken on the mellow, seductive tones he used when he wanted to be particularly persuasive. "You've got to trust me on this, Devon. I'm trying to help you here. I'm trying to be a friend . . ."

O'Neill's voice came tinnily into her ear. "We're clear." Devon thought her legs would go weak and watery at the words, but they surprised her by staying firm and rigid, holding her upright to the deck as though she'd been riveted there with the rest of the hardware. She felt powerful in a way that bore no resemblance to the pseudo-power she had once wielded.

Her eyes held Blalock's with the same intensity he'd tried to use on her, which he *had* used on her more times than she cared to recount. She was gratified to see sweat break out on his brow. Looked like he wasn't the only one who could throw weight around. "One thing I've learned, Dison." She leaned over and placed a hand on the vid screen. "I'm all out of friends."

"Don't go off li—"

A flick of her fingers killed the monitor. Suddenly his voice sounded behind her and she whirled, having forgotten about the smaller monitors on the other console. Blalock's expression was murderous now, and she couldn't help but think how apt that was. "I can't do any more," he declared firmly. "I can't protect you. I wish you'd listen to me . . ."

A massive explosion lit their front screens with an eye-watering brilliance, brightening the entire cockpit and leaving everyone momentarily blinded. Alonzo whooped with loud delight, bouncing in his seat with joyous, frenzied excitement. Martin was curled into a ball on the floor behind the pilot's chair and looked as if he just might have wet himself.

Devon turned to watch the remnants of the explosion dissipate in all directions. Satisfaction stole across her face and settled into a subtle smile. Her headgear signaled and this time she was free to swing in the opticals. "You do very well with those sentimental good-byes," O'Neill praised her with a smile.

She snorted. "How long before they realize they didn't get us?"

"Oh, I'd say they know now," he replied, confirming what she'd already guessed.

Morgan's head turtled up from the floor. "They're not coming after us." He sounded as if he wanted to make it a question, but didn't quite dare.

Devon glanced at the rear monitor, showing the massive space station receding into the distance, and sighed heavily.

"We're already dead to them," O'Neill said, answering Morgan. "They're firing up that newscast as we speak. We're on our own now. There's no turning back."

The familiarity of that condition settled over Devon like a comfortable, well-worn coat. She'd traveled this road many times before and no longer feared it. "Was there ever?" she asked with a tired smile. She placed a hand lightly on the back of Alonzo's chair. "Just get us out of here," she ordered quietly when he glanced round at her.

"Yes, ma'am," he responded promptly, and she heard the engines fire with the sound of freedom.

Chapter 4

• • • • • • • ● ●

The quiet scuff of Devon's boots sounded against the metal catwalk as she quickly crossed above the cold-sleep chamber and headed toward her stateroom to check on Uly before returning to the cockpit's controlled, celebratory chaos.

The momentary break was more than welcome, not just because it gave her an opportunity to reorganize her disordered thoughts, but also because it got her away from Alonzo's cocky exuberance and O'Neill's insufferable smugness. Granted, they had a lot to be proud of, but still . . .

The sudden need to move out early and the discovery of a bomb (dear God, a *real* bomb!) was enough to rattle her nerves quite sufficiently, no matter how good she might be at not showing it. And thanks to whatever gods there were that, after a thorough search, no bomb had been found on the Colony ship as well. Right now, Devon wanted nothing more than to crawl into bed beside her son, pull the covers up over their heads, and let someone else handle things for a change.

But it wasn't over yet, not by a long shot. She wondered if it ever would be, really. She'd never been one to stand aside and let someone else run the show. Could she do that once they reached New Pacifica, or would she place herself in the middle of things? She knew herself well enough not to have to answer that question.

A wry smile tugged at the corner of her mouth. She couldn't imagine what it would be like to allow herself the luxury of having nothing to do but drift blindly through each day, enjoying what came without worry or care raising its ugly little head. A blissful lifestyle would probably drive her nuts far faster than the normal run of her life seemed to be doing. After all these years, Devon had no choice but to suspect she thrived on stress. Still, as much as the pattern of her life had been irrevocably changed by Uly's being born ill, she wouldn't have changed one iota of it if the only other alternative was not to have had him at all.

Striding along, she turned a corner and nearly collided with Yale coming from the opposite direction. Every motherly instinct went on alert. "Is Uly all right?"

The Teacher nodded. "He's fine, Devon. Stop worrying."

"You don't break old habits so easily, my friend." She ran a hand through her hair and suddenly realized how dirty she was from sweating so much. She wanted a shower desperately. "Where's Dr. Vasquez? I can't get him on gear. He should be prepping Uly."

"Devon—" Yale glanced around at the other people passing by, each face intent, every pace hurried. He took her arm in one large hand and steered her into a small alcove around the corner. "Vasquez is not on board."

"What?" she demanded in disbelief. It only took one straw to break the camel's back, and she was already carrying a full load.

Yale nodded. He looked ancient all of a sudden and she couldn't tell if it was from general tiredness or having to deliver this news. "Apparently, he went over to Colony for a final check on the children."

"We'd boarded for departure!" Devon exclaimed angrily. "No one was supposed to disembark without—" The pit of her stomach dropped away as the ramifications hit home. "My God . . . We have no doctor."

"Dr. Heller is on board," he corrected her.

Devon snorted. "Heller? She's the most junior member of his team. She's barely qualified to be his intern."

Yale cleared his throat sharply, eyes darting over Devon's left shoulder. She pursed her lips, knowing she was going to hate this, and turned to find Julia Heller standing behind them, having just come around the corner. The look on her face, before she quickly schooled her features into their usual professional mask, said she'd heard every denigrating word.

"Dr. Heller has come to prep Uly for cold sleep," the old cyborg said needlessly, his voice gently chiding.

Devon was annoyed by her indiscretion, but that wasn't about to get an apology out of her. Everything she'd said was true, even if it was indelicately put. She nodded and left it at that.

When it became apparent Devon wasn't going to be the first to speak, Julia nodded deferentially. "I should monitor his cryo-sleep for twenty-four hours before the rest of us go down for hibernation," she explained.

Devon already knew all that. Vasquez had told her. She nodded stiffly, unhappy with this latest cast of fate's dice and unhappier still that there wasn't a damn thing she could do about it except dream of wringing Vasquez's neck the next time she saw him. "I agree. You should get started."

"I assume Dr. Vasquez explained the risks a child like Uly faces going into cold sleep, even under optimum conditions."

"Which we no longer have," Devon replied tersely. "Yes, I'm aware of the risk." Did the other woman think Devon was blind to the dangers facing her son? "But we don't have much choice, do we?"

Julia blanched slightly at the faint sarcasm in Devon's voice, but held her ground. "No, ma'am."

"Then you'd better get to it, hadn't you?" Her eyes slid over the doctor dismissively. "Yale, I'll be in the cockpit with O'Neill. Tell Uly I'll see him in a little while." She turned and walked away before he could say anything, either in rebuke or encouragement. She didn't want a lecture on bad manners right now. What she wanted was to see her son by herself, just the two of them, not with Heller hovering around checking things. But it was true Uly needed prepping and truer still that he needed twenty-four hours of monitoring before the adults who were in Heller's care lay down for their own long rest. Her wishes were, *had* to be, superseded by those needs. It was enough to make her want to scream, but she didn't. There were too many people around. Maybe she'd give herself the luxury of a good yell later on.

She strode into the elevator and slammed her palm hard enough to hurt it against the button to close the door. Dammit! Wasn't anything going to go right around here today?

Apparently not, as she discovered upon returning to the cockpit. O'Neill and Danziger stood almost toe to toe, staring into each other's eyes. The Commander's chin was thrust out aggressively, and he looked about as annoyed as

Devon had ever seen him. For his part, Danziger looked cool as ice. How the hell did he manage it after everything that had occurred?

"Listen," O'Neill snapped. "You can tell everyone from Mechanical to Kitchen crew, we stick with the original contract: Transit To and Deposit On Planet."

"I'm not asking for the crew," Danziger said quietly, his voice tightly restrained with impatience. How many times had he already gone over this? "I'm asking for myself. Contract didn't say much about bomb scans or leaving under a No-Go. After we drop you off, I still have to do business with that port."

"Twenty-two light-years there and back?" O'Neill scoffed. "How many administrations do you think that'll be?"

"Just tell everyone the hazard pay clause has been invoked," Devon said, wanting to end the argument before it got out of hand, and disappointed by this obvious bid for more money.

Danziger's head bobbed once in a curt nod. "Fine. That's all I wanted to know." He left the cockpit without further remark.

O'Neill shot Devon a look that spoke volumes, and she returned it with a commiserating grin. Oh, yeah, they both knew Danziger's type. Well, at least he wouldn't be staying with them in New Pacifica.

One of Alonzo's monitors sprang to life to show Shelia. "Eden Advance, Colony ship prepped for disengage."

Alonzo sighed theatrically. "You're breaking my heart."

"I'm sure it'll bounce back, Lonz," she said and grinned.

O'Neill slid into the vacant copilot's seat and leaned over the monitor. "Tell those passengers of yours to hang tight. By the time they're out of cold sleep, we'll have set up their new home at New Pacifica."

63

"I'll tell them, sir," Shelia confirmed.

Devon watched Alonzo's expert hands work the ship's controls. The view on their front screens changed as the two spaceships split apart, the push bars withdrawing into Advance's hull. The Advance ship snaked around the larger vessel and began pulling away under increased power.

"Thanks for the push," Shelia added. "Hope you all sleep tight."

"Good-bye, Shelia," Alonzo said with a heartfelt sigh, one hand splayed against his chest, but the woman was obviously already as good as forgotten as the vista of space opened up in front of him. "Wish we could bring you along."

"Now, when have I heard *that* one before?" she countered wryly, and cut the transmission. Alonzo blinked in mild surprise, then chuckled and settled back in his seat.

"Well, gentlemen," Devon said. "I'll be in the cold sleep chamber if you need me." She stepped toward the door.

O'Neill half rose out of his chair. "Adair, we need to—"

She held up a hand, forestalling anything he had to say. "Maybe so, Commander, but it will have to be later. I let myself get pulled away from putting my son to bed, but I'm *going* to be there for him when he goes into cold sleep. No arguments." She stressed it in a pleasant enough manner, but her tone let him know he'd have a fight on his hands if he wanted to press the point.

He nodded sagely and lowered himself back into the chair. "Later, then," he said and nodded.

She returned the salute and left the cockpit, feeling for a moment as though all her paths led back to this small, activity-filled room.

The tiers of cold-sleep bunks lined the wall one after another like little cars ready for a journey. Devon smiled over that image, finding it much more appropriate than her former one of them as coffins. These "little cars" were about to provide twenty-two light-years of safe transit for their passengers. And when they awoke . . .

A cold hand crawled into hers, drawing her back to the present. She looked down at Uly lying in the open capsule she knelt beside, and gave him as confident and courageous a smile as she could muster. "I love you, Champ." She brushed his hair back out of his eyes, her smile broadening as he scowled at her for doing so and momentarily forgot his fear. She leaned forward and kissed his cheek, his skin cool against her lips and his scent, eight years familiar.

The fingers of his other hand caught her collar, holding her down so close that their breath would have mingled if it hadn't been for his respirator. He rubbed his cheek against hers in a gesture that had been theirs forever, then released her so she could sit back and he could look up into her eyes. "I won't wake up for twenty-two light-years, but it'll seem like tomorrow, right?" he asked nervously.

"Just like any other night," she agreed.

His gaze never wavered. "You don't think I won't wake up, do you?"

How much bravery it took to voice that question! Pride in her son swelled through her. "You'll wake up, Uly," she said with unflinching faith. "I promise. And when you do, we'll be looking at a new home." She smiled and tweaked the end of his nose. "Then you can tell me the end of that story about that beast of yours."

He nodded and let himself share her smile now. "I will," he promised.

Eyes still locked with his, she nodded and rose. *Let me be as brave*, she thought, trying hard not to give him any hint of all she was thinking, all of the conflicting thoughts and emotions running pell-mell through her brain.

Julia stepped forward from where she'd been waiting at a discreet distance, bent to place a sedi-derm against Uly's neck, and pressed the activator. Almost immediately, his eyes fluttered closed and his shallow breathing slowed.

Devon felt footsteps through the decking and knew without turning that Yale was behind her. "Good night, Uly," the Teacher said, warm affection making his deep voice mellower than usual.

"Night," the boy murmured, fading swiftly into sleep. He rallied suddenly, his eyes fighting to open lids that would only grant him a crack. "I love you, Mom," he whispered, and was gone.

Swallowing around the hard, sudden lump in her throat, Devon reached out and stroked his cheek, so soft and downy beneath her fingers. He was still such a very little boy, but look at all he had endured and all that still lay before him, shining with possibilities. Could she do any less than face it as bravely as he?

She stepped back and nodded briefly at Julia, immensely comforted when Yale placed both warm hands upon her shoulders and drew her against his chest. Julia took her cue and began to close and secure the bunk, readying her equipment to closely monitor his sleep for the next twenty-four hours before she, and all the others, sought rest in their own capsules.

"We are pioneers, heading into the great unknown," Yale murmured, his mouth close beside Devon's ear. "We bring with us only questions. Will this new planet hold the key to healing humankind? Will the frontier hold the same promise for us that it did for our ancestors?"

Devon's eyes flooded with tears as something deep within her clenched with love and fear. She'd spent the last eight years of her life fighting for this moment. If New

Pacifica didn't cure Uly, she would still have to stand by and watch him die.

That could not be a consideration. She believed in this dream, she *had* to, or she would never have been able to bring it this far.

The capsule door lowered and was secured. She watched Uly's face through the window, so placid in sleep, but separated from her for the first time for what, at this end, felt like an eternity.

"And, most important of all," Yale continued, his voice even lower and pitched for her ears alone, his hands tightening on her shoulders, turning her to look up into his eyes, "will Uly ever get to slay his monsters?"

Fear and worry and insecurity fled into the dark as Devon Adair threw back her head and laughed.

Chapter 5

Twenty-two Light-years Later

Alonzo never knew for certain which sense impinged first upon his slowly growing awareness of the world around him. He'd done the cold sleep routine so many times that it had become rote by now, something that just sort of *happened* to him without him really being cognizant of the process. Which was probably just as well, and he should thank his lucky stars for it. He'd heard tell of some people who never learned to cope with the side effects—both physical and psychological—of cold sleep. If he'd been one of those poor SOBs, he never would have been able to enjoy this career as a pilot—and God knew he *did* enjoy it. Worse luck, he would have died a long time ago, probably of old age. How could anyone think of dying when there was so much still out there (women included) left unexplored?

So, whatever and however it occurred, he was just suddenly aware of sensation creeping back into his limbs, of neural synapses sputtering and firing like spark plugs used to in old cars before catching and humming along at their normal pace. He took a long, deep breath, coughed to clear his throat, and opened his eyes, blinking at the dim lights on the ceiling. He was poignantly aware of a desperate need for coffee, a quality of the human race that didn't seem to change no matter how many centuries passed.

The containment seal on his cold-sleep capsule had slid gently open, the computer being programmed to wake him first upon arrival at their preset orbital coordinates above the surface of G889. G889! He snorted. What kind of name was that for a planet? Couldn't they be a little more original? Everything was either numbers or "New" this and "New" that, like their continent of New Pacifica, in memory of a place they'd left behind because they either hated it there or it was already dead. Alonzo couldn't figure it out. If it was left up to *him* he'd give a planet a name it could live up to. Something like . . . like . . .

Like Solace. Yeah! That was the sort of name that would have the tourists flocking in by the droves, searching for exactly what the name implied, something they couldn't buy at the local space station commissary or on the black market. There was money to be made in a name like Solace.

He chuckled and reached to pull away the diodes stuck to his temples, shoulders, chest, the inside of each arm, and his groin. His fingers sought and found the fingerpad near his left hand. Without looking, he tapped a sequence of numbers and letters to let the computer know he was awake and functioning, and then he sat up.

A long stretch was the first thing in order after such a long cryo-sleep, and Alonzo took his time about it, glorying in the sensation like a cat after a long nap. He cracked his knuckles, popped one wrist joint twice, scratched his short, bristly growth of beard, and sprang out of the cold-sleep tube with the agility of an elf.

"Yeow!" His voice echoed in the vast sleeping chamber. The damn floor was *cold*! He danced his bare feet up and down for a few minutes, getting used to it, then padded across the metal decking to check the computer readout on the other passengers. A quick eye scan proved everyone was just fine.

Now came the first serious question of this portion of the journey. Who to wake up first? As pilot, it was something of his prerogative, though it was pretty much taken for granted that the head honchos, meaning O'Neill and the Adair woman, should be woken first. But *should be* had never meant *must be* in Alonzo's book.

He frowned as he gave the question serious consideration. O'Neill was okay, for being military, and certainly no worse than anyone else Alonzo had known and worked for in his long and colorful career. And Devon Adair seemed to be an all right lady with a lot of moxie and savvy. But he felt like he owed Danziger something for the mechanic's quick discovery and removal of the bomb that would have ended everybody's careers damned precipitously. And then there was that pretty doctor . . .

The pilot grinned, tapping his fingers on the computer screen. What the hell? He'd wake up both Julia and Danziger and see which one joined him first in the cockpit. He rather hoped it would be one over the other, because it had been a *long* sleep . . . and he was feeling frisky.

His forefinger jabbed the appropriate buttons to begin waking the chosen ones, then he rigged the computer to start the waking sequence in one hour for the remaining passengers. That gave him plenty of time to work out the kinks, use up all the hot water in the shower, and get to the cockpit for an orienting look around before entertaining visitors. Cool.

"C'mon, man!" a cheerful voice enthused from somewhere deep inside Danziger's brain. "It's show time!"

"What?" he asked muzzily, confused, and licked his lips. His mouth felt as if it were stuffed with cotton.

"Show time!" the voice repeated and began singing reveille. "It's time to get up, it's time to get up, it's time to get up in the moooooooooooorrrrrrrrrning!"

Danziger jerked fully awake, almost dropped back into the deep, alluring pit of sleep, then forced himself to stir and open what had to be the heaviest eyelids in history. He blinked a couple of times in an attempt to banish sleep's final, coaxing fingers, and frowned at what he was hearing. The idiot he'd thought was part of a dream was still singing reveille, only now Danziger *knew* he was really awake. Groaning, every joint stiff with twenty-two light-years' worth of being motionless, he slowly sat up and steadied himself with a hand on the capsule rim.

True's tube lay next to his, her sleep-smoothed features visible through the window. Beyond her, stacked in rows, were bunk after bunk of cold-sleep tubes, each with its somnolent occupant. Beyond the last stack, Alonzo Solace was doing clapping push-ups as he sang.

Danziger stared at him, convinced that maybe he *wasn't* so awake after all. This *had* to be part of a dream. No one, *no one*, had any right to be that chipper first thing in the morning. The pilot was shirtless, the well-defined muscles of his shoulders and chest bunching and relaxing with the force of his exertions. He'd barely broken a sweat. Danziger decided he hated him.

"Ninety-eight," Alonzo broke off singing to count. "Ninety-nine . . . one hundred!" The last push-up flipped him almost effortlessly onto his feet and he stood, barely out of breath. He grinned hugely when he saw Danziger watching him. "Hey! Welcome back, man! I gotta catch a shower before things start hopping. See you later!" With that, he trotted away among the racks of capsules and was soon lost to sight.

Danziger shook his head, contemplated going back to sleep, then decided against it and slung a leg over the side of the tube. He'd slept long enough. It was time to get moving.

Alonzo whistled while he worked, running a diagnostic program through the control panel and finding everything in working order. His second cup of coffee steamed at his elbow and he snatched brisk sips of the searingly hot brew from time to time.

He paused, one ear cocked as the elevator arrived at the cockpit hallway. Now, if fate were kind to him . . . The door opened and he pursed his lips, biting back a smile. Oh, lady fate was kind indeed! It seemed that she just *loved* her boy Alonzo.

Julia's image reflected off the cockpit's front windows. Even after such a profound cold sleep, with her hair slightly disheveled and her eyes bleary with the aftereffects of the prep-drugs, she was still a knockout. She stood in the doorway and silently watched him for quite a while. He enjoyed the scrutiny and worked on, letting her think he didn't know she was there until she shifted and stepped farther into the room, letting the door close behind her.

"It's standard op to have me verify position," he said without turning. "So you and me can hop back into the big cold sack if we're a couple hundred million miles off course."

She nodded. "That's right." She stepped closer, sliding a

diagnostic glove onto one hand as she did so, and placed the flat of its palm against the back of his neck. He liked the feel of that, but would have been happier if it were her bare hand instead. She shifted position slightly to better check the readout as the numbers and lights flashed their cryptic medical code at her.

Alonzo smiled engagingly, trying to meet her eyes in their joined reflections. "Well, you'll be happy to know that my record's intact. Haven't missed yet."

"I know," she said absently, and slid her hand along his throat to press over the carotid artery.

He raised his eyebrows in his best endearing little boy look. "You know . . . I could postpone everyone's defrost so we could celebrate life a little . . ." He left the sentence hanging suggestively.

She met his gaze then, eyeing him coolly. "Is that the only come-on you sleep jumpers have these days?" she asked with disgust.

His smile broadened. A common thread of experience gave them something to talk about, something to share, something he could use to ease into other things. "You've worked cold-sleep runs before?"

She snorted. "Let's just say your reputation precedes you."

Alonzo swiveled his chair around to face her, enjoying the closeness of those beautiful features. She refused to meet his eyes, but placed her hand flat against his chest and studied the readouts. "I don't have a rep," he assured her guilelessly. "I'm not around long enough to make one." This earned him a small, cold smile in response. She moved her gloved hand toward his wrist and he caught her chin with one hand. "You know," he murmured. "You still have some sleep in your eye." He reached out to gently remove it.

Julia leaned away from him, the soft skin of her jawline

74

sliding past his fingers like fleshy silk. "What're you doing – ?"

"Oh, *man* . . ." Danziger groaned, voice raspy with disuse. He leaned his way into the cockpit. "Please tell me I can go back to sleep."

Julia sprang away, stepping well out of Alonzo's reach. The pilot's irritation flared only briefly, squelched by the humor of Danziger's appearance. His hair was clumped in an unruly patch to one side of his head, and packed bags sagged under both of his eyes. Without a doubt, the man suffered from a twenty-two-light-year-old hangover.

"Sorry, pal," the pilot said commiseratingly. "We are *right on course*. I win the betting pool. Tell your guys to fork it over."

Danziger blinked slowly at him. "Lemme guess," he said sourly. "You're a morning person." He leaned back against a console as Julia approached to scan him with her glove.

Alonzo grinned, feeling good and happy to be awake. "Twenty-two light-years is a bitch, huh? First cold sleep?"

"Third," he said and yawned, scratching his hair into further disarray and blinking somewhat stupidly at the starry vista beyond Julia's shoulder. "Never more than nineteen months standard time. I think I had a bizarre dream or something."

The pilot shook his head. "Not me. Been under so many times, I lost my dream button." He shrugged. It was no big deal to him. "Never really get used to how much the world changes, though." Leaning forward, he peeled the photo off his dashboard and studied it for a moment. She had been such a pretty girl, too. Not a knockout like Julia Heller, but a down-home beauty nonetheless. "One long night's sleep," he mused. "And everything you knew . . ." He looked up and smiled wryly, catching Julia's eye. "She's probably a grandmother now anyway," he added with a sigh and tossed the picture into a nearby compartment with only the subtlest sense of regret. You win some, you lose some. "'S why we get the heavy pay, huh?"

He felt eyes other than Julia's on him and looked across at Danziger, who studied him with an intensity bordering on fixation. "How old *are* you, man?"

Alonzo shot him a dazzling smile. "Helluva lot older than you, kid," he responded, leaving both the mechanic and the doctor to wonder whether or not he was telling the truth as he turned back to his controls.

Twenty minutes later, confident that Danziger and Alonzo were functioning just fine (or maybe too fine, in Alonzo's case), Julia returned to the cold-sleep area, summoned there by Devon because Uly would not wake up, would not respond to the sound of her voice. On her knees beside the boy's open capsule, with both hands clasped firmly around one of his, Devon flicked her eyes between her son's pale, unresponsive face and Julia's hands as she ran the diagnostic glove over Uly, checking his vitals at all the necessary points. She tried to be patient when Devon angled her head into her line of sight to take a reading of her own. She appreciated Devon's worry, but why couldn't she let Julia just do her job?

"He's still at ninety-seven," Devon said worriedly.

"That's fine," Julia assured her and moved onto the next point, her glove soft against Uly's neck. The digital readout on his suit confirmed what the glove was telling her.

"He should be responding by now." Panic edged those words, and Devon rubbed her child's hand between her own, watching closely for some sort of response to the contact.

"His cardiorespiratory's improving," Julia read from the glove. "EEG's on target."

"He's taking so long," Devon almost moaned.

"He's also a lot sicker than anyone else aboard," Julia reminded her. "We have to be willing to give him a little extra time to compensate."

"I think a stimulant is indicated." Devon didn't make it a question or a request. There was no "please" attached to it. This was an order.

Julia's eyes met hers over Uly's body, locking for several moments before the doctor took a deep, measured breath and turned toward her bag. She didn't much like orders. She'd bend over backward for someone who asked her for something, but demands ran straight into a stone wall. Devon was the boss, but . . .

Her hand strayed over the bag's contents, choosing nothing from her meager stores, and she turned around again. "Devon," she said with more patience than she felt. "I *do* know what I'm doing. Before apprenticing with Dr. Vasquez, I—"

"Graduated cum laude in Diagnostic Analysis," Devon finished for her. "I checked."

The doctor paused, finding herself not very surprised that Devon knew. It seemed right in keeping with her personality, and what had Julia expected anyway? Did she honestly think Devon Adair would let just *anyone* tend her child? Well, maybe so in this case, when she was the only doctor aboard and Devon didn't have any other choice. "Then you also saw my parents had my chromosomes skewed toward the medical arts," Julia added guardedly.

Devon nodded. "Your background compensates for your lack of experience," she conceded. "But at the moment, my son—"

Julia was saved from any further slings by the sound of coughing. Uly's coughing! She dropped to her knees beside him and ran the glove over him again. Every vital sign showed marked improvement. "Uly? Can you hear me?"

Devon's hands tightened around his as Uly's eyes fluttered open briefly and then dropped closed again. "Uly!" she cried. "Honey, I'm here."

His eyes opened again and tracked around blankly before settling on his mother's features. "Are we there yet?" he asked.

Tears flooded Devon's eyes. She pressed her lips against their joined hands and shot a look of such profound appreciation and gratitude at Julia that the doctor couldn't believe the woman had just been questioning her abilities. Working with Devon was like riding a roller coaster.

"We're almost there," Devon told her son. "We're getting close."

Julia hated to intrude on the reunion, but she needed to get her patient up and moving around. Surprisingly, Devon didn't argue. She even smiled at Julia as she released Uly's hand and sat back out of the way. Bizarre. Just when Julia thought she knew how to handle Devon, the woman did an about-face.

"Uly?" Julia slid one arm under his shoulders. "I'm going to need your help, now . . ." She smiled into the growing wakefulness of the boy's eyes as he slowly sat up and took his first groggy look around.

In another part of the cold-sleep chamber, Danziger leaned against the wall and grinned with amusement as he watched True regain her equilibrium after the long sleep. She was literally running into walls, but it didn't seem to bother her much. She just rebounded off them like a bad billiard shot, and ricocheted in a different direction, to bounce off another wall. It was pretty funny to see, and he probably could have continued watching her for a while, but that didn't seem to be the appropriate fatherly response to her sleepy disorder.

Shoving off the wall himself, he came up behind her, took her shoulders in both hands, and steered her toward the washroom. "C'mon, honey. Buzz your teeth. You gotta help me up top."

She was so out of it, she didn't even ask about breakfast, a subject near and dear to her heart, as was anything having to do with food. Her head lolled backward, her hair brushing his hands. "I'm getting a cat, right?" she slurred, still half-asleep and drooling slightly out of the corner of her mouth. "I dreamed I got a cat."

Her father nodded, humoring her, and stuck a small, sonar toothbuzz into her hand. "A *real* cat?" He smiled. "Did you dream we won the Tran-Station Lottery, too?"

"Hey!" True exclaimed, fighting her way out of sleepiness. "You said we were gonna be richer."

"I didn't say we'd be billionaires," he teased. "Do you know what a pet allotment costs?" He turned her around and once again gently shoved her in the direction of the washroom. "Now, c'mon. Meet me up on deck." He let her go and turned away, only to have her suddenly spin about and grab his sleeve hard enough to nearly yank him off his feet.

She drew him down until their faces were almost touching and stared him straight in the eye, wide awake and completely lucid. Her breath was *bad*. "Lemme make this clear, Dad," she said seriously, biting the words off and piecing them together in little chunks so he couldn't miss a bit of what she had to say It was a habit he had himself when he was particularly pissed off. "After we drop them off, and we get home, I get a cat. Not a cheap-o synth cat. A real cat. No discussion. Un'erstand?" Her nose and eyebrows touched his, and her eyes all but bore into him.

He stared back, knowing from hard-earned experience

that this was not one of those times to mess with True, whether or not he was her father. Besides, he *had* sorta-kinda promised her they might get a cat when this trip was over. *Might*.

She read the look in his eyes correctly and smiled with the satisfaction of someone scoring a point. Stepping back, she released his sleeve. "Good," she said nonchalantly, all of the challenge gone. "I'll meet you on deck." She vanished into the washroom.

Danziger watched her go, momentarily stunned once again by the force of his daughter's personality. Then a slow, happy, and undeniably proud grin crossed his features. He had a lot of respect for that scrappy kid of his. Whistling, he headed toward Ops to collect his gear.

"I can't believe I'm doing this," Morgan said in a grousing tone, sticking his legs into clean slacks and pulling them up. Fresh from the showers, his hair stuck up all over his head in damp little tufts. "I mean, I hate travel, I hate that Devon woman—Miss Stop-The-World-My-Son-Is-Sick-My-Cyborg-Tutor-And-I-Want-To-Get-Off." He rammed his arms into his shirtsleeves and pulled the garment on over his head, then paused reflectively with his head half-out of the collar. "How could I be so stupid? Two-year salary, level-four upgrade . . . They were going to kill me, Bess—*me*." He tugged the shirt on the rest of the way and pulled it straight. "I've practically given them my *soul* . . ." He thrust a finger at his wife. "I'll tell you what we're gonna do. We're gonna stake ourselves a little mining claim on good old G889. And we're gonna catch a ride home on that Colony ship, sell those rights, and . . ." He flung his hands into the air. Well, the rest was obvious!

When he got no response to these terrific plans, he looked more closely at Bess. She was sitting on the bed staring into a wall-mounted mirror. One hand was against her face, moving almost wonderingly over the skin, and she didn't look as if she'd heard a single word he'd said. "What?" he asked irritably, not liking the way she stared at her reflection. "What're you looking at?"

Bess's expression was bleak. "I feel older," she murmured quietly, studying her face from every angle.

Morgan rolled his eyes. "You're not. We went over this. We were in suspended animation. We *didn't* age. It's *impossible*. Okay?"

His wife nodded, still staring into the mirror. Her unhappy expression never changed. "I didn't say I *was* older. I said I *feel* older. You can't suspend feelings." Her eyes met his in the mirror, pain-filled and lonely.

Morgan stepped closer and took her hand away from her face, bending to gently kiss the top of her head. "Sweetie, I'm sorry. I'm just under a lot of pressure. You *know* you're my whole world."

She looked up at him, clearly scared, confused, and uncertain about so many things. He smiled confidently at her, finally won a shaky smile out of her in return, and bent to meet her lips with his.

Anything that might have followed from the kiss was interrupted by O'Neill's voice coming over every intercom and echoing throughout the entire ship. "Our destination isn't just some dim dust point in the distant universe anymore, people. It's near." Somewhere, thrusters activated, and Morgan felt a subtle difference in the ship's movement. "Those of you who are just dropping us off, our flight crew—arigato. The rest of you, have your fun now. Upon touchdown, the *work* begins!"

The comm line went dead. In the moment of silence immediately following, Bess and Morgan stared at each other with wide eyes, romance forgotten; then they suddenly flew into a frenzy of activity, shoving everything within reach into the nearest carrying case in anticipation of the drop planetside.

Morgan's mind churned as he worked, hardly paying attention to what he was doing, Bess's silly age worries forgotten. What a *deal* he was going to squeeze out of the mining company back on Earth for the rights to this place! He hadn't been the government's top negotiator for nothing. In just a short while, he and Bess were going to be fixed for *life*!

Chapter 6

· · · · · ● ● ●

True frowned when she worked. She always had, from about the age of eighteen months on, immersing herself so deeply into whatever oddity currently captured her fancy that little lines and ridges furrowed her brow like an old woman's. The two between her eyes had become permanent a long time ago. She couldn't decide whether she liked that or not. At times, staring in the mirror every morning as she buzzed her teeth, she thought they gave character to her young face, made her look older, wiser, and more like her father, which she usually didn't mind in the least. At other times, she despaired that she was already beginning to look ancient and a lot like her father, which, if they'd just had one of their tiffs, she most certainly did *not* want to have happen.

Right now she was cramped into an extremely narrow

corridor, kneeling on legs beginning to stiffen from being in the same position too long, and from taking a meticulous inventory of the ship's mechanical tools. She frowned as she worked, well aware she was doing it and knowing there was nothing she could do about it. A habit was a habit. She logged each tool's bar code and quantity into a monitor strapped around her slender wrist.

Her mind was half on what she was doing, and half on what she would name her cat when she got her. Him? It was hard to say. Not that it mattered. She'd take whatever was available. She'd waited so long and worked so hard to convince her father to let her have an animal, that she wasn't about to quibble over the cat's gender. It would just be nice to have something to cuddle and hold and talk to and have sleep on her bed . . . besides a stuffed animal, of course. *Those* couldn't respond except in your imagination. True sometimes felt that her imagination was losing some of its zing and becoming a little dry and brittle at the edges. She wondered if that was one of the warning signs of encroaching adulthood.

She was so immersed in a name search for her cat that she didn't realize there was anyone else around until a mechanical clanking impinged on her awareness. She sneaked a peek past her shoulder and then raised her hand to stare openly at Uly approaching from the far end of the corridor. He walked with painstaking care and slowness, trapped in the confines of his immuno-suit and braces. It was the braces that made the clanking noise on the bulkhead with every carefully precise step the boy took.

What True had meant to be a passing, negligent regard of whoever was there became a transfixed perusal of macabre fascination. She'd never been this close to a Syndrome kid before, and it was a lot different from seeing them on vid (she always changed the channel anyway).

Though he was only a little kid, and skinny besides, he was a lot scarier up close than she'd have believed possible. His skin looked bleached, paler than any she'd ever seen before, and without a single hint of the healthy color that bloomed in her own cheeks. It clung to his bones in a gaunt, hollow-eye-socket sort of way that made him look like she thought a corpse might. The immuno-suit made him appear as if he were something from another planet.

He caught her watching and clanked to a halt just a few feet away. The only sound in the sudden silence was his pronounced, heavy breathing as he drew air through the suit's respirator. True wondered if the suit was doing the breathing for him, whether or not he already might be just as good as dead.

Dead or not, he still had a voice. "Please don't stare at me," he asked, his tone polite but more weary and full of age than the voice of an eight-year-old child had any right to be.

"I'm not!" she challenged, lying, but preferring to die rather than admit it. Blush heated her cheeks with guilt, but she wasn't about to look away now and have him think . . . What? Well, have him think anything he liked.

Her staring probably made him uncomfortable, but he was damned if he was going to show it. His eyes met hers in an almost blatant challenge, and the time for a friendly salutation from either of them was past, if it had ever been there at all.

True might have gone on staring forever if she hadn't looked past Uly and seen Yale approaching, pushing a wheelchair before him. Curiosity squirmed again. She wanted to check *him* out almost more than she wanted Uly to drop his eyes first. Something like the old cyborg was foreign to her, and she was fascinated by him. Imagine something so old still working as well as he (it?) did! Every one of the Yale series of Teacher Class had been recalled a long time ago and reprogrammed or dismantled . . . except for him. She didn't know why, but she figured it must have something to do with Uly's mother. Now Yale was outdated, a relic from another era, an antique, whose failing human anatomy had been replaced with robotics in an age when something was immediately recycled when it outlived its usefulness.

That thought gave her pause. Yale's still being around might be Devon's doing, but that meant the old man was still useful, to Devon at least. Why that was so, True couldn't imagine, but the concept of advanced age and usefulness had never come together for her before. They were supposed to be mutually exclusive terms, weren't they? Still, it was a new, complex, and intriguing idea, and one she would mull over later, after the kid was gone and she'd decided on a name for her cat.

Yale's broad smile, directed right at her, told her she'd been staring again. Unlike Uly, he looked more amused by it than bothered, but he'd probably had a lot more years to get used to it than the kid.

She dropped her eyes immediately, uncomfortable in his presence, and focused on the open case of tools by her knees and the wrist monitor blinking patiently, waiting for the next row of bar codes to be input.

"Uly? Don't wear yourself out now." The wheelchair hummed quietly at True's back as Yale brought it to a halt. "Well, hello," he said, directing the remark at the top of her bent head. "We'd heard there was another child on board."

Child?! Who was he calling a *child*?! Insulted as she was, True kept her attention focused on her knees and the open container of tools, trying to remember where she left off so she could do more than look like she was just sitting there. "My dad's on Operations," she mumbled toward the tools, not wanting to be completely rude but trying her best to give the impression that she was too darned busy to be interrupted right now, sorry and thank you.

"Well." She heard the humor in the Teacher's voice and it goaded her. Her back stiffened. Was he making fun of her in some way, or was her own embarrassment worrying her? "Too bad we'll be parting ways soon," he finished.

"Mm-hmm." She bent her head lower over her work, scanning the tools and knowing she'd have to recheck the numbers to make sure she hadn't entered something twice or made some other stupid mistake. Thanks to these two, she'd end up doing double duty.

A silent moment passed, and then movement made her hazard a glance over her shoulder. She watched with interest the invalid *and* the cyborg. Yale helped Uly get comfortable in the chair and then turned him down the corridor, back the way they'd come. His head bent to pick up something the boy said, and he chuckled deeply, but True didn't waste time wondering if the remark was about her. Wait until she got back home! There would be a whole new slew of mechanics' kids to impress. Between the Adair kid and Yale, she'd have enough story fodder to last her for *months*. No one was going to *believe* this!

The other half of the Adair family sat in their room studying architectural drawings of the soon-to-be Eden Colony on the wall monitor. Even after hundreds of hours of perusal and deliberation and changes and modifications, Devon still found the blueprints both fascinating and worrisome. Even more amazing was the knowledge that soon these "mere"

87

drawings would become a tangible reality, a new place to live, a home, a haven where Uly and all the other Syndrome kids could grow and thrive the way they were supposed to.

At least, that was the dream. And she'd kill herself to make it a reality for her child.

She reached out and hit the keyboard to change the angle of the drawings, for the umpteenth time needing to make sure they were just right. As the current drawing circled around, O'Neill's florid face unexpectedly appeared in miniature in the corner of the vid screen. He was brimming with the self-satisfaction he hadn't put aside since their run from the space station. "You better get in here, Devon!" he enthused, eyes shining with delight. "You're going to love this!"

She knew at once what he meant, what he *must* mean. Flying out of her chair, she burst out of her stateroom, bounced off the wall, and raced down the corridor. Anticipation built to an inferno within her as Devon wove through the narrow space, barely avoiding other crew and passengers as she passed, whipping off quick apologies to those with whom she momentarily collided.

She took a corner too fast, fouled her feet, skidded into the wall, and kept going down the corridor toward the elevator to the cockpit. A door opened on her right as she blazed past. "What's going on?" someone asked. She recognized the querying voice as Morgan's. Beyond that, she didn't give a fig. She slammed into the elevator, watched the doors close on Morgan's astonished face, and all but danced a jig during the short trip to the cockpit. Why was everything moving so damned *slowly*?

When the doors opened, she streaked out of the elevator and charged into the cockpit. There she was brought up short, stumbling to a stop, her eyes transfixed by the sight of their hard-won goal.

It was gorgeous. It was *beyond* gorgeous, but she didn't have any words for that. It was so much more than the sum of its parts, all those surveys and reports and satellite pictures. They were hypothesis and conjecture. This was the real thing.

O'Neill glanced at her, clearly loath to tear his eyes away from the gemlike planet in the center of the screen. He shifted to make room for her behind Alonzo's chair. "Check 'er out, Devon," he murmured with undisguised pride. Well, let him. He had every reason to be proud. They all did. Turning dreams into reality is a heady sort of miracle making when it's actually achieved. She was just having a hard time believing they'd actually done it.

Their new home was no longer a holographic image shot from the end of Yale's arm. No longer was it just a speck in the distant somewhere, sometimes seemingly no more than a willful woman's conjecture. Now it was *real*, a magnificent blue, white, and green orb floating in the near distance against a backdrop of constellations she didn't recognize now, but would have time to learn over the years of showing them to Uly and, God willing, her grandchildren. Discernible land masses, banks of swirling clouds, and massive oceans defined the planet's contours and made it, without a doubt, the second most beautiful thing Devon had ever seen (next to her newborn son, of course). She didn't know what to say, or how to say it if she managed to find the words. She just watched it, openmouthed and utterly awestruck.

O'Neill grinned, and his big chest rumbled with laughter as he wrapped an arm around her shoulders and pulled her close. "I never thought I'd see the day when Devon Adair was at a loss for words," he said and chuckled. "There you go, Dev. Just what you ordered. A new place to call home."

Home. Somewhere deep inside, a dam burst. Devon

threw back her head and pealed laughter with sheer exhilaration. She startled the hell out of O'Neill when she threw her arms around him and squeezed the daylights out of him. She even bent down and gave Alonzo a hug that he was more than willing to accept, his soft laughter warm against her ear. Behind them, Morgan, who had followed her in his single-minded quest to be the nosiest person in the universe, went up on his toes and squinted past the jumble of their shoulders. "We made it," he breathed in amazement.

O'Neill nodded, hands planted firmly on his hips, and looked every inch the conquering hero he probably felt like. "Other side of the stars," he agreed.

Alonzo released Devon to let his experienced fingers catwalk among the controls, touching where needed and leaving alone what was fine. "Take a gander at the landmass you folks call New Pacifica," he invited. The line of monitors directly in front of them bloomed with a variety of aerial images: lush landscapes green with vegetation, jagged coastlines being alternately caressed and bludgeoned by bright blue waters, and serene mountain tops, their summits dusted with a white so pure and pristine it was almost blinding as the sun reflected off of it.

O'Neill thumped his fist into the headrest of Alonzo's chair. "We did it," he growled. "Let Dison Blalock chew on this for a while."

Emotion as painfully clean and sharp as a scalpel's blade sliced through Devon, silencing anything she might have added. Suddenly she didn't *know* what to say. What to do came easier, though, as a desire to escape overwhelmed her. Turning blindly, her eyes filled with sudden tears, she feverishly pushed past the others. Behind her, O'Neill called her name, voicing a question, but she ran on, unheeding, out of the cockpit and back through the ship, retracing her steps as swiftly as she'd first made them, weaving through the narrow hallways and trying hard, trying oh so hard, to contain her erupting, overflowing emotions in the face of so many curious stares from so many strangers.

Uly was hovering just outside their stateroom, obviously trying to work the lock and not having a very good time of it. He looked up at the sound of her running steps. His face lit with relief, instantly replaced by concern as he *really* saw her. "Mom? Are you all right, Mom?"

She brushed past him without replying, hoping she could apologize later, hoping she could make him understand she could not stop, not right now. At this very moment, and for the first time since Uly's birth, she had nothing to give him, nothing she could spare. She needed it all, every resource she had, just to make it inside the stateroom and close the door behind her before she burst into tears.

She was in her chair, though she couldn't remember crossing the room. Emotion that had built for years suddenly found an egress. Shoulders shaking, she sobbed harshly, but not with sadness. With pride. What Devon shed were tears of success.

Their exhilaration temporarily spent in a euphoric satisfaction, it was time for Alonzo and O'Neill to get back to work. As the Commander watched, Alonzo triggered a switch he'd been itching to use ever since waking up. A massive incendiary blast cut loose a portion of the ship. The communication dish separated as cleanly and prettily as anyone could want and tumbled into the planet's gravitational pull.

"Communication dish released," Alonzo reported, watching it spin out of sight and tracking it on the ship's monitors. "Commencing aero-capture . . . three, two, one . . .

Entry. Gravity gradient four-dash-five and rising. On target for New Pacifica."

The ship's cameras followed the enormous dish as it pierced the arid, cloud-covered, blue atmosphere with ferocious force and plummeted toward the ground below and its targeted landing point.

"Okay," the Commander murmured soothingly, almost seductively. He crossed his arms and leaned on the back of the pilot's chair. "Easy does it there, girl . . . Drag and stage . . . Make Daddy proud. Propulsion *shift*. Oh, yes . . ."

On the video screen, the comm dish thrusters engaged. The landing gear slowly lowered, and three chutes opened to slow the rapid descent of the dish. "Propulsion entry has been initiated," the pilot reported and sharpened the cameras' focus. In the next few crucial, heartbreaking moments, the comm dish made an utterly perfect landing, as beautiful as anything Alonzo had ever seen or done before. He brushed his hands together. "That was one perfect touchdown."

O'Neill's beaming satisfaction made the pilot grin and shake his head. Evidently Papa was proud of his baby.

Her composure regained, Devon sat shoulder-to-shoulder with Uly in front of the vid screen in their stateroom, their eyes fixed upon an orbital image of their new planet. Devon could not seem to pull her eyes from the screen. There it sat, and still she couldn't quite believe it, couldn't quite comprehend they were really *here*, G889 and New Pacifica weren't just elusive dreams anymore.

Fixed as her gaze was, she was not unaware of Uly's presence, his breathing heavy but hushed, as though he might be afraid of breaking the moment by breathing too loudly. His hand slowly slid into hers and curled beneath her fingers. A flick of her eyes showed he wasn't looking at her, but at the image on the screen. When he spoke, his voice was barely audible even with him close enough to hug.

"Thank you, Mom," he said softly. Suddenly everything was as perfect as Devon could ever hope it to be.

Chapter 7

Commander O'Neill settled into the vacant copilot's seat and hunched closer to the vid screen microphone. "We all set?" he asked.

Chin propped indolently in one hand and his elbow firmly planted in the one space on his control board that didn't contain a button, a switch, a microphone, or a screen, Alonzo nodded. "All's ready and waiting, Commander. You're set to air anytime you're ready."

An anticipatory grin lit O'Neill's features. "Then there's no time like the present."

Alonzo knew a cue when he heard one. "Aye, aye, sir," he replied, and flicked a switch with one long finger. His nod told O'Neill the channel was clear for transmission, that it would beam his message not only to every vid aboard ship, but back home to the Earth system as well—the *entire* Earth system.

"Sector Seven, this is Commanding Officer Broderick O'Neill of the Eden Project. I know it'll be a few years before you pick this up, but guess where we are? Transmitting from none other than our fully operational dish at New Pacifica on Planet G889." He rubbed his hands together, warming to his role, and wished mightily that he could be there to see the look on Dison Blalock's face when he got the news.

"And I just want to say to all of you who haven't retired by now—Blalock, Adam, McMann, and everyone else I butted heads with at Pluto Six over the years—and I mean this from the heart, you can all kiss my star-spangled butt!" Supremely smug and satisfied as hell, O'Neill flipped off the comm mike with a flourish and leaned back in his chair. The techs in the cockpit cheered, having given up trying to control their laughter, and he wished the same for everyone else on board. They could all use a good, hearty laugh after everything they'd gone through to get here, and if it was at the expense of those bastards back on the station, then so much the better.

He glanced at Alonzo, who eyed him with an extremely wry expression. "What?"

The pilot pursed his lips and shrugged innocently. "Feeling a little cocky, huh?"

O'Neill snorted. "Just a little." He stood and patted him on the back. "Solace, you put that cargo down as nicely as that dish, we're in business."

Alonzo popped a nod. "You say stack 'em, I'll say how high," he singsonged and poised his hands over his board.

"Commence at your discretion, pal. I'll be in the head." He rose and headed for the door. They had endured betrayal and sabotage to get here and it felt damned good to thumb his nose at those who tried to destroy their dream and them along with it. If he could have sent back more than just a verbal transmission, he might have been tempted to moon the bastards besides. Let them eat *that* for breakfast, along with a hefty helping of crow!

Behind him, Alonzo initiated the cargo release sequence and then said something softly that earned him delighted laughter from the rest of the cockpit crew. Good. Laughter was the right thing to have happening right now, and the more the better.

O'Neill left the cockpit and traversed a short angle of hallway before stepping into the bathroom and closing the vacuum door. From inside this tiny space no larger than the proverbial broom closet, outside sounds were muffled and all but inaudible. Not really needing to relieve himself, O'Neill put down the toilet seat and sat on it, taking a moment to bask in the brief luxury of utter privacy. Finally content and at one with the universe, he reached into the inner pocket of his jacket and pulled out a thin glass tube containing a single perfect Earth Cigar. He turned the slender capsule in his hands, admiring its beauty, and then the beauty of its contents. Buying it had cost him dearly, but it was guaranteed genuine and to taste every bit as wonderful as it looked, and that made it all worth it.

He slid the tube back and forth between his hands, enjoying the sleek feel of the glass against his skin, then uncapped the cylinder, slid the cigar out between two fingers, and placed the empty tube on a shelf over the sink. He ran the cigar under his nose, inhaling its fragrance like a rich perfume, then placed it between his lips. Savoring the bitter taste of dried tobacco against his tongue, he lit the cigar from the tiny flame of his Swiss army knife. The tobacco crackled; he puffed and it caught, flaring brightly for a moment before succumbing to a rosy glow that increased to a ruddy hue with every inhalation. Smoke lifted on the exhale and circled around his head, wreathing him like a woodcut of Santa Claus with his pipe, before being drawn upward through the ventilator. He breathed evenly, pulling the smoke deeply into his lungs and holding it there a moment to appreciate the full enjoyment of this particular blend. Yes, sir, it was certainly worth it, just as the black marketeer had promised.

For a while, time stood still. The only things that existed were the little cubicle, the cigar, and O'Neill. It was one of the few truly perfect moments in the Commander's life, and he couldn't remember the last time he had been so happy. The only thing that could make this day any better would be if—

A slight rumble shook the bathroom. O'Neill glanced around curiously and watched the empty cigar tube roll slightly back and forth. The shaking increased slightly. Before he could catch it, the tube rolled straight off the shelf and shattered on the floor, exploding into a thousand tiny shards. O'Neill blinked around in confusion and half stood—

—and the entire ship rocked with a violence that almost threw him to his knees. O'Neill slammed hard against the wall. The cigar went flying, leaving behind an ash mark as it bounced off the opposite wall and disappeared behind the toilet. He grappled for the door handle, slipped, and grabbed for it again, turning it the wrong way first and fighting to get it open as a deafening alarm began to blare from the loudspeakers overhead.

The corridor beyond swarmed with panicking passengers and crew, all of them asking what and why in a babble of frenzied, frightened voices. The sheer press of bodies almost forced O'Neill back into the bathroom. Fighting hard to keep his balance against the swarming mass, he breasted the flood like a large animal swimming against the tide. The ship shook uncontrollably as he pushed his way along the corridor and burst into the cockpit.

Alonzo, his face devoid of color and his clothing soaked with the sweat of his terror, struggled with the ship's controls, fighting with them manually to retain mastery of the ship.

"What the hell's happening?!" O'Neill roared over the noise.

"Cargo pods won't release!" Alonzo yelled, his grip so tight on the controls that his knuckles were white. "They're dragging us down!"

O'Neill's eyes darted to the window beyond the pilot's frantically shaking shoulders. The first pod was only half-disengaged, glowing orange as it buffeted the atmosphere, pulling them down with it. In the background, G889 loomed toward them, coming on *fast*. He lunged for the intercom. "Ops crew! Disengage the damn cargo pod! Dump it! Now!"

The screen at his elbow flared to life with Danziger's ashen face. He waved a bloodied hand at O'Neill. "Release mech is jammed!" he yelled. "We picked up a heavy magnetic charge—"

"Then blow 'em off!" O'Neill roared, thoroughly pissed off and scared as hell. They had come this far, *so* far, and it wasn't going to end like this, dammit! It wasn't! "Do it—"

"Charges are ineffective!" Danziger spat back, fury and fear warring in his eyes. "You think I haven't tried?! It's not working! If you think you can do better—!" His line went dead, leaving O'Neill staring at a blank screen. All around him, passengers screamed.

If she'd been asked, Devon would not have thought she could run so long or so fast with Uly in her arms. Alone, he was a featherweight. The added poundage of the immuno-suit made him a heavy armful, but it was an armful she would not relinquish under any circumstances.

She pushed her way against the flood of panic-stricken passengers and crew as they squeezed past her, fleeing in every direction with no rhyme or reason, in a desperate hunt for safety and escape. Behind her strode Yale, a steadying presence at her back, his arms full of whatever had been nearest to grab in the last instant before they fled the stateroom.

"Everything will be fine!" he shouted to anyone with the wits to listen and take heed. "There are three e-vac pods with enough room for everyone! Do not panic!"

He'd have better success whistling down the wind. Panic ruled these people's lives right now, a panic which might see them all dead in a few minutes if someone didn't take charge.

But that someone was not Devon Adair, not this time. This time she refused to answer that familiar siren's call. All that mattered was getting Uly to safety. The others were on their own for now. She was surprised she didn't feel more guilty about it, then forgot about that as well as she fought against the surge of bodies forcing her back from her goal.

Morgan shoved Bess out into the corridor, pushing her along with his hand crammed into the small of her back and practically running her over in his frenzied search for some avenue of escape. "We're not going down with this thing, Bess!" he vowed, more terrified than his brave words would allow. Rank fear followed him everywhere. "We're not dying on this thing!"

"But our stuff!" she wailed, trying to turn back despite the overnight bag she clutched to her chest.

Morgan grabbed her roughly by the elbow and kept her

going forward, dragging her along in his wake, pulling her so fast that she nearly stumbled and fell. Unlike so many of the others aboard, Morgan knew exactly where he was going. He proudly acknowledged the fact that he was the sort who routinely searched out an avenue of escape from wherever he was, be it a trundle-cab, a conference board-room, or a neighbor's kitchen. It always paid to know the quickest route out of a situation, in case things turned nasty. He knew where each one of those escape pods was located.

Even so, he was more than a little surprised when they reached the one he had in mind and found it empty, with not another single, solitary person in sight. Great luck! They wouldn't have to fight to get on board!

Bess ran a hand through her disheveled hair. "Morgan, how did you know this was here?"

Without preamble, he opened the door and shoved her inside. From somewhere down at the other end of the corridor, he heard a voice call out, "True! True, where are you?" It was that mechanic, Danziger, looking for his snotty kid. Well, if he was thinking about coming with them, he was out of luck. This pod was taken, and it wasn't as if there was time to hang around waiting for people. The damn ship might break up at any second.

Morgan climbed in after Bess, slammed the door closed behind them, dogged the catch, and locked it. He heard Danziger cry out. "Hey! Hey, don't leave yet! Hey!" He looked up and met the mechanic's eyes through the door window. From the expression on Danziger's face, it seemed that it was clear to him who Morgan was and what he had just done.

"Morgan, help me!" Bess wailed, searching for her seat harness. She was too petrified to do anything with it once she found it. "I can't fasten this thing!"

Morgan could not tear his eyes away from Danziger's.

"Bess, hold on!" he snapped at his wife with enough force to silence her. "Don't worry! We're not gonna die!" He held Danziger's gaze for a moment longer, feeling it practically sear onto the back of his brain, then turned away and yanked the release lever. The pod disengaged with a loud *phoomp!* and they fell away, spiraling down from the vessel and hurtling toward the planet's atmosphere, with Bess's scream following them down like a vapor trail.

Alonzo knew it was a disaster. There was no way to win with controls that would no longer respond to his command. The ship was going to shake herself apart around him and send him drifting into space. Well, there were probably worse ways to go . . .

He shook himself. Screw that! There was nothing on *his* personal agenda that said *anything* about the captain going down with his ship.

Beside him, O'Neill threw his hands up in futility. "Forget it, Solace! Abort! Now!" He grabbed a weapon and shoulder holster from the rack near the door and raced out of the cockpit, leading the rest of the crew toward the pods.

Desperate, hating to see a well-built, responsive vessel go down without a good fight, Alonzo tried one last maneuver. For an instant, he thought it had caught, but then it fizzled like all the others. Somewhere, he thought he heard fate give a triumphant laugh. Heart wrenching with despair, he flung a final glance around the cockpit, wishing the ship well and checking for any stragglers, then followed O'Neill.

He couldn't *believe* it!

Rage fueled Danziger, sending him hurtling back the way he'd come, frenziedly searching every crevice and corner for his missing daughter. He couldn't believe Morgan was so . . . so . . . Words failed him. There wasn't an epithet

102

anywhere in the universe foul enough to describe what Morgan had just done.

Danziger felt sorry for Bess, sorrier than he'd ever felt for another human being. He wished her no harm, but if there was any order to the universe at all, Morgan's pod would break up into a million tiny pieces on its way to the planet's surface. Better yet, let them crash-land with Bess surviving and Morgan reduced to a pile of jellied goo that looked like something True's hypothetical cat had coughed up. Yeah. That would work. That would suit Danziger just *fine*.

He burst into the cold-sleep area, his eyes darting from place to place. "True!" He flung open the first locker, slamming its door back against the row. Nothing and no one inside. He moved on to the next one. "True! C'mon! We gotta go!"

As Murphy's Law always postulates (and quite accurately, too), what you're looking for is always in the last place you look. He found her in the final locker, frozen with fear and cowering on the floor, with her arms wrapped around herself in a tight hug, her face against her knees, and crying harder than he'd ever seen. He grabbed her arm and hauled her to her feet. She was unresponsive to his touch, spaghetti-like and listless under his hands, hardly able to stand even as he pushed her ahead of him, starting her in a staggering run toward where the other pods were berthed.

In the corridor ahead, people raced toward them in a bid for safety. Danziger waved his arms in warning. "No pod down there!" he shouted. "It's gone! Gotta turn back!"

They back-stepped, halting, turning, surging back on a steady flow of people down the corridor, the two groups slamming into one another like the waters of a river converging with the ocean. Some fell, disappearing under the tramping swell of so many feet. Danziger breasted that surging human surf with his child pushed before him, breaking a trail and leading the way to what he hoped would be safety for them all.

It wasn't. They reached the second pod only to have the door slam closed in their faces. This was too much like the first time! Danziger pounded furiously on the door, peering in at the closely packed confines and the terrified faces of the passengers.

"No room!" the ship's navigator screamed at them through the portal. "Too many people already! Take the other one!" *Phoomp!* That hated sound, and the pod was gone.

Take the other one. *So simply said,* Danziger thought. *Let's just hope there is another one.* He turned and ran, his heart laboring in his chest, and the others followed blindly, sheep behind the only one who seemed to know where he was going.

Racing for the pod, borne along on the rushing tide of people whether he liked it or not and trying not to be crushed in the process, Alonzo heard a woman scream. Canting his head back and forth, trying to see beyond the surging roll of heads and shoulders, he spied Julia on her knees in the middle of the corridor. An empty medical satchel lay open beside her, and she was frantically trying to gather up its strewn contents as the panicking passengers trod blindly on her and her supplies, breaking them, stepping on her fingers and tripping over her, knocking her onto her side and threatening to trample her to death in the blindness of their fear.

Alonzo pushed toward her, back-stepping so as not to overshoot his mark. Reaching her, he bent down, grabbed a handful of whatever lay nearest, crammed them into the bag, and shoved the whole thing into Julia's arms. "C'mon! We're out of time! The ship's breaking up!"

Clutching the bag under one arm, Julia struggled to grab more of her supplies, stuffing them into her pockets as fast as she could. "No!" she screamed. "Not without my equipment!" Overhead, compartments popped open like gaping mouths and spewed their contents, raining detritus down on their heads.

"Stupid, stubborn woman—!" Alonzo swore. He almost left her, then and there. In fact, he let her think he would, dancing on the balls of his feet, as if to flee with the others. Suddenly he turned and grabbed her around the waist, hoisted her into the air and carried her, kicking and screaming, toward the open portal and the waiting pod.

Somewhere ahead he heard O'Neill yell the impossible words "Leave it! We're giving her up—" He didn't know if the Commander meant Julia or the ship, but a cry of rage and horror welled out of him as Devon's voice sliced through the cacophony and countermanded the order with one of her own.

"Not yet! C'mon! Hurry, everyone!"

Ahead of him, Danziger and his daughter dove through the doorway. Well, Mama Solace had raised no idiots. Adair didn't have to tell him twice. Clutching Julia, not caring if he broke every bone in her body, Alonzo began to run.

He hurled Julia inside the e-vac pod, thrusting her far enough into the overly crowded compartment so that she couldn't try to make some stupid break for it and go back for her trashed supplies. Danziger was backed against a wall, clutching True, her eyes wide and frightened over the false security of his arms. Devon was on the floor, holding her boy for all she was worth, with the old Teacher standing like a protecting god over them both.

Alonzo spared Devon a brief nod of thanks, his gratitude enormous, and vacuum sealed the portal behind him. A flick of his eyes over the crowd showed them all to be as secure as the crowded confines would allow. His heart broke a little at the ship's cries as she creaked and groaned around him, breaking up, dying. He reached for the release lever. "Everyone inside?" he asked.

"Disengage, man!" O'Neill ordered from the back of the pod, his voice thunderous. "Disengage!"

"I said—" Solace repeated clearly, yelling to be heard over the outside noise, "everyone inside?!" His eyes were not on O'Neill, but on Devon. He hadn't really given any thought before to which of them was his boss. It hadn't seemed important. The Eden Foundation had contracted him for a lot of money, and that was all he cared about.

Or rather, that *had been* all he cared about. Things had changed subtly with Devon's order to wait, and if there was a question in anyone's mind as to whom Alonzo considered his boss to be, this should answer it.

Devon nodded, her face strained and white over her son's bowed head. "Go," she said quietly.

He returned the nod and pulled the lever hard. *Phoomp!*

It was awful. Worse than anything he could ever have imagined and far worse than any training he had ever undergone. The pod rattled violently, shaking them from side to side as they fell, like loose stones in a can. They were a dead weight careening toward the ground, clutching at whatever support they could find, even one another, bracing themselves for the dreadful impact and all of them too petrified to cry out. For an instant, Alonzo glimpsed through the window the Advance ship tumbling end over end, spewing cargo pod sectionals.

". . . Father who art in Heaven." Yale's voice rose above the racket. "Protect us with your strength as we are guided—"

"Dad!" True Danziger shrieked. Raised on her toes, she stared out the single port-side window. "We're gonna hit!"

Chapter 8

· · · · · · ● ● ●

O'Neill had known battles and their aftermath. It was brought home to him, in the stunned moments directly after their crash landing, that one battle was much like another. Whether or not you had armaments had very little to do with it, really. People fought battles of all sorts every day, and the aftereffects were the same no matter what sort of warfare was waged.

The interior of the e-vac pod was dark, the lights having blown on impact with a flash of almost eye-boiling brightness. Thin fissures of natural light filtered in through cracks in the pod's carapace, lending just enough eerie illumination to the scene to allow O'Neill to make out the humped and huddled shapes of those thrown about by the impact—Alonzo's bright eyes, Devon's cheekbone etched with a fine line of light, Uly in her arms and Yale crouched over them,

Danziger and his kid flat on their backs, Julia blinking about in confusion, Baines and two more of the crew, Walman and Magus, and four colonists whose names he didn't know. Two of those were crying uncontrollably, torn by fear or pain or perhaps both. Others swore, using phrases which even the Commander, with all his past military experience, found unfamiliar. Slowly, they began to shift, jostling back and forth, fighting to collect and orient themselves. Her medical satchel still clutched under one arm, Julia slowly rose and began moving from person to person, asking if anyone needed her help. O'Neill didn't think she was getting much in the way of coherent responses.

Shoving his way through the tumbled jumble of people sorting themselves out, O'Neill headed toward where he remembered the hatch being. "Everyone!" he ordered, pitching his voice above the rising noise of impending panic and using the tone that never failed to gain him an appropriate response, from recruits on up through the higher echelons of the military. The garbled conversations and weeping fell to a low hush. "Shut up and stay calm," he urged them. He bent close beside Baines, who had beaten him to the door and now sat with his head bent over a series of gauges set into the bulkhead. "Do we have a reading?"

"I'm processing." He shook his head after a moment's consideration of the readout dials. "Can't get anything," he said with disappointment.

"What do you mean, can't?" the Commander countered, not willing to accept that conclusion. "We need an atmospheric reading—"

"I understand that, sir," Baines replied, voice edgy with a testiness O'Neill decided was prudent not to challenge. They were all stressed, and any of them was likely to fly off the handle at a moment's notice "But I'm not getting

108

anything. The sensors are down, probably trashed. I'm getting no reading at all."

No reading at all. Crapshoot. They needed to know if the atmosphere was safe before opening the door, but now they needed to open the door in order to check the atmosphere.

"Open the hatch," Devon said quietly from the rear of the pod. O'Neill looked over and found her on her feet beside Yale, who had Uly in his arms. His eyes were shut, his head pillowed against the big man's shoulder. It was impossible to tell in this light if he was injured . . . or dead. If he *was* dead, it would kill Devon as well.

Every eye was on Devon—hopeful, watchful, trusting her to make the right choice since it was because of her that they were all here in the first place. It occurred to O'Neill (and not for the first time) to wonder just who was really the commanding officer of this project.

They shared a long look and then she shrugged. He glimpsed bare skin through a rip in the arm of her shirt as the cloth moved. "There's nowhere else to go," she said. "We can't stay in here."

She had that right. Despite the fine-line hull cracks, the air was already becoming thick and stale. O'Neill cleared his throat and elbowed Baines out of the way. "Brace, people. Hatch opening." Gears twisted beneath his hands. He thought for a minute it was going to stick, then the hatch slid smoothly aside and light flooded in, bringing with it a rush of foreign air.

Everyone held his or her breath. Even as he also succumbed to the uniting, all-too-human fear of death, O'Neill heard it—the silence of pent breathing. Who would be the first to inhale and run the risk?

Disgusted by his fear, O'Neill was about to do it himself when Devon suddenly beat him to it, exhausted from holding her breath so long. She sharply inhaled . . . and nothing happened.

Breaths exhaled in a puffing rush. Conversation rose anew, punctuated by crying and colored with fear, concern, curiosity, and excitement. O'Neill let it all drift into the background as he stepped out of the pod and placed his feet firmly on the soil of their new world.

His eyes teared, squinting against blown dust and dazzled by sunshine that dappled green leaves dancing and soughing in the gentle wind. Here and there, little standing whirlpools of dust, miniature twisters, moved over the ground, collapsing when the wind momentarily died and arising again as it returned. The others stirred behind O'Neill, emboldened by his move, and followed him into the light.

Awe and wonder were short-lived. Those emotions could be richly entertained at another time. For now, there were injured to attend to and reconnaissance, tallying of supplies, and security measures to initiate.

Emergency triage came together under Julia's hands, though she couldn't remember a time in her entire life when she had felt less in control or more overstressed—not even when she had learned Vasquez wasn't aboard the Advance ship, and not even when that ship had begun breaking up.

The stunned awe and amazement among the passengers, left in the wake of their mostly safe landing in new surroundings, lasted just until the first of the injured parties made their miseries known. Julia responded instinctively— but her hands were tied in so many ways. She was only one person—the only one here with anything more than a rudimentary knowledge of medicine—and she hadn't been able to salvage even one tenth of her supplies. How was she supposed to administer to the medical needs of so many people without adequate supplies?

Trying to maintain a demeanor of control when it might have been nice to give in to a little panic, Julia rummaged through her pockets and her medical kit in a frenzied tally of what she possessed. Relief punched a tiny hole in her fear when she discovered a small plastic diagnosis inhalant bag in her right pocket. Clutching it, she hurried over to where Uly sat beside Devon in the shade of the wrecked pod.

He lay unmoving in her arms, eyes open and fixed on the suit wrist monitor. "I'm at one-thirty over ninety!" he shrilled. "It's too high!"

"You're okay, Uly," Julia said soothingly, hoping she was right and that the child had suffered no further damage in the crash. "You're still just scared and nervous. I need a big breath, now, c'mon . . ."

He obediently inhaled and breathed into the monitor bag. Immediately his body clenched like a curled fist, caught in a spate of coughing that doubled him up with his head bent over his knees.

"What is it?" Devon asked worriedly, her eyes on the inhalant monitor, one arm across her son's chest while the other hand rubbed circles on his back trying to ease the seizure. "How's he doing?"

Before Julia could reply, Yale approached, wending his way between the three or four huddled groups of survivors. *Please, God, no,* the doctor prayed, fearing he might need her services as well. It wasn't that she didn't like the Teacher. She didn't know him well enough to have formed an opinion either way, though Uly and Devon both seemed genuinely fond of him. The problem was she hadn't a clue how to treat a cyborg. For some reason, that seemed to be something more along Danziger's or Alonzo's line of work, something for a mechanic to do, but neither of them was in sight at the moment to even field a question if she had one to ask.

Clearly upset, Yale knelt beside Devon and spared a brief smile of encouragement for Uly, his big hand smoothing back the boy's hair. "There's no signal from the other crafts," he said, his voice pitched low. The message was clearly for Devon's ears only, but Julia was close enough to hear, and his words made her glance up quickly. She caught him looking at her and dropped her head back to Uly's monitor. Damn! Did he think she was eavesdropping? It was kind of hard not to when they were all so close together.

Devon's shoulder shifted slightly in what might have been a shrug. "Keep trying," she replied simply. Yale nodded, gave Uly a comforting pat on the leg, and moved off.

The monitor finally beeped, and Julia looked up to meet Devon's strained expression and worried eyes. "No sign of trauma. He's clear."

"Thank God," Devon breathed in relief and closed her eyes briefly to hide away behind her lids. It was a tactic Julia knew well. Seeing it on Devon made something inside her warm to the cooler, older woman. Maybe they weren't so different after all.

She squeezed Uly's leg through the immuno-suit and rose. "You're doing great, Uly. I have to check on the others now, okay? I'll be back to check on you again in a little while."

He nodded, content for the moment to be out of the pod, safe and alive in the circle of his mother's arms. "Okay, Dr. Heller. And thanks."

"My pleasure, Champ," she replied, indulging in his nickname for the first time and liking the smile it drew from both him and his mother. Suddenly she didn't feel nearly so wrung out as before, and she turned toward the other waiting patients with a new confidence.

O'Neill scrutinized the crash site, not quite able to put a name to what he was feeling. Excitement, certainly. Relief and elation that they'd all survived impact. Concern over the whereabouts of the other e-vac pods and the condition of their passengers. Curiosity about the locations of any cargo pods that might have survived the dump. Running over, under, and through it all was a sense of . . .

Of thrill. Of anticipation. Of elation. This was something he'd always dreamed of, something he'd always wished for in the back of his mind. The chance to start again, to hack out a life among an uncharted wilderness, bringing a frontier under his sway and dominion. Mankind had plumbed the depths of the oceans and the vast reaches of the stars. They'd tamed Everest and Kilimanjaro and the suitable escarpments of every other planet in the solar system. But here . . . *Here* it was all new, all raw, completely untried—wide open, untouched, untamed. And O'Neill was just the man to tame it.

He sidled up to Yale, trying to look nonchalant, and glad the others were too wrapped up in their own concerns to pay him much attention. His eyes tracked the movement of trees in the wind, watching to see if the tossing boughs masked the motion of an unseen adversary. He knew what the survey reports said about G889—knew that the planet was reported as showing no civilizations of any kind—but even that assurance didn't let him put down his guard. There were plenty of *uncivilized* things in the universe, and he wasn't keen on being attacked by any of them.

"Listen, uh, pal." He nudged Yale's arm to get his attention and unobtrusively slid one of the weapons he'd taken from the ship into the cyborg's big hand. "Do me a favor and keep an eye out for anything that moves, will ya?"

Yale hefted the weapon, handling it like a pro, shifting his fingers around like he knew what it was for. O'Neill's swell of relief at the cyborg's obvious experience fluttered and sagged as Yale smiled slightly and handed the weapon back. "I . . . uh . . . can't," he said somewhat regretfully.

The Commander's hand curled around the small gun, hiding it inside his palm. Eyes narrowed, he gave the Teacher a long look. "Weapon aversion in the Yale program?" he asked with thinly veiled disgust.

Yale nodded, his eyes still on the gun hidden in the curve of O'Neill's hand. His expression, embarrassingly clear and obvious to the military man, said it all. This was something known, something of the past, something the cyborg had once had and that was now lost to him. Whether the memories of guns were good or bad was impossible to fathom. But there was more going on under Yale's surface than O'Neill had ever guessed. Before, he had viewed the cyborg as something antique, something archaic, an object Devon carried on from her childhood. Now the look on the old man's face made O'Neill wonder just how deep still waters ran.

He nodded once. "Okay." There was no point in arguing. Yale couldn't fight against programming. O'Neill moved away, angling across the crash site toward Baines, who had just emerged from a stand of trees where he'd gone to relieve himself. The Commander knew the younger man had a military background and would be well versed in arms. He'd know how to use the gun and would gladly take it, O'Neill was certain, if for no other reason than to make points with the Commander. As he quietly haled the technician and drew him to one side, his mind was still partly on Yale—the sudden unknown quantity and wild card in their deck.

Danziger was trying to wrap a blanket around True, trying to give her some faint sense of comfort in the aftermath of the crash, but she wouldn't hold still. She kept squirming in

114

his grasp, finally snaking one hand free of the blanket to touch the ground and scoop some up into her hand.

She stared at it wonderingly, watching with fascination as it trickled and sifted through her fingers, leaving them faintly brown. "Is this dirt, Dad?"

He nodded at her briefly lifted face before she returned her attention to the ground, touching it here and there, exploring how it felt against different parts of her hand, rolling pebbles between her fingers, then holding the small rocks to her nose to smell and rubbing them carefully against her face. Danziger was touched by her wonder and amazed at the change wrought upon his child. It stilled his movements, and he let her be, let the blanket fall away. Sometimes she seemed almost terrifyingly grown-up for her years, and other times, like now, she was back to being the little kid who was easily amazed and delighted by each new discovery she made. For a brief, flashing instant, Danziger was almost glad the ship had broken up. It might be kind of nice for True to have an opportunity to grow up in a place like this.

"Dad, are these *rocks*?"

The question made him grin. He tucked the slumping blanket back up around her shoulders and spent the next few minutes with his arms around her, just enjoying his child and the wonder of her life, the wonder of them all still being alive and able to ask such questions.

Julia's confidence, buoyed by her success as she treated the minor cuts and abrasions suffered by most of the e-vac pod's other passengers, shattered like glass when she finally reached Alonzo. She'd been wondering where he was, and confused by trying to figure out how to convey her gratitude to him for saving her life, without having him construe it as a come-on. She was still annoyed at having been dragged away from her supplies, but that was far preferable to what her fate would have been otherwise. But if she just could have taken a few more things . . .

She found him sitting in the pod's hatch opening, dazed and confused by the crash, both legs dangling in the air. A trickle of blood seeped from a small wound on his forehead. "I, I *tried* to hold her," he mumbled, staring down at his hands. "I couldn't shake the unit. Never," he shook his head. "I never . . ."

His rattling dissertation didn't bother her half so much as the look of his legs. A twist in her guts told her something wasn't right. "Hold still a sec!" she ordered and ran the diagnostic glove (one of the few really useful things she'd been able to grab in the rush for escape) over both legs. The readout made her bite her lip hard.

He waved her off, flapping his hands in irritation, his pupils dilated with shock . . . and pain? She rather thought so, given the results. "Hey, I just wrenched 'em! Please! Gimme a minute and I'll be fine!" He rubbed his temple, smearing blood across his forehead and fingers.

"Make that twenty-four hours," she countered unhappily. "You've got multiple fractures of the left tibia and the right knee. You won't be walking till tomorrow."

He snatched at her hand, hurting her as he wrenched the glove around to see the diagnostic screen and read the results for himself. His disbelief and dismay were clear as she pulled her hand away and ripped each pant leg to the thigh, exposing tanned, well-muscled legs that were bruised and oddly canted. He suddenly began swearing in Spanish.

Julia, conversant in the romance languages, blushed and tried to ignore what he was saying. "What's the matter?" She frowned, and then another thought made her eyes go wide. "You *did* take a bone healer vaccine, didn't you?"

Alonzo shook his head, eyes wide with panic. "It was for

the colonists!" he wailed desperately. "I wasn't even land-ing!"

She stared at him, stunned by a set of circumstances she'd neither encountered nor anticipated. Old-fashioned medi-cine wasn't exactly part of the curriculum at medical school anymore. What was she supposed to do now?

Busy helping any of the others who needed assistance, finding useful work for himself that beat just standing around, Danziger felt a surge of annoyance when he looked up to check on True and found her blanket heaped in an untidy pile and her nowhere near it. He straightened and craned his neck in every direction, finally spotting her beyond the last edge of huddled passengers. She was about ten yards out and starting up the rise out of the clearing where the pod had crashed.

"True!" he called. "Come on back here!"

She either didn't hear him or, more likely, pretended not to as she continued scaling the embankment, headed toward the rise. He recognized her shoulders and figured it was probably the latter. She'd gotten wind of something, and curiosity was an enticement that True could never refuse. Shaking his head with good-natured annoyance, he started after her, his boots crunching pleasantly on the gravelly ground.

She wasn't hard to catch up to, for she didn't move from the rise upon reaching it. The posture of her shoulders changed, however, straightening to rapt attention, and Dan-ziger went instantly on alert, ghosting up beside her to see what threatened.

It was nothing. Or, rather it was *something*, but nothing that, as far as he could tell, posed any danger. It was the landscape that held True enthralled, nothing more than that. Unlike anything Danziger had ever seen on vid or dreamed

117

of in the vastness of his mind, it stretched away as far as the eye could see, reaching to the horizon and beyond. It would be a long time before he found the right words to describe that first look. Words like "panoramic," "scenic," and others of that ilk didn't exist much anymore in the English language, at least not when it came to describing their planet. But this . . .

This was a vast, spectacular landscape that defied description and took away his breath. His heart pounded with anticipation, eager to see what lay beyond the range of his eyes. Not a single building or structure broke the leafy canopy of the trees below, not a single bridge spanned the distant river, and the only thing crossing the beauty of the flat plain in the distance was the thrown shadows of the fluffy clouds overhead. To one side (calling it east seemed the thing to do, though Danziger hadn't a clue yet of directions on this planet), two moons were just beginning to breast the horizon.

He didn't realize they'd been followed until he heard the indrawn breath of amazement. He glanced back at Devon, her face bearing the same stamp of rapt wonder and disbelief as his own. A smile touched his lips, and he moved forward to stand beside his awestruck, slack-jawed daughter. He put an arm around her shoulders and squeezed her up against his side. "Sure you're okay, pal?" he asked.

Eyes wide, True looked as if she'd forgotten how to blink. Her arm came up around his waist and snugged around him firmly. "Is . . . is it all *dirt*?"

John Danziger laughed, and the sound of his voice echoed out over a land that had never seen their kind before.

Chapter 9

Two huge moons eased up over the horizon, moving with the imperceptibly slow grace of an ancient galleon. They were enormous and utterly majestic when compared to the memory of the sorry little satellite circling what was left of Earth.

Morgan would have given anything he possessed to be staring at Earth's moon again, from the safety of the space station lounge, rather than be here, shipwrecked and alone on an alien world, exposed under an open, unfamiliar night sky of incomprehensible vastness.

He lowered his eyes from the spread of unidentifiable constellations to stare, unhappily and mistrustfully, at the fire his wife had kindled. "I . . . I don't think this is a . . . a good idea, Bess."

Huddled beside him in front of what remained of their

e-vac pod, as bruised and dirty as her husband, Bess shook her head. "I feel like we're gonna get arrested." She smiled slightly at the look he gave her. "Burning wood's been illegal on Earth since I was a kid," she explained. "Even though we burned everything else." She tugged absently at a torn sleeve.

A log snapped, throwing a shower of sparks into the air in a lurid, scarlet spray. Morgan jumped halfway to his feet. "What's that? It's spreading!"

The planes of her face lit from beneath by the flames as she leaned forward to prod the logs with a long stick, Bess had the temerity to laugh gently at her husband's fears. While he usually looked down his nose at—or tried to ignore entirely—where and how she had grown up (native Earthers being born on the "wrong side of the tracks" as far as those on the space stations were concerned), it was at times like this that he suspected there was more to her manner of upbringing than met the eye. For instance, he hadn't even known she knew how to make a fire . . .

"Don't worry, honey," she assured him, putting aside her poker and patting him on the leg. "It'll stay put. And if anyone else is alive," she added encouragingly. "Maybe they'll see our flames."

Morgan nodded morosely. "Yeah, *if*." He glanced over each shoulder at the encroaching night. He'd never liked darkness. Hell, he'd never *known* darkness, at least not *real* darkness like this. This stuff was *dark*! He gritted his teeth and wished fervently for a bank of floodlights with which to pierce the night and render it harmless and tame. "I think we might be the only ones who made it, Bess. I . . . I . . ." He took a deep breath and shook his head remorsefully. "I feel awful about leaving them . . ."

Bess inched closer and put her hand on his arm. "Stop blaming yourself, Morgan," she ordered gently. "You explained it. We just broke away. The wind sheer ripped the pod right off." She squeezed his arm and settled her shoulder against his. "Thank goodness you got the door closed in time, y'know? You're a hero actually."

He'd been enjoying her words, basking in the relaxing balm of her voice as he often had before, but that last remark brought the starch back into Morgan's spine with a vengeance, because he knew it was a lie. In his mind's eye, he saw once again the look on Danziger's face just before the pod dropped away from the ship.

He shifted tensely, rocking side to side on his rump, and felt a sudden, sharp pain in his neck. His hand slapped down, stinging the skin. When he checked his fingers, there was a tiny dot of blood on them. "Yow! What was that?"

"It's just a little flea," Bess replied placidly, staring musingly into the flames. She smiled sweetly at whatever it was she saw in the dancing movement of the fire. "They've been biting me since sundown, love. It's no big deal."

"No big deal?!" Morgan jumped to his feet, almost in tears. "You mean there are *bugs* here?! This is horrible, Bess! What're we doing here? What're we going to do?!"

She reached up and coaxed him back down beside her, holding him close in the warmth of the fire's glow with his head pillowed against her breasts. "Shhh. Shhh. It'll be okay," she said soothingly, gently rocking him back and forth. "Maybe you should close your eyes and get a little sleep."

Morgan clutched her, his eyes wide over the warm protection of her arms. "I can't sleep out here!" he whined. "It's too . . . *big!*" He struggled to rise free of her embrace. "C'mon, help me. I gotta get our beacon working."

"No," Bess countered with gentle firmness, pulling him back against her. "Tomorrow. In the light. The sun will come up. We'll feel better."

Her words began to have their desired effect. Morgan slowly relaxed, his body blending to the rhythm of her rocking, her voice soothing in his ears. Little by little, his eyes began to close.

"We've got our fire," Bess murmured, smiling beatifically down at him. "It'll keep us warm . . . Keep animals away . . ."

Morgan's eyes popped open as if he'd been goosed. "Animals?!" he squeaked. "What animals?"

True sat on the long grass beside the sprawled form of her sleeping father and glanced idly around the darkened crash site. Once everyone had been reassured and their injuries attended to, a temporary camp had been constructed using tarps and blankets. Some of the crew and passengers were already asleep, falling into unconsciousness with an almost palpable sense of relief. Maybe the crash wouldn't exist in their sleep, in their dreams. Maybe there, things had gone differently and they landed when and where they were supposed to. Others sat around the ruddy embers of a small fire, afraid to go to sleep in this strange world, afraid they might not wake up again.

True wasn't afraid of sleep; she just wondered at her ability to do it. How could anyone sleep, how could anyone even *want* to, when there was so much going on, so much *out there* beyond the immediate boundaries of their camp? So many sounds, so many smells, so many . . .

A flash of light drew her eyes to the sky as a few bolts of lightning erupted in the distance with short, static wrinkles of energy. She listened closely, but didn't hear any thunder following. Her father had once told her how to count the time between the lightning and the thunder to determine the storm's distance, but she couldn't remember the formula now. Her brain seemed too muddled and full of stuff to think of something like that. Besides, she was hungry. She began rummaging among the blankets for the semolina bar someone tossed her a while earlier.

Devon, Yale, and Commander O'Neill stood together a short distance away, close enough for her to overhear their conversation. They broke off for a moment, their eyes turning toward a second flare of lightning and following the brief, jagged spikes as they danced across the sky. Then they resumed, Devon and Yale watching intently as O'Neill moved in a slow circle, working a transponder receiver.

"Definitely our cargo pod sectionals," O'Neill said confidently. "The other fifteen pods are probably scattered all over this planet."

Yale leaned in to take a look over the Commander's shoulder. "Pod twelve. Inventory has it with vehicles, VTO aircraft, probably some clothing, maybe some weaponry . . ."

Devon interrupted. "What do you guess—ten more hours of darkness?" She glanced at the sky.

O'Neill nodded. "We'll move on at first light," he said.

Her head dipped in acknowledgement and she stared out into the darkness. After a quiet moment, Yale touched her elbow. "Devon . . . ?"

She shook her head sharply, bringing herself back from wherever she'd gone. "It's . . . just hard to believe. If this is anything like Earth was hundreds of years ago . . ." Her voice trailed away.

"It's a second chance," the cyborg agreed. "The odds are unbelievable, but here it is."

O'Neill leaned toward them and smiled. "Let's try not to go all weepy, huh?" he teased. His smile broadened when they grinned in return. He slapped Yale's shoulder with a familiarity True wasn't certain the cyborg shared. "Rest up." With a decisive nod, he moved away.

True's eyes followed the Commander's broad back as he crossed the encampment, and came to rest on Uly, sitting with a blanket drawn up around his hips and looking, in the shiny sheath of the immuno-suit, like something out of her worst nightmares. At the same moment, her fingers encountered the searched-for food bar. She shifted around to sit cross-legged on her blanket and ripped off the foil wrapping with her teeth. She broke off a piece and crammed it hungrily into her mouth. Right now the gray stuff tasted like the best food in the world!

"Better save some for tomorrow, pal," her father warned sleepily, eyes shut, with a blanket folded half-under and half-over him against the vague chill of the night.

She should have figured he wasn't sound asleep yet. "I am," she garbled around a mouthful of food, and looked up at that moment to catch Uly watching her. She felt like a disgusting pig, getting caught shoving food into her mouth like an Earthside refugee! Her face flushed crimson with shame, and she stared back, bugging her eyes at him.

He tried to meet the challenge, tried to keep his eyes locked on hers, but nerves got the better of him and his gaze dropped. He sat up to cover his discomfort and made a big show of fixing his blanket around him. A semolina bar suddenly dropped into his lap, and he looked up to find O'Neill settling onto the grass beside him. While True watched, Uly flicked the bar back into the Commander's ample lap with two fingers, as though he didn't want to touch it.

O'Neill tossed it back, landing it squarely between the boy's legs. "It's all there is, son," he said firmly, but not unkindly. "Eat."

That last word was almost an order. True was intrigued to see what the kid would do with that since the Commander wasn't his parent or anything. To her disgust, the little weeny gave in, picked up the bar, and reluctantly peeled back the wrapping to expose the flesh-colored oblong. He sniffed it, clearly disgusted, and was about to take a bite when O'Neill's voice interrupted him.

"C'mere. I want to show you kids something."

True was startled to find the Commander looking straight at her, motioning for *her* to come over, and she felt a flush of embarrassment at having been caught watching. What could he possibly have to show her that would be of any interest? She thought about ignoring the invitation, then glanced at her dad. He seemed to be really, truly asleep this time, so she got up and started across the grassy verge. She inched forward cautiously, feeling like O'Neill might take a bite out of her instead of the semolina bar he was eating with gusto, and found herself unaccountably unable to meet Uly's gaze.

O'Neill glanced at them both, then shifted onto one hip to reach into his pocket and pull out a small silver-colored disc. "Know what this is?" he asked, holding it out on his open palm.

Hunkering down across from him, True shook her head. Uly aped the movement and pretended she didn't exist.

"My good luck piece," the Commander continued proudly. He rubbed the coin between his thumb and forefinger. "A relic from another time."

"What is it?" Uly asked curiously, cocking his head sideways and leaning closer to get a better look.

"Money. Currency. People used to trade these things for goods down on Earth. Before everyone got fund transfer codes." He flipped the coin off his thumb and caught it in his hand, eyeing it with an expression that could only be called love. "One side a buffalo head, the other side an Indian. Celebrating another era, when men still hunted out on the frontier. The vast unexplored."

"What . . . happened to the frontier?" True asked cautiously, suddenly afraid of what the answer might be.

O'Neill shook his head. "Nothing happened to the frontier, little girl. Happened to the men. They got lazy. Got scared. Like our government back on the stations. Decided it was easier to sit on their butts and stop anyone from looking to see if the frontier still existed." He held out his hand again, palm open with the nickel lying brightly against his skin. "Go ahead. Touch it. It's part of history."

One after the other, each kid reached out to gingerly touch the coin, being careful not to brush each other's fingers. Uly was just about to ask another question when a voice haled O'Neill from across the campsite.

"Commander?" Baines called. "You wanted to chart tomorrow's journey."

O'Neill waved a hand. "Right away," he called back. He rose and started to pocket the coin, then turned and tossed it to Uly. "You hold on to it for a while," he suggested. "A little good luck on the new planet." He walked away.

Suddenly they were alone together. There were adults no more than ten or fifteen feet away, but as far as True was concerned, she was alone with this brat. Her jealousy over his having been the one to receive the coin from O'Neill went to bay, superseded by something else.

She gestured idly at Uly's dinner. "You don't like semolina, huh?" She made a face and nodded with understanding, leaning forward confidentially. "I heard about a kid who *choked* to death on it once."

"Really?" Uly asked, fascinated.

She nodded. "Uh-huh. Went all blue in the face and everything. So, if you're not gonna eat it . . ."

She immediately realized she'd pushed too hard, too soon. Young as he was, Uly was no patsy and no pushover. He sat back warily, eyeing her with suspicion. This sudden interest in his welfare must have smelled pretty bad, judging from the look on his face.

"I get it," he said with a sneer. "You want something, so you decide to be nice to the freak."

"You're crazy!" she retorted, furious at being found out, but feeling even more furious and shamed at herself because she realized that was almost exactly what she'd been thinking. But it wasn't her fault he was weird looking and had The Syndrome!

Her emotions must have been a beacon on her face, and they angered Uly. He picked up his bar and held it out in his hand. "Want it?" he offered sweetly.

She eyed him, watching for the trick her sixth sense told her was there, but not seeing it. Uly's expression was utterly guileless. In spite of her intuition, True decided to trust in luck after all and reached for the bar. Their fingers were nearly touching when Uly suddenly whipped the bar over his shoulder and sent it sailing behind some rocks.

He gifted her with a smile of hollow triumph. "Help yourself," he suggested and turned away, thudding down onto his makeshift bed and pulling the scant covering up over his head.

True shot to her feet, standing over him. Her first inclination was to kick him sharply in the side and run like hell, but she didn't do it. Breathing hard, she stared down at him for a minute, feeling torn and all mixed up, angry for what he had done but feeling like she ought to apologize or something. Not being one who gave in easily, she hated the thought of apology and ended up just walking away. *No,* her brain niggled at her. *It isn't your fault he's weird looking and has The Syndrome. But it isn't* his *fault, either.*

She wandered away, feeling lousy for what she'd said and tried to do. That lousy feeling lasted until she remembered the discarded semolina bar. Her stomach growled a demand.

No one else was going to want it now, after it had been thrown away. Anybody who found it would think there was something wrong with it . . .

She glanced around the campsite. Almost everyone had gone to bed, though she couldn't be certain they were all asleep. But it didn't appear that anyone would see what happened, so . . . Moving quietly, trying to seem nonchalant, she circled the campsite and soft-footed in among the rocks where Uly had flung his dinner.

The foil wrapping shone brightly in the light of the two moons and was easy to spot. Looking around once more to satisfy herself that she was really alone, True ripped open the package and took a bite. Ah, bliss!—even if it did taste like crap. Leaning back against a tall rock, she grinned hugely. All her conflicting feelings about Uly were momentarily laid to rest as she savored every bite of the fruits of her scavenge.

She ripped the package further down its side, opened her mouth to polish off the bar . . . and froze. Solid. No motion. She was a block of ice because something in her, some innate sense drilled into her by her old man, had just told her she was not alone anymore. Something else was very close to her, and it wasn't something human. Mouth gaping and head rigid, she rolled her eyes slowly to one side . . .

"Yow!" She leapt away from the rock wall, spinning to face her adversary. The creature leapt down from its rock and did exactly the same thing, spinning in a circle as she had and landing on its squat hind feet. It arched upright to its full eighteen-inch height and stared at her, bug-eyed.

What the heck was it? It sort of looked like a lizard, except she'd never heard of any that stood on their hind legs. Slightly potbellied, the creature had no hair and its skin was a dry-looking brownish-yellow, parts of it scale-like and other parts looking more like plates of armor. A standing crest of angled plates went down the middle of its back to a tail it seemed to use as an aid in balancing. Its front and rear paws (hands?) were broadly splayed and almost paddle-like, with no discernible digits, but the front ones had four thick, broad claws while the rear had three. The creature's eyes were round and wide, the pupils black and the irises yellow ringed with purple. The bottom and top lids met in the middle when it blinked at her. Its ears stood out straight from the sides of its head. Its snout was short and broad, and it wrinkled across the top when the thing inhaled deeply, scenting her.

True stared, captivated by this amazing thing she'd discovered (or that had discovered her), and took a careful step forward. The creature stared back and then did the same, inching its little feet in the dirt. Cautiously, True repeated her approach and so did the animal. She grinned with delight, and darned if it didn't bare its teeth in what was probably supposed to be a friendly manner, but which looked a little frightening even on something so small.

She suddenly remembered the semolina bar still clenched in her hand. Weren't most animals usually hungry? Moving slowly, she broke the remainder in half and scooted part of it across the ground toward the creature. "Here kitty, kitty, kitty," she called soothingly.

The animal, or whatever it was, eyed the treat suspiciously, then inched forward, picked up the bar, gave it a good sniff, and broke it in half to inch a portion across the ground toward her, hooting quietly as it did in clear parody of her call. Every ounce of resolve melted away inside True in an overwhelming wash of love for the little beast.

"I know you're not a kitty," she murmured. "But what are you?" There was no reply beyond the blinking of two surprised eyes. She gingerly held out her hand. Dad would never forgive her if she got her arm ripped off, but she couldn't resist trying to touch it. "Can I . . . ?" Slowly, she leaned down and gently stroked the animal's head. It scared her by springing onto her shoulder, almost knocking her down as it ducked to nuzzle under her hair. She reached to catch hold of it, not sure if she was going to pull it off or cuddle it back, and—

"True? What are you doing?" her father asked out of the darkness.

She whirled. The unexpected sound of his voice almost made her wet herself, but it also gave her a great excuse. Trying not to look guilty of anything, she smiled at him as innocently as she could manage while trying to keep one side turned away from him. "I . . . had to pee," she said.

Danziger nodded. The look on his face said he wasn't sure he believed that explanation, but he'd accept it for now. "Well, don't stay out here too long. Come get some sleep. We're starting out early in the morning."

"I'll be right there as soon as I'm done," she promised. She kept smiling at him until he left, then reached up to carefully free the animal from beneath her hair and tuck it under her jacket. It immediately curled into a ball and snuggled against her as if she were its mother. Was its mother dead? Is that why it had the bravery to come so near? Had she just been adopted?

Her heart swelled with pleasure at the thought. The animal's presence was a warm bundle against her side as True waited a few moments for the sake of performance, then started back to camp with her face lifted toward the stars. It was turning out to be a lovely night after all.

Chapter 10

· · · · ● ● ● ●

A jab in the ribs woke True earlier than she would have liked. She grunted sharply and rolled over, burying her nose against the elbow of the arm cocked under her head. A part of her semi-conscious brain was aware of the tiny beast curled against her chest inside her jacket, and she shifted carefully so as not to squash it. Beneath the blanket, her arm curled protectively around the small lump of warm flesh housing the tiny heart that beat against her skin. This was better than a cat. Cats didn't hug back.

"C'mon, True." Her father's voice somehow managed to sound both patient and insistent at the same time. "Rise and shine." He poked her again, this time in the butt and not half as gently as before.

"Uughrk!" She sat up fast, trying to keep the blanket around her to hide the telltale bulge of the animal, while at the same time not scaring it into sudden flight and blowing her cover. She glared up at her father from beneath a fall of hair that all but obscured her eyes. "Very funny," she said and yawned.

"I can see you're amused," he remarked dryly and smiled. "C'mon, pal. Up and at 'em. O'Neill wants us on the move pretty damn soon. I let you sleep as long as I could, but you need to pitch in getting things together and I want you to eat something before we start out. You're going to need the energy. It looks to be a long haul."

"How far are we going today?" she asked, shifting more firmly onto her butt. As it started to squirm, she held the animal securely, praying her father wouldn't notice and that the beast wouldn't bite her.

"I don't know yet, but if I'm any judge of O'Neill, it'll be a fair piece." He tossed a semolina bar into her lamp. "Munch that down and then get things packed up and stowed, all right? I'm going to see if I can help any of the others get ready to move."

"Okay," she agreed readily. She managed to stand up without revealing the animal hidden inside her clothing, and started away with her blanket still wrapped around her shoulders. "I'll just go take a pee . . . ," she called over her shoulder.

"Make it quick," he countered seriously and started across the campsite toward the small huddle of Devon, Uly, and Yale.

"Make it quick, make it quick," she mimicked. "How fast does he think a person can pee?" Not that she had elimination on her mind. What she needed was a little privacy to work out a better way to carry the animal with her. (What were these things called, anyway? Did they even have a name? Could she name them, since she'd found them first? She thought that seemed reasonable and spent the next few moments trying to come up with a suitably scientific sounding name for the small creatures. This might even make her famous!)

She finally decided her knapsack would make the perfect hideaway and spent the next few minutes making it as comfortable as possible before picking up the whatever-it-was and placing it inside. It immediately made itself at home, staring up at her from the dark confines of the canvas carryall with a warm look of contentment in its eyes. It blinked sleepily, then curled around, tucked its head against its chest, put its front paws up over its head, and promptly went to sleep. Were they nocturnal, then, these little creatures? If so, her evenings were going to be pretty busy from now on.

"Sleep well, Kitty," she murmured lovingly, then loosely closed the knapsack and slung it onto her back.

Things were hopping by the time True returned to camp. Almost everything was packed, and she hurried to complete her share of the work, hoping her father hadn't noticed how long she'd been gone, and cramming her semolina bar into her face with one hand while she packed with the other. She stood at a respectful distance, keeping back out of the way as she watched two of the heftier crew members hoist Alonzo onto a makeshift stretcher. The pilot's legs stuck out straight in front of him, trussed securely into two makeshift splints. He scowled darkly, not meeting anyone else's eyes for more than a few seconds at a time, and looking for all the world as if he wanted to rip someone's head off and chew it up whole. The skin around his eyes and mouth was drawn tight with pain or worry. She'd seen the same thing happen to her dad when he had a lot on his mind and needed her to stay out of his way.

The imposing bulk of Commander O'Neill strode between her and Alonzo, occluding her view of the proceedings as the pilot was settled in for travel. "We've got to cover 27.8 kilometers to reach cargo pod number twelve by sundown," he told everyone, gesturing with the beacon receiver in his hand. "Cargo manifest indicates we should be fairly well supplied there." He swung around the stuffed backpack in his other hand and slung his arms through the straps, shifting it to sit comfortably across his broad shoulders as he strode to the head of the forming wagon train. "We'll set up a base, try to contact the two other escape pods. Cargo twelve does have a VTO aircraft—we can at least airlift ourselves to New Pacifica," he called back.

Alonzo didn't look impressed. In fact, he flipped a rude gesture at O'Neill's back, then caught True watching him with wide eyes. He smiled ruefully at her, patently embarrassed, and shrugged. She grinned, averting her eyes, and hurried to catch up with her father, who stood waiting for her not far behind the Adairs.

O'Neill glanced back at the assembled group stretched out behind him in a scraggly line. "You okay there, Adair?" he asked.

Devon nodded sharply, standing beside Yale, the two of them holding pull straps attached to a sled of sorts which had been rigged for Uly. He lay prone upon it with his head cushioned on a wad of folded clothing that looked like someone's jacket. "No problem," Devon replied and gifted her son with a courageous smile.

"All right, then, people." O'Neill faced front and, master showman that he was, waited a moment before raising his arm over his head and swinging it forward. "Let's move 'em out!" he called, and the train started forward across the vast terrain.

The going might not have been so bad had the day not turned hot. The ground was scrubby and gravelly, with not much purchase on the hillier sections, but it would have been easy to deal with except for the heat. The midday sun blazed down a torrent of molten light the likes of which True had never experienced. She was used to the different climates programmed into the space station's hydroponic and land gardens and a few of their recreational areas, and she'd "experienced" other climates thanks to the auspices of virtual reality, but none of that was anything like the real thing. In a short time, her skin was red and tight where it lay exposed to the merciless heat, and bathed in sweat where it was covered. Her armpits were soaked, and sweat beaded and ran down the small of her back and the inside of her thighs. Her feet were hot and itchy inside her boots, but there was no pausing to take them off and nowhere to do it comfortably anyway.

She lagged behind the vanguard of the group, falling farther and farther back until she straggled along with the last few. It was not tiredness that drove her to this, but a need for a few moments of privacy. Watching to see that she wasn't observed, she unslung her knapsack from her back and carefully unzipped the bag. The little critter inside peered sleepily at her and tried to stick out its head for a look around. She smiled at it, giving it a chuck under the chin which it returned before she gently tucked it back inside the sack and hurried her pace to catch up with her father before he got worried and started looking for her.

She found him where expected, toward the front of the group and marching along with an almost tireless ground-eating motion that belied the fact that he'd been born and raised on the space stations and never hiked a mile in his life. Sweat rolled down the planes of his face, and his soaked clothing stuck to his body. His cheeks, forearms, and the back of his neck were frosted an angry, sore-looking red.

Danziger glanced at her as she pulled abreast of him and

tried to match her stride to his own. "Need to take a pee again?" he asked.

So he'd noticed she was gone. She should have figured. She shrugged and kept her eyes on the ground in front of her, watching for holes. "I had a stone in my shoe and didn't want everyone behind tripping over me, so I fell back to take it out."

His gaze measured her thoughtfully, and he nodded. "That's a good way to do it, True. I'm proud of you. Next time let me know, though, will you? I was starting to get worried."

His concern didn't rankle her. Rather, his love made her feel a warmth that had nothing at all to do with the sun. "Okay, Dad. Sorry."

"No problem." His eyes flicked forward, and he frowned, sweat puddling in the creases of his face. She followed his gaze and saw Devon and Yale struggling with Uly's sled. Evidently what had looked like a good idea in their heads was proving to be otherwise in reality. They really looked as though they were having a hard time of it.

"Back in a bit," Danziger murmured, moving ahead of True almost before she realized he'd spoken. What was he up to? What did he want with the Adairs?

Without preamble, Danziger fell into step behind the sled. "Lemme give you a hand," he suggested mildly, not asking permission or, seemingly, wanting it. In one fluid movement, he unslung his knapsack and flung it onto the sled, then grabbed Uly's straps and hauled the child up to carry on his back. Uly's eyes were huge with startlement and a little fear, and True snorted under her breath. The big baby. Her father was the last person anyone had to be frightened of. He'd never hurt anyone. Of course, the Adairs didn't know that. She wondered if it was cooler inside the immuno-suit or hotter. Knowing the brat, it was probably climate controlled.

Devon turned as all this was taking place, moving slowly compared to the swift economy of Danziger's motion. She flung out one hand. "Careful!" she warned.

Danziger shifted his shoulders, making the load more comfortable and glanced up at the boy peeking over his shoulder with a grin of delight plastered all over his face and his eyes as wide and round as dinner plates. "You okay up there, son?"

Uly nodded. "Yes, sir," he assured him, breathing hard through the ventilator. "I'm fine."

It was easy to see how much it cost Devon to stand back, to stop her forward rush, to let someone help, to lower her arm and unclench her hand, then raise it to dash the sweat out of her eyes. She reached out almost nonchalantly and adjusted the front of Uly's immuno-suit. "Just watch his tubing," she said quietly, her eyes never reaching Danziger's face. She licked her lips. "Thank you."

He glanced at her, but didn't reply. He just kept walking, face forward, hands up and holding Uly's straps securely against his shoulders.

True sneered, feeling jealousy trickle through her veins at seeing her father do something nice for another kid. Let the weirdo get his own father, if he ever had one. Hers was taken.

Marching to the side of the advancing group as the afternoon wore on, O'Neill took a good look around him. They were still moving at a reasonably decent clip, but the group had fanned out slightly and he was constantly concerned over stragglers or someone becoming lost in this unknown territory. He'd have to get them bunched closer together pretty soon, or risk having someone fall behind and vanish altogether as evening came on.

Damn, but it was hot! He'd felt heat before, but it had been a long time since he'd been subjected to it on a march of this kind. Not that they'd expected or anticipated having to do any of this. Things were supposed to have gone off without a hitch. Well, so much for overconfident cockiness and Viva Murphy's Law!

He smiled and nodded greeting as Devon fell into step beside him. Up ahead were the broad backs of Yale and Danziger, their heads close together as they talked. Uly slumped over the mechanic's shoulder, his head lolling as he slept, rocked to sleep by the gentle roll of the older man's gait.

"I can't get used to how the air moves around all by itself," Devon said by way of greeting, fanning one hand in front of her face. "And it's vaster than I expected."

"What is?"

"The sky," she replied. "I mean, I tried to imagine endless blue . . ." She shook her head over her own sense of wonder. "I guess you've seen skies before . . ."

"My '64 tour on Earth." He shook his head, turning his face up to peer at the white-hot disc of the sun. "But it wasn't like this. The sky down there was rusty, thick stuff." His eyes tracked along the horizon, and he sighed. Had Earth ever really been like this? If so, what made mankind behave so stupidly as to let it turn into a dung heap? He shook his head again, remaining silent. He knew the answer to that as well as anyone.

Some hours later, and several yards ahead of the main body of marchers, O'Neill crested a ridge and stopped, staring into the broad valley below with a sense of satisfied contentment washing over him like a soothing balm. Everything was going to turn out right, after all. From here on out, things were in an upswing. He could feel it!

"There she is, people!" he called out without turning, and waited while the others caught up with him and took in the view.

The valley was broad and rolling, an admixture of long grasses, short scrub, gravelly areas, and small stands of trees, as though whatever passed for Mother Nature around here couldn't make up her mind when it had come time to exterior decorate. At the near end of the valley lay their cargo pod. The massive structure was canted over onto one side, but looked to be relatively intact and otherwise okay.

A ragged cheer went up from the exhausted group. O'Neill had time to share a triumphant look with Devon before caution was flung to the four winds and everyone spilled over the ridge at a whooping run.

It became a race, a grand and glorious race in which no one really cared who won or lost, it just felt good to run, to feel softer ground under their feet, to have a break from the monotony of the march. Exhaustion evaporated in the heady rush of good feelings and excitement as they neared the cargo pod.

O'Neill nearly killed himself making sure he was one of the first to reach it. His reviving lungs heaved for breath as he swatted the metal hulk with the flat of his hand, feeling like a proud papa, and stepped around the side of the container to activate the door. His euphoria instantly vanished as though it had never been.

His expression staggered the others to an abrupt stop, halting them in a ragged semicircle around the pod, suddenly hesitant and scared to approach any closer. "What the hell—?" O'Neill couldn't believe it. He just couldn't believe it.

One side of the massive construction had suffered serious

damage in the crash. That was not unexpected and nothing which they couldn't handle. But this— O'Neill gestured futilely, unable to speak. The pod's loading doors had been ripped open and were swinging in the wind with the tiny, tiny creak of agonized metal. The interior of the container was almost as pristine as it had been coming off the assembly line, or however it was they manufactured these things. It was empty of all but a few items, and none of those worth much. Every important piece of equipment had vanished.

Devon shoved her way through the crowd with Danziger and Yale close behind. She rounded the cargo pod and stumbled to a halt as she saw what O'Neill and the others were looking at. "Oh, my God," she panted breathlessly. "We've been robbed."

O'Neill straightened and turned in a circle, eyeing every rock, every cranny, every crag and tree shadow, not wanting to believe the evidence of his eyes, but being forced to because there was no intelligent alternative. This was not right. This was not how it was supposed to be, or how the surveys had said it was. "We're not alone," he murmured and turned, with all the others, to stare at the woman whose dreams and schemes had led them to this world.

Chapter 11

• • • • • • • ●

Devon didn't know what to say or do. She felt as if she didn't know anything at all, except she didn't like the looks on the faces staring at her. She didn't like their fear and worry, but most of all, she didn't like what she read as betrayal. From the look on some of those faces, there were those in the group who had already played judge and jury, condemning her to life-long guilt if not outright death.

Her mind whirled. Had some animal done this? Survey after survey had been done on G889, and not one of them showed anything more advanced than some birds and a few large mammals. Nothing ever indicated advanced sentient life, if ransacking a cargo pod could be termed proof of sentience. Nothing in the reports ever indicated anything even remotely humanoid.

If this thing was humanoid, she reminded herself, annoyed at what felt like a touch of conceited xenophobia. She had thought herself beyond all that. Certainly, there was nothing written in stone that said whatever lived on this planet had to fit her biased view of what it should or should not look like. The trouble was that for too long she'd been thinking of G889, and New Pacifica in particular, as hers, filling in the details in her head without a clue as to what the reality might prove to be. Well, now reality had kicked her soundly in the teeth, and what was she going to do about it in the face of several bewildered, confused, frightened, and angry people?

From off to her left, Danziger cleared his throat, drawing the attention of the others. He carefully swung Uly down from his shoulders and settled him comfortably on the ground, then elbowed his way past the few people standing between him and Devon so he could take up an easy stance at her side. "Before someone suggests a lynching, I recommend we set out sentries in case whatever pilfered our stores is still around. Some of you others can take inventory of anything that might be left in the pod's other bays."

"That's a good idea," O'Neill agreed, somewhat belatedly. Devon thought he sounded a little jealous.

"And what are *you* going to do?" a petulant voice asked from the back of the group.

The mechanic smiled coldly at the female Advance colonist who had spoken. "Anything I have to," he challenged quietly. "How about you?" The others backed down then, stepping away and managing to find themselves useful things to do.

Devon wiped her sweaty hands against her pants and tried out a smile that didn't quite make it. "I could have handled that on my own."

"I know." Danziger shrugged, his expression closed and guarded.

"Yes . . . well . . ." She held out a hand. "Thank you for backing me."

He glanced briefly at the hand, but didn't take it, and she ended up having to self-consciously stick it back into her pocket. "Don't thank me. If it was backing, it was temporary, at least until I figure out what's really going on here. If you just made a mistake, fine. I can live with that. But if I find out you knew there were other . . . creatures . . . here who might pose a threat—if I find out you risked the lives of hundreds of people without their knowledge just to fulfill some dream of your own making—rest assured I'll be leading the pack when they come for your blood." He turned and walked away, leaving her a little stunned and very thoughtful over what he'd said and the quiet vehemence with which it had been delivered.

Needing something to do besides standing there feeling confused, and seeing that Julia was tending to Uly, she trailed along behind Danziger and ended up beside O'Neill at the foot of the ramp leading into the cargo pod's empty main bay. With her eyes, she followed the movement of Yale and Danziger as they crisscrossed inside, now appearing, now disappearing, checking for clues and hoping to find something useful left behind. Light beamed from the end of the cyborg's arm as he illuminated the empty interior.

"Something really picked this place clean," Danziger remarked, his voice echoing in the large, empty space.

"VTO aircraft. Titanium building units. Probably a land vehicle—" Yale shook his head at the tally of loss.

Danziger ran his hand along the edge of the loading door that was jammed about a third of the way up. "How 'bout the bay they didn't get into?"

"We're not sure. No individual bay manifests were available."

"Great." It was a growl of disgust, and Devon could

hardly blame him. She felt like snarling herself. He stepped out of the bay and into the vestibule where Baines and one of the colonists were on their knees investigating the partially wedged-open bottom of the only unpilfered bay. "You guys get a look inside there yet?"

Baines shook his head and paused to use his shirtsleeve to mop the sweat from his top lip and his forehead. "Couple more inches, maybe."

Walman nodded toward the open, vacant bay behind them. "I'll tell you something—we better hope whatever ripped that thing open isn't coming back." The three of them paused, meeting one another's eyes with a look that said it all, even from where Devon stood. Almost as one, they took a careful look around. If the situation hadn't been so serious, it would have been laughable.

Danziger gave himself a shake. "Let's see if we can find something to wedge that open. I want to see what's in there." He followed Yale down the ramp, passed Devon and O'Neill without so much as a look or word, and went off with the cyborg in search of something to use as a pry bar.

O'Neill's fingers flicked Devon's wrist to get her attention. He nodded at the ground where a set of scuffed, three-toed tracks led from the cargo pod into the surrounding trees. "Not one piece of probe info showed even an inkling of civilization," he said quietly, voice pitched low so no one else would hear. "No structures, roads, agriculture—"

Her eyes were still on the trees. She started strolling toward them, leaving O'Neill with no choice but to follow if he wanted to carry on their conversation. "Well, whatever it is must be interested in manufactured goods." What the hell were they going to do with an *airplane*?

"Devon." O'Neill hissed her name, his hand under her elbow stopping her a few yards from the treeline. "We

144

checked the last twenty-five years' worth of probe reports. There was nothing above flora and fauna . . ."

Devon didn't know why he was trying so hard to be circumspect. The tracks were no secret. Even if they were, the evidence of the pod was right there before everyone's eyes. They'd all seen it. They all knew there was something else, something they hadn't anticipated, living on G889.

O'Neill's remark made her recall her own thoughts of before, only now she saw them in a new light and with a new lucidity. How could she have been so naive? "Yeah, *government probes*, Broderick. For newscast. We saw what everyone was supposed to see. We saw exactly what they *wanted* us to see . . . and nothing more."

His eyes darted toward her, sizing her up critically, and he snorted. "Let's not go off the deep end here, Adair."

She raised her chin. "Then you tell me I'm wrong," she challenged.

O'Neill met it from another angle, though she could tell by his eyes he was giving what she'd said serious consideration. Maybe he was arguing because what she postulated was readily believable and he didn't want to believe it, didn't want to give credit to the evidence of his eyes. But strange things happen. Dison Blalock had wanted her dead. After that, after the betrayal of his supposed friendship, Devon was confident just about anything could occur.

"Anthropologists have been yammering for years about the possibility of intelligent life elsewhere in the galaxy. But did you ever notice that no matter where man's gone, or how many light-years he's traveled, all anyone's ever found is a couple variations on plankton?"

Devon swung an arm at the violated pod, angry at his patronizing tone, no matter how well intentioned it might be. "Broderick," she said tightly. "Plankton didn't loot our cargo." Anything else she might have said, or any argument he might have raised to counter it, broke off as someone behind them cleared his throat. They turned to see Yale approaching with a good-sized crate in his arms.

"Two of the colonists found this back in the bushes, Commander. Evidently, the looters couldn't get it open. It has your code on it."

O'Neill's face brightened with more relief and delight than Devon would have thought him capable of. "Well, well, well . . . I guess there's a cosmic balance out there, after all, isn't there?" He motioned for Yale to set the crate on the ground, then stepped forward to thumbprint the lock and heave open the lid.

"Have they found anything else?" Devon asked as she watched, curious to see what O'Neill was so thrilled to have regained.

The Teacher shook his head. "Nothing of importance," he said regretfully. "A few odds and ends. That's about it."

She sighed in frustration. "No aircraft, no vehicles of any kind, no neural net computers—"

An exclamation of delight grunted through O'Neill and he lovingly lifted an antique hunting rifle out of the crate. He sighted down the barrel, then propped the stock against his knee with the gun held upright, gleaming in the sunlight with an oily sheen.

That was *it*? That's what he was so excited about? After a moment's consideration, Devon supposed she could see his point. They were facing an unknown adversary. Better to be safe than sorry, and if weapons made you safer . . .

Before she could ask him about it, True's sharp, high voice called out. "Hey! Over here! We found someone! He's locked in!"

Devon darted away, hearing the cadence of O'Neill's and Yale's running steps close behind her as they raced back to the cargo pod.

• • •

Stripped to his T-shirt and sweating like a stuck pig, Danziger struggled to open the door of the undisturbed bay with a makeshift pry bar made from a large piece of metal cast off by the nameless so-and-so's who'd looted the pod. He paused in his efforts only long enough to wipe stinging sweat out of his eyes with a bare forearm. "Hang on. Any lock releases inside?"

"Wish I could say so," came the oddly enthusiastic reply. The voice sounded distinctly masculine. "But, then, if wishes were—"

Danziger cut him off. "Right. How 'bout a hand to help force it up a couple more inches."

"If I had a hand, I could give you two feet."

The mechanic swore tensely. What'd this guy think he was, some sort of jokester? If they didn't get this open, and pretty darned soon, that poor bastard inside would suffocate. Didn't he realize that? Or was he just trying to put on a brave front in the face of such adversity? If so, did that make him braver than hell or an idiot?

"Somebody help me with this," Danziger ordered. Several of the men and women standing nearby immediately hopped to, bending their strength with his toward prying open the door from the bottom. After a handful of tense moments that seemed like forever, the bar finally caught and bent back a small portion of the hatch to expose a gap of darkness. Danziger reached inside, hunting around, and came up with . . .

The mechanic looked down and blinked in surprise at what was obviously a robotic head in his hand, complete with neural net intelligence. Danziger shook his head bemusedly and felt a grin tug at one corner of his mouth on a day when he'd have bet he couldn't find much to grin about. "Looks like we've got ourselves a Zero unit . . . or part of one, anyway."

"Part nothing," the head piped up with enthusiastic assurance. "I've got an entire body in there. Construction Worker series. Ready to give New Pacifica full one hundred percent, sir."

Danziger's tiny grin broadened into fullness. He turned the head this way and that in a quick inspection for damage. "Well, I can't speak for New Pacifica, but we could sure use the rest of your unit." He tossed the head toward another crew member, who caught it deftly.

"Easy there, pal," the head warned, and flicked a few lights along its "face" for good measure.

"My apologies." The mechanic picked up his pry bar and, with a nod to his helpers, set to work once again in an attempt to force open the recalcitrant bay door.

Julia was growing more and more worried about Alonzo. She was able to keep the brunt of his pain at bay with the use of sedatives—it was not her chosen method, but broad-spectrum painkillers seemed to be in the minority for now, at least until the Colony ship arrived. That was too many damned months in the future for it to make any difference to Alonzo. She just prayed to God no one else suffered serious injury before then. The sterile precision of her lab back on the space station seemed far away and almost dreamlike.

What worried her more than the pain was the pilot's frame of mind. He had seemed relatively okay before—understandably angered by his injury and frustrated over his inability to save the ship from destruction—but basically all right, wide awake and lucid. Now he seemed to be in a dreamworld and hardly aware of her presence at all. His stretcher bearers had left him lying in a low-slung hammock under a makeshift sun shelter from where he could watch the others work on the cargo pod, but he hadn't once looked in their direction and, in fact, behaved as though they didn't exist. He seemed oblivious to any of the activity going on around him, even down to Julia's careful ministrations. Offhand, she could think of a dozen serums that, when injected, would probably have booted him out of this lethargy or whatever it was he'd fallen into and back into the real world. Without them, and without the diagnostic tools to tell her precisely what was wrong with him, she felt at a loss. It was a new sensation and there wasn't a thing remotely pleasant about it. To top it off, how was she going to break the most recent bit of news to him?

She glanced at him from the makeshift table where she was inventorying the depressingly small amount of medical supplies, and stretched to ease the kinks out of her bent back. "How's the pain?" she asked.

Unmoving. Listless. Was he staring at his toes, beyond them at the ground, or at something neither she nor any of the others could see? He blinked, and that was at least something, though she didn't for an instant let herself think it was in response to her voice. "I should've rocked her," he said simply.

That again. How could she ever hope to convince him none of this was his fault? "Alonzo . . ." She rose and moved around the table to kneel beside him. The cut on his forehead was bleeding again, and she quickly dabbed it with some ointment she'd found in her pocket, then held her finger there, a point of coolness against the heat of his skin.

"If I'd rocked her like hell," he continued, apparently not having heard her. "The pod might've knocked loose."

The fingers of her other hand spread across the top of his wrist and squeezed in sympathy. "You did all you could, I'm sure. You're a natural pilot."

His eyes flashed suddenly, inexpressibly lucid and clear, no more than a few inches from her own and filled with all the anger he possessed. His hand twisted in her grip, capturing hers inside the curl of his fingers. "Right. What do *you* know about it?" he demanded sarcastically.

Feeling the bones of her wrist grind together, Julia didn't even attempt pulling away. She removed her finger from his face, glad to see that the ointment had done its job. There was nothing left of the wound but a thin, hair-fine scar. "About nature? A lot. Enough to know that feeling sorry for yourself doesn't do any good."

He stared at her, studying her features with an almost minute intensity. Suddenly his fingers relaxed from around her wrist and he set her free. "You're a chromo-tilt, aren't you?" It almost sounded like an accusation. When she nodded, he hissed through his teeth. "Oughta be illegal."

Her eyes widened. Of all the—!

He saw the look and read it correctly. "Oh, I'm sure you're a good doctor—" he began.

She held up a hand to stall him. "Yeah, but not good enough to fix your confidence."

Again that unnerving, dark-eyed stare, so enigmatic on one hand, and so billboard-brilliant on the other. "You know, where do you get your figs—telling me to stop feeling sorry for myself?" He hitched himself up a little straighter. "Huh? You don't have the slightest idea what I went through up there." One finger punched toward the sky. He glowered when she ignored him, going through her pockets instead. An idea had just occurred to her and she was about to implement it. There's no time like the present, as the Ancients used to say.

"Well?" He obviously wanted an answer of some kind.

"Well what?" she asked, leaning forward to rest one hand

briefly on his neck. When she sat back, a small silver disc remained adhered to his skin.

Alonzo's hand clapped over it. "What're you doing? What's with the derm-app—" His eyes fluttered, drowsiness stealing over him no matter what he might have preferred. He pawed futilely at her with his free hand.

She smiled slightly as she captured it and lay it back across his stomach. "Sorry, Alonzo. I don't want you to be alarmed. I have some bad news. We've got no bone healer. Med crates were looted. Your legs'll have to heal the old-fashioned way."

He was fighting so hard to stay awake, fighting to rekindle his anger from the bank of embers it was rapidly being reduced to, fighting a battle he was inevitably going to lose. "Old way? What—weeks?" His eyes fluttered closed and he sighed deeply.

Julia sat back on her heels, with her hands dangling between her knees, and sighed heavily, watching the steady rise and fall of the pilot's chest as he slept. "No, my friend. Months."

Back at the cargo pod, things had progressed to Danziger's satisfaction. The gap through which Zero's head had been retrieved was slightly wider now. Flat on his stomach, Danziger helped True wriggle her pinkie-thin body through the narrow opening and into the undisturbed bay beyond.

"Careful, sweetie," he cautioned. Hands firm around her knees, he slid her farther inside. Her body shifted from side to side, bringing her knees into play and scooting along like some commando in an old movie. The light strapped to her wrist bobbed and weaved so much with her jerky movements that he couldn't grab a single clear look of the interior beyond the thin sprawl of her body. He tried to ignore the sick sensation in the pit of his stomach as her legs slid from view. "Can you see around in there, True?"

"Dad . . ." Her voice, distorted by the acoustics of the inner chamber, held wonder, excitement, and incredulity. "They've got one of those TransRovers in here!"

"Old solar-powered job from Earth, huh?" From the floor, her light dipped around the interior, briefly highlighting several pieces of strewn cargo before swinging around to illuminate the large, archaic piece of equipment. Brightly lit by the stark bulb, the TransRover looked like nothing so much as the skeletal remains of a dinosaur or whale set up for exhibit in some museum.

Danziger beat his head softly against the pried-up edge of the door. "Guess they really went all out for us," he remarked with humorless sarcasm to no one in particular, but hoping Devon was somewhere nearby to hear him.

True was still talking. "I can spot at least one ATV . . . and there's a DuneRail! And—"

Danziger cut her off as murmurs rose around him from the waiting group of people clustered just beyond his splayed feet. "You see the unit, sweetie?"

She slowly got to her feet and cast the light around in a swerving arc. It took her two swipes to find the rest of Zero's body. "Yeah, I see it." She hit the ground with a thud and, shoving her body along with her feet, scooted under the TransRover on her stomach. From Danziger's small vantage point, the robot unit looked to be in decent shape—its compact "muscular" frame, mostly white but painted here and there with red, blue, and yellow, was familiar to anyone who'd ever spent time working the docks. "Okay, see if you can get to its collar control pan—"

She was way ahead of him, sliding under the TransRover like she was greased, and crawling her way over to closely inspect the prone, headless body. After a moment's careful consideration, she touched a light on its collar. Instantly, the unit came to life, rocked onto its side, and stood.

True's eyes were huge in the refracted light from her wrist lamp. "Whoa!" she exclaimed, staggering back out of the way. "It's humming—"

Danziger glanced back at Zero's head couched securely in the crooked elbow of one of the crewmen. The guy looked about ready to go out for a forward pass. "You hum when you're not around, is that right?"

The head gave the impression of somehow having shrugged without the use of shoulders. "Can't say that I know, since when I'm not around, I'm not around . . ."

The silence following that remark lasted all of three seconds. Suddenly the entire cargo pod rocked. Danziger had just enough time to scramble back out of the way before the door was thrust up from the inside, grating in its socket with an unpleasant grind of metal that hurt his ears. Zero's body, the purveyor of this escape, teetered precariously on the edge of the sill for an instant before catching its balance and standing there like a conquering hero, with True riding its back as she had her father's so many times before.

But not lately, Danziger couldn't help but think, and he wondered fleetingly just how much his little girl was already grown up and out of his reach.

True's laughter bubbled up as she relaxed her legs and arms and slid to the ground. The gathered assemblage gave a ragged cheer, their voices babbling excitedly. Reaching to take the offered head and place it on the robot's vacant shoulders, Danziger saw Uly out of the corner of his eye, watching the entire proceeding with undisguised envy. A twinge of unexpected pity passed through him for the handicapped child. It must be a helluva thing to be born with something you know will ultimately kill you. What would his own life have been like had True not been born her hale and hearty self?

His mind shuddered away from that thought. He did not wish to jinx what had been, for the most part, a pretty darned happy life so far between father and daughter. "Good work, sweetie," he praised her, making her proud as punch. He fit the robotic head home in its niche and tightened down the latches holding it in place.

Reassembled, Zero raised a hand and made a circle with his thick mechanical thumb and forefinger. "A-OK," he affirmed with a gung-ho heartiness to his voice that Danziger felt certain would drive him around the bend if he had to listen to it for any protracted period of time. "Feel like a new man."

"Great. Then let's get—"

O'Neill, a vintage hunting rifle slung affectedly over one shoulder, shoved past them and peered into the cargo bay's dim interior. "Hey! Anyone have a clue how to get that old TransRover charged up?"

A great, weary, reluctant sigh welled up from inside Danziger. He glanced at True and smiled faint recognition at the knowing look she cast his way. "Sure," he sighed, raising his hand to get O'Neill's attention. "I think I can do it." It looked like there would be no rest for the weary. But as True stepped up beside him, clearly planning on giving him a hand, it suddenly didn't matter. It appeared she wasn't so far away after all.

Chapter 12

Morgan thought now might be a good time to just throw his hands up and go insane.

Somehow, through the grace of a benevolent God or good karma or because he changed his underwear daily, he and Bess had managed to survive their horrible night alone and unprotected in the wilderness. It was an experience that he hoped never to repeat for as long as he lived. He'd hardly slept a wink all night, fearful the fire might spread despite his wife's assurances to the contrary, or go out, if he so much as closed his eyes. Not that he could have slept anyway, having been kept awake and fretfully twitchy by the stinging, whining presence of billions of biting insects. Then there were the sounds of *things, bigger* things, sneaking along furtively in the underbrush. Lastly, there were the twin moons which, at full, shone into his eyes like two searchlight beacons, making it impossible to relax. All the while, Bess had the unmitigated gall to sleep on undisturbed at his side, as if she did this sort of thing every day. It had to come from having been brought up on Earth. Those people down there were a bunch of savages anyway. Everybody knew that.

Now he sat by the ashes of last night's fire with the beacon from the emergency pod disassembled on top of a rock. It was a confusing array of bits, pieces, and components, and he was fervently committed to making it work. The sooner he was out of here and off this godforsaken hunk of dirt for good, the better!

"Okay . . ." He licked his lips, brow furrowed in concentration and dripping sweat into his eyes. It was hot in the sun, but the insects seemed to avoid the heat, preferring to accost only those foolish enough to seek the sheltering shade beneath the trees and bushes. He'd suffer in silence if it meant he didn't have to deal with anything crawling on him. "Reverse polarity on the code unit . . ." He lapsed into mumbling, squinting along the lines of two wires he held in his hands.

Bess came out of the pod and stood in its meager shade with the sweat running down her neck and under the soaked material of her shirt. "Look at us." She wiped a hand over her forehead and cheeks and down her throat, then swiped the sweat onto her clothing. "No wonder we can't think straight. Honey, let me get you some fresh clothes out of what we brought. A clean shirt'll do wonders."

Morgan sighed tightly, his teeth clenched in frustration at her, at the sun, at the beacon, at himself, and mostly at the whole *damn universe*! "Bess, *please*. I'm very close to getting a read on one of our cargo pods. This is very difficult."

A whistle sounded among the bushes off to their right. To

Morgan's disinterested ears, it was just more of the strange background noise of this hateful place, one of those stupid birds, probably.

"Morgan . . . Did you hear that?"

"Hear what?" he asked, not even looking up from his close perusal of the beacon's interior. Why wouldn't she go away and leave him alone to work?

Another sharp note sliced the air. There was a moment of silence. (Blessed silence! This world was much too noisy to suit him.) And then the bushes rustled directly in front of Bess. Morgan froze and slowly raised his head to stare at the offending shrubbery.

"There's something in here . . . ," Bess murmured, and horrified her husband by stepping closer to the bushes, her eyebrows pitched upward in curiosity. A thin, high whine of air escaped Morgan's lips, forced out by lungs that thought they were screaming. Before Bess had moved more than a few paces, the bushes rustled harder, shaking from side to side. She took the warning to heart and stopped, tilting her head and weaving slightly from side to side as she tried to peer between the concealing screen of foliage. "Morgan . . . ," she whispered quietly.

He wrenched his frozen gaze from the middle of her back, and his eyes tracked jerkily, laboriously over her shoulder to . . .

Two eyes, all but hidden by the surrounding greenery. Two eyes, piercing in their intent scrutiny as *something* stared back at them from the bushes.

Bess let out a squeal, grabbed up a log from their cold fire, and fled to Morgan's side. His mind warred with the surprised conflict of a body desperately wanting to flee and legs that were frozen into place. He cowered behind his wife, holding her like a shield in front of him with her makeshift weapon and trying not to look like he was doing it. "Don't . . ." He swallowed hard, unable to work up enough spit to talk. He hazarded a look over her shoulder and saw that the eyes had vanished. "Don't be scared," he managed in something a little closer to his normal tone. "Whatever it was, it's gone."

Another whistle, this one even closer, belied his remark and assured them of the creature's continued presence. Suddenly the eyes were back, closer this time, with only a screen of gently moving leaves separating *it* from them. The eyes didn't blink, and Morgan wasn't certain his ever would again, either.

"I, I say we charge it," he suggested, barely moving his lips as he whispered into Bess's ear.

"No, no, no," she countered with emphatic certainty, one palm up and open in warning. "Wait."

"I *am* waiting, Bess," he pointed out testily. "And the thing isn't going anywhere."

She shook her head slightly. "You don't make the first move with an animal."

Morgan stared at her, utterly bamboozled by the remark, and then sighed irritably. "What animals have you ever seen?" he questioned.

Bess shrugged, her shoulder blades moving a scant inch or so from his nose. "On Earth," she explained, shrugging again, patently uncomfortable with the memory. "There were rats."

Disgusted, Morgan made a face, then took a deep breath and placed his hands firmly in the center of her back. "Count of three, Bess. On your mark, get set, *go*!"

Whooping and hollering, they charged the screen of bushes with Bess brandishing her log like a broadsword. They crashed through the stand of shrubbery and emerged on the other side in time to see a weirdly hunched, squat little creature sprint lickety-split into the woods on the far side of the next clearing.

"My God!" Morgan gasped, clutching at his wife for support as he tried to catch his breath. "Did you see that? It was . . . It was . . . wearing *clothes*!"

Bess shook her head, chest heaving. "Maybe it was skin," she suggested dubiously, mouth agape and snatching for air.

"With a hood?" Morgan countered archly.

Another whistle sounded, this time from directly behind them, back at their camp. Without even thinking, they plunged back the way they had come, tearing through the bushes, heedless of slapping branches and puncturing thorns. They caught themselves up short just before reaching their campsite and progressed slowly the rest of the way, setting their feet down as quietly as they could among the tangled undergrowth. In the heat of the moment, Morgan was actually able to forget about insects for a while.

They found the creature, or another one just like it, sitting on its haunches in the center of their campsite, staring intently at the broken emergency pod. Morgan decided he just may as well have heart failure right here and now and save everyone a lot of trouble.

The creature lifted a bony hand to its lips and blew across the ridge of its knuckles. At once, an eerie melody tainted the air, its strange tone and cadence both oddly alluring and as disturbing as oil floating on water. From far in the distance, the melody was repeated, but this was no echo. This was something else, another one of these creatures, repeating the message back or carrying it on. A message. Morgan was dead certain it was a message of some kind, but *what* kind? What could these creatures possibly have to say to one another about his escape pod? And how many of these animals were around—if they *were* animals? And just exactly *where* were they, so he could do his best to avoid them? If they were talking about the pod, were they also communicating about him and Bess? He liked that thought the least of all. And why hadn't Adair or O'Neill said anything about other life-forms on this planet? What were they doing out here attempting to colonize a world that was already taken?

The creature stood suddenly, freezing the humans where they sat hidden among the bushes. It stared at the emergency pod for quite some time, then began to rapidly bob up and down on its crookedly bent knees, alternately kicking up its legs. Morgan noticed that it had only three toes.

"What's it doing?" Bess whispered incredulously.

"I dunno," Morgan answered in kind. "Exercising or something."

Any further extrapolation on the subject was curtailed as the creature stepped forward and fit its hand around the door frame. With a nonchalance bordering on laziness, it ripped the heavy metal door right off the pod, swung the ponderous sheet of metal onto its back with effortless ease, and toddled away into the forest, leaving Morgan and Bess staring slack-jawed at its retreating back.

Morgan eventually shuddered out of his stupor. Face front, he darted his eyes sideways to his wife. "I gotta fix that beacon, Bess," he stressed. "And I gotta fix it *now*."

Danziger paused in the shadow of the ransacked cargo pod to study Uly. He lay in a hammock under the sheltering screen of some nearby trees, stretched out on his back, with his arms listlessly crossed over his stomach. His eyes moved back and forth in tiny darts and dashes as he followed the dance of leaves, tracked the movement of insects and birds, or followed the serene pageantry of the cloudy procession high overhead. Danziger had never in his life seen anyone look so bored. It must be absolutely hell to be so sick everyone just automatically assumes you can't do anything for yourself, so you're never even given the opportunity to try.

That last thought gave him an idea. He strolled around the pod and approached the convalescent with all the nonchalance of not having known Uly was there. "Hey, kid," he said by way of greeting, lifting one hand briefly in salutation. "Can you give me a hand here?"

Features slightly distorted through the immuno-suit, the boy looked as though he couldn't believe what he'd just heard. He certainly wasn't used to having people ask him that question. "What can I do?" he asked warily, with all the forlornness of someone left out of every game ever played.

The note of resigned self-pity in the child's voice put Danziger's teeth on edge. He hated that in people, that woeful sense of having no control over their own lives, but he guessed he could understand it in Uly's case. He'd been taught to believe he couldn't do anything, so why think otherwise? When was the last time he'd been given a chance to find out what he could do physically when he put his mind to it? And how did he expect to get better if he didn't put a little effort into it?

"I'll show you," he replied, and bent to hoist Uly into his arms. The kid was a lightweight and less of an armload than True had been at his age. Danziger carried Uly around to the other side of the pod and placed him in the driver's seat of a small, four-wheeled ATV excavated from the wreckage. He bent and adjusted the seat, scooting the child a little closer to the controls. "How's that for size? Can you reach the handles?"

Not easily, not in a million years . . . but Uly wasn't about to admit it and risk jeopardizing what was happening. Silently he stared at the control panel, then leaned forward and reached for the controls. Scant inches of air waved between his seeking fingers and the controls that could mean freedom. Gritting his teeth, jawbone popping into prominence beneath the pale sheath of his skin, he stretched forward, reaching hard, fighting to win . . .

His fingers brushed the handles, skimming across them like the fleeting kiss of a lover, and away. Inching forward, leaning away from the comfort and security of the back of the padded seat, Uly reached farther and carefully, wonderingly, curled his slender fingers around the ATV controls.

O'Neill strode by at that moment, the rifle slung up across both shoulders as if he were some sort of big-game hunter going out to bag an elephant. He paused and frowned at the tableau of man and boy. "Reckon Rail's your top priority, friend," he told Danziger sternly.

The mechanic met his gaze squarely, unimpressed. *I don't need reminders on what my job is,* he thought. "I thought *everyone* should be mobile," he said pointedly, forcing the words to emerge calmly from between clenched jaws. *Maybe the rest of you think this kid is luggage, but I'll be damned if I'm going to . . . and neither is he.*

Surprisingly, O'Neill took a moment to think about that rather than go off half-cocked at being challenged. And, really, there was nothing to challenge. Considering their circumstances, and the unpredictable nature of their situation, everyone *did* need to be mobile . . . in case of the need for a quick getaway, if nothing else.

The Commander bobbed his head in a quick nod. "Good idea." He conferred the phrase like a blessing and walked away with his head held high.

I feel so honored, Danziger thought scornfully and turned back to the boy, hoping his face didn't show what he was feeling. He stepped back to get a good look at Uly atop the vehicle, and gently slapped a tire guard. "She ain't much to look at, but a guy's gotta have wheels, right?"

Still no reply, though Uly's eyes had grown even wider at the older man's implication.

"What?" Danziger continued, staring at him in mock surprise he hoped was convincing. He swung an arm at the ATV. "Did you think I was gonna keep carrying you everywhere?" he asked. Then he added shrewdly, "Did you *want* me to?"

The boy's head shot up and he stared at Danziger with an intensity that almost made the mechanic laugh. "No, sir!" he assured him quickly and with almost feverish emphasis. "No! This'll be fine."

"Okay, then. Now listen." He took Uly's hand and placed it precisely on the ignition handle. "If she won't start, fiddle with this and spit on her." He stepped back and waved one arm in a gesture to give it a try. For a minute, he wasn't certain the kid had the guts, despite his eagerness. But then his fingers flexed around the handle and the ATV suddenly lurched forward, almost over the mechanic's toes.

"Easy!" Danziger danced out of the way, and the vehicle ground to a halt. Uly's face was aflame with embarrassment, his eyes bleak with the certainty that he was about to be permanently evicted from the driver's seat. "There's no rush," Danziger said soothingly, remembering what it was like when he learned to drive, and trying not to wince at the memory. "Take your time."

Uly nodded intently, then carefully started the ATV more smoothly. It trundled away, moving slowly on its big tires.

"Hey!" the mechanic called after him. "Don't forget to steer!"

The boy shifted the stick over, executing a somewhat shaky 180-degree turn, and came back toward Danziger with the biggest grin on his face that the older man had ever seen. Uly was mobile, under his own power and direction, for probably the first time in his life! The world had better get ready to stand back in wonder!

Stretched out on the ground on one side, True checked inflation levels in the DuneRail's tires preparatory to it's being taken out by her father and Commander O'Neill on a reconnaissance run to see if they could locate the items looted from the cargo pod, or the whereabouts (and, more importantly, identity) of whoever took them. She was trying to decide which she felt more—angry or worried. She'd watched her father rig the ATV for Uly, seen the way the kid looked at him, and jealousy had flared. John Danziger was *her* father, and he had his hands full just taking care of *her*. He didn't need some other kid.

Unless maybe he *wanted* some other kid? That hardly bore thinking about. Had she done something particularly bad lately that he might think about trading her in? He used to tease her about that when she was little. Maybe he hadn't been completely teasing.

On the other hand, she wasn't thrilled to think of her dad going off with no more protection than O'Neill and his antique gun, but she supposed he could take care of himself. He'd somehow managed to do it before she came along. It was just that there were so many *unknowns* out there.

Speaking of unknowns, she hadn't seen her pet all day, not since letting him (her? it?) out of the knapsack this morning for a pee and something to eat. She knew it was around here somewhere, but she didn't know where and was worried that someone else might grab it up and claim it as his or her own. Like that kid, Uly, for instance.

Something thudded against one of her boots and she looked up. A tool lay there, tilted against the sole. She was certain she'd left it up on one of the seats. She glanced around surreptitiously and whistled lightly, hardly making a sound. "Here, kitty," she called softly. Nothing.

The sound of approaching voices cut short her search. Unhappy for many reasons, and concerned over the creature's whereabouts, True hunkered down beside the tire and resumed working, glancing up as the footsteps drew closer.

Even at her young age, True knew boredom had a lot of faces. Devon wore one now as she walked toward the DuneRail beside O'Neill, who still carried the rifle like it was stuck to his body. Every few steps, he trained the weapon on various rocks and bushes, sighting down the barrel and pretending to squeeze the trigger. He'd seemed inordinately content since finding the thing in one piece, and carried it everywhere with a cocky assurance True didn't find at all reassuring.

"Two tons of supplies and equipment, Devon," he said, squinting along the gun's sight. "And it's nothing more than shiny beads and trinkets to some stunted, tri-toed hominids."

"I'm not second-guessing you, Broderick," Devon said in a voice that sounded tired from arguing over the same old thing. "It's just—"

"Then don't." He cut her off, his voice nearly sharp. "It's ours, Devon. As is this planet—sitting here, waiting for us to take it."

What next? True wondered sourly from her place on the ground as she tightened the last loose bolt. *Elect you emperor?*

True recognized her father's boots from beneath the vehicle as they scuffed to a stop a few inches from her face. "True?" he called into the air. "She ready to roll?"

She slid out from underneath the buggy, startling Devon who hadn't had a clue she was even there. The woman's face flushed, and the girl wondered if she was embarrassed that her conversation with O'Neill had been overheard. True dusted off the seat of her pants. "Yeah," she said distractedly, still uncertain whether or not she was mad at her dad for the attention he'd paid to Uly. She glanced around. And where in heck was her kitty? "Yeah, ready to roll."

"What are you looking for?" her father asked curiously.

"Nothing," she assured him and stuck both hands in her pockets so she wouldn't have to hug him good-bye. Yeah, it looked like she was mad at him after all.

He eyed her knowingly. "It better not be one of my tools, and it better be back in place when we return. *Capishe?*"

She nodded. "Sure, Dad. Gotcha. Have fun."

He watched her a minute more, clearly divining that she didn't want a hug, and letting her get away with it a lot easier than she wanted him to, darn it! His eye twitched in a brief wink and he turned toward O'Neill. "Ready when you are."

The Commander slung a leg into the passenger side of the buggy and settled onto the seat. "You drive," he ordered preemptorially.

Irritation pinched the skin around Danziger's eyes. He shared a look with Devon over the Commander's head, and she smiled faintly in commiseration. "Just be careful," she said and tapped her fingers against the vehicle's side before stepping clear.

Shaking his head slightly, Danziger climbed into the driver's seat and revved the engines. With a final check all around to make sure everyone was standing clear, he threw it into gear and they started off. True waved perfunctorily and then resumed her careful quest for the kitty, all too aware that Devon still stood nearby, watching her.

"You see what Uly's driving?" True asked nonchalantly, inherently sensing just which buttons to push to get the response she wanted.

She wasn't disappointed. Devon spun around to face her, eyes wide. "What?" she asked. "Uly's *driving* something?" Her eyes darted to the place under the trees where Uly should have been in his hammock—and wasn't. A hand to her mouth killed the gasp in her throat. Without waiting for a response from the girl, she trotted off in a hurried search for her missing son.

True grinned to herself and bent to collect the rest of her father's tools before resuming the hunt for her new pet. Uly Adair wasn't laying claim to her father without a fight. His mother would probably be so angry over the ATV that she'd never let Danziger near her kid again. And that was a good thought.

True smiled and flipped down the latches on the tool kit. It was nice to know she hadn't lost her touch.

Chapter 13

· · · · • • • ● ●

The man who never dreamed, was dreaming.

Alonzo was back inside the Advance ship, strapped into the familiar seat and fighting the unresponsive controls as the vessel bucked against the drag of the unjettisoned pods and hurtled toward the planet far below. The surface rushed to meet them, growing larger and larger through the orange glow of the cockpit's viewport as the ship careened downward on its destructive course. They were going to crash! They were going to die! Fighting with the belt that held him in, he wrenched it loose and ran to flee the cockpit. Behind him, the control board exploded in a shower of fiery sparks. With a last, desperate bid for escape, he flung himself at the doorway, dove through the open portal—

—and rolled to a stop across an earthen floor. No dust puffed up from the ground, hard-packed by the passage of many feet over many years. Puffing for breath, he rested on his hands and knees and stared about in startled wonder.

He was in some sort of cavern. It was hard to tell its exact dimensions as the lighting was not very good, but he got the sense of great openness around him. He settled back on his heels and ran his hands over the ground in front of him. It was cool against his fingertips and gave up a slight film of dirt when he pressed against it hard. He held his hand to his nose to breathe in the scent as air fluttered against his face; it was cool and soothing in his lungs after the scorched scent of burning components. The air smelled cleanly damp, rather than unpleasantly musty and close. The smell of the ground was in his nose and his brain and his blood. It was an odor he'd never known before, and yet he had somehow been born knowing and understanding it. It was the smell of a rich world, a giving world, a world that cared for and succored its children. He felt oddly drawn to this ground, this world, as though he intimately knew it.

A sound or some other faint intuition made him look up. A tall, thick-waisted figure stood menacingly before him, upright on two legs with misshapen calves, backlit by tenebrous light from somewhere within the deeper recesses of the cavern.

Alonzo shot to his feet, whirling to flee the mysterious and terrifying apparition, and ran head-on into something that stood where he thought there was only earthen wall. He staggered, catching himself against something, and looked up. A scream welled in his throat as the thing—tall, muscular, carapaced in leather, and horrific—lowered its flat, almost noseless face toward him and—

Alonzo's eyes popped open. For an instant, he didn't know where he was and he thrashed frantically for escape, hardly noticing the pain this caused his legs. Then the sights and sounds of the campsite—Julia tending someone's scratched arm, True searching through the underbrush for something, strangers' voices that were already becoming familiar, the sound of machinery being worked on, that stupid work robot's strong voice raised in some sort of cadence song—rushed back in on him and he blinked with full awareness.

He sagged back into the comfort of his hammock with profound relief and swallowed hard. His heart thudded against his ribs, and he heard the subdued rushing of his blood in his ears against the insistent throb of his injured legs. He wasn't certain which was most frightening to him: the leftover image of whatever that creature had been—the leathery creases of its face deepening and splitting as it bent toward him—or the fact that he had dreamed.

He dreamed! But, he *didn't* dream. That was the worst part of it. He just did *not* dream. It wasn't that he wasn't supposed to, he just didn't. Hadn't in more years than he could easily recall, or cared to. He'd told Danziger the truth about that. His dream button had become disconnected a long time ago, and he'd found he didn't miss it.

But he had dreamed. There was no doubting it, for the creature was nowhere to be seen in the bright light of day. As though to make up for all the lost years, the dream—nightmare—had been a whopper. He breathed deeply to slow the racing of his heart. There was no way this side of hell he was going back to sleep. Not right now. Maybe not ever, if that's what awaited him every time he closed his eyes.

He shifted over uncomfortably onto his side, glad for the discomfort, the pain from his legs a welcoming distraction as he tried to forget what he'd just seen.

Danziger wondered if suicide was an option. If he had to listen to much more of O'Neill's spouting, he might just take the first opportunity to slash his wrists or run his head full-tilt-boogie into a tree. Then again, he could always kill O'Neill instead. *That* was a tempting thought.

Bad joke, Bucko, he told himself, giving no outward sign of his thoughts as he drove the DuneRail along the dry riverbed, following the clear trail of the three-toed whatever-they-weres who had rifled the cargo pod and made off with the colonists' supplies.

The gun barrel wavered into his line of vision, and he tried not to cringe. God, but he wished O'Neill would put that thing away! He glanced at the Commander, who was aiming the weapon at the wide bole of a nearby tree. Danziger wondered if he would threaten to kill the tree if it didn't immediately divulge the whereabouts of their supplies.

"See that? Simple laser aim. Not one of those pansy heat seekers. This gives your prey a fighting chance."

Macho wilderness bullshit was a rarity in an age when there was no longer any wilderness to explore—at least not back home, and Danziger wasn't one for going out and conquering other worlds as a way of passing the afternoon. Still, and against his better judgment, he found himself intrigued by the antique weapon. "That real wood?" he asked, eyeing the stock's dark color.

O'Neill lowered the gun into his lap, releasing the trigger, and ran a covetous hand along the entire length of the rifle as if he were caressing the long length of a woman's body. "Walnut," he replied proudly. "They stopped making these in the twenty-first century. I haven't fired this beauty in years." His eyes met Danziger's "Officers' Hunting Preserve, you know."

Danziger nodded, unimpressed by the name-dropping, but he pursed his lips as though he were. "You must have earned a few medals to get *that* invitation."

The Commander nodded, his mouth quirked wryly. "A few," he replied modestly. "I figure I've got a few more coming, even way out here."

Hearing the rising tension in the other man's voice, the mechanic gave O'Neill a sidelong look. His eyes were on the far horizon, but unfocused, looking back at a place and time that no longer existed.

"That why you came?" Danziger asked curiously.

"Last frontier, son," O'Neill replied in a paternal tone that set Danziger's hackles rising. "Last one." O'Neill startled him by suddenly springing to his feet. Danziger slammed on the brakes, jolting the DuneRail to a grinding halt as the Commander jerked the rifle up to his eye and assumed the firing position. In the silence, there was nothing to hear but the sibilant purr of the vehicle's motor.

After a long, tense moment, O'Neill lowered the weapon without firing it and calmly sat back down. Sweat beaded his upper lip and the portion of his forehead not sheltered by his cap. "Some men don't have it," he remarked coolly.

Danziger wasn't prone to falling for the alpha-male schtick, but he thought about killing O'Neill anyway, just as a matter of course.

Devon wasn't happy to find Uly on the ATV, and now she couldn't get him off it despite all her entreaties—heated, pleading, or otherwise. Julia wanted to check his vitals, and he insisted upon her doing it with him sitting astride the damned machine Danziger had rigged for him. While on the one hand she appreciated the man's repeated kindness to her child and his concern for Uly's welfare, on the other hand she wished he would butt out and mind his own business or at least ask her opinion about the things he did with her kid!

"Mom," Uly explained in the patient tone of a child

letting his parent know she was being an idiot, "it's as safe as my wheelchair."

"Really?" She didn't bother trying to hide her skepticism, though she was almost certain Danziger wouldn't put her son on something dangerous. "I'm not so sure."

Julia leaned over, breaking up the argument as she disconnected the tubing from Uly's immuno-suit for the very first time. "Okay, keep breathing," she ordered. He took a tentative, shallow breath, his eyes riveted on the doctor's face, hunting for worry. Julia raised the diagnosis inhalant bag up to his mouth and he closed his lips around the short neck. "And . . . give it your best shot."

Devon watched the bag as Uly exhaled into it as hard and thoroughly as he could. The results were not what she had hoped for, but she tried hard to hide her disappointment. "Good job, Uly." She gave him a hug.

"Yes," Julia followed, picking up her cue. "Not bad at all. Good peak."

"My personal best?" he asked with bright hope.

"Almost," Devon assured him and watched his face fall with disappointment.

"Aren't I *any* better?" he asked. "I thought I was going to get better here."

"You *will*," Devon assured him, annoyed by the whine in his voice even as she prayed she had told the truth, and hadn't condemned her son to dying far away from the only home he had ever known. "Besides," she continued, rallying. "Did you think you weren't going to have to work at it?" She chucked him under the chin reproachfully and bent to touch her nose to his. She waited, eye to eye with him until he smiled in response and nodded a little to acknowledge that she'd guessed correctly.

She straightened. "Now, let me see you drive this thing—carefully. Down to that tree and back."

"Time me!" he said enthusiastically and took off on the ATV, bouncing from side to side in excitement as it trundled along. As soon as he was out of earshot, Devon's face fell.

"He's no worse," Julia said encouragingly, watching her. "Considering all he's been through, that's . . . not a miracle, no, but it's something."

Devon listened with half an ear, most of her attention on the distant figure of her son as he reached the tree, circled it with the ATV, parked it, and waved at her. She waved back, her hand curling into a fist and dropping to her side as Uly husked a single cough. She stepped forward, wanting to go to him, *needing* to go to him—and then stopped herself. There were things they both needed to learn and this might be as good a place as any to start. "All I want is to save him."

Julia's hand was light on her arm. "Nothing today suggests you can't."

That much was true, and it gave Devon a lot to think about. One day did not necessarily make up a lifetime.

Uly recovered from his bout of coughing without their help and started the ATV moving again. In a moment, he pulled up beside them and parked. "Want to go for a ride?" he challenged his mother.

Never before had she seen his eyes sparkle quite like this. For that, if nothing else, she thanked Danziger a thousand times over, apologizing for her angry thoughts and wishing him well on his trek with O'Neill. "Think it can hold me?" At Uly's happy nod, and convinced she was about to get herself killed, Devon swung up onto the back of the ATV and leaned forward to hug her son. "No speeding," she cautioned, so of course he took off like the wind.

Standing on the hood of the DuneRail, Danziger swept the horizon with a telescanner and couldn't help thinking Devon had found them a planet loaded with scenery, that much was certain. What else it might be loaded with remained to be seen, but the scenery was magnificent enough all on its own.

They'd moved from the tall grasses, trees, and low shrubbery of the cargo pod site and stopped atop a ridge leading into a land of desert with flat, sandy soil and nothing but scrub vegetation. It made for excellent viewing through the telescanner, and he hoped True would get a chance to see it or something like it.

O'Neill was stationed twenty feet ahead, down on one knee and checking the three-toed tracks that now fanned out in all directions as though the group of scavengers had exploded. Surprisingly, he'd left his gun behind. Evidently he was fairly confident the tracks wouldn't need to be shot or threatened.

Danziger lowered the scanner and wiped his forehead with his sleeve. "Nothing for miles," he reported. "No movement anywhere." He hopped down and crossed toward O'Neill, offering the scanner in case the older man wanted to take a confirming look for himself.

He refused with a shake of his head. "We won't be bested by this, Danziger," he said determinedly. "We won't."

Bam!

For an instant, ducking in reflex, Danziger didn't know what had happened. Then he realized O'Neill's gun, alone in the DuneRail and propped against the dashboard, had gone off. But that was impossible! He spun in unison with O'Neill and saw a small, potbellied lizardy sort of critter bound away from the gun with one gigantic leap and back onto the front seat.

"What the—" O'Neill drew a side-arm pistol from a holster Danziger hadn't even realized he was wearing. What did he do—sprout weaponry? Wear one to bed every night? It was all too easy to believe. O'Neill sighted on the creature as he slowly started forward, and the little animal held out its arms in perfect parody, even down to having one little digit cocked as though around a trigger.

Danziger's heart slowed its pace. It was just a critter, just some little beast True would probably fall head over heels in love with the first time she saw it. Besides, its mimicking of the blusterous Commander was kind of funny. "Hey, O'Neill, relax. Maybe we oughta hold off a little here—"

The Commander curled his lip, clearly disgusted, but Danziger didn't know if it was directed at him, at the beast, or both of them together. "If I wanted to hold off, I would have stayed on the station," he said, slowly moving into position to get a clear bead on the animal. Before Danziger could react or even think of a way to stop what he knew was about to occur, O'Neill squeezed off a shot. The animal let out a whooping cry and jumped from one seat to the other as the backrest it had been sitting on blew apart. Eyes wide and unblinking, it slowly craned its neck around to inspect the damage, then turned and leveled a frighteningly intelligent-looking gaze at O'Neill.

Something deep down in Danziger's gut told him he didn't like the look in those wide yellow eyes. He wished O'Neill would take a serious look at the situation and put away the damned gun *now*. "Hey, O'Neill, you don't even know what we're dealing with here—"

The Commander straightened, momentarily distracted by the comment. "It's the frontier," he explained simply, as though that explained it all and Danziger were an idiot for not having realized that fact. "Leave it at that." He turned back on his quarry and sighted along the rifle again, his finger squeezing gently on the trigger . . . squeezing . . .

The animal flicked out its arm in what, in any space station bar, would have been called a rude gesture. O'Neill flinched and slapped a hand against his neck. "Ahh," he hissed.

"You all right?" Danziger asked anxiously.

Pinching his fingers together, O'Neill yanked something from his neck and held out his hand to display the tiny, curved, quill-like claw that had been embedded in the skin. "Damn thing just stings like a son of a . . ." He wavered, then staggered. The claw dropped from his shaking hand and landed in the dirt. "Jeez, the little bugger's got a . . ." He gasped, his mouth opening and closing on words that would not come. "Holy . . ." He wheezed and dropped to his knees in the sand.

Danziger rushed to him as he fell over onto his face and lay still. "Hey, hey . . ." The mechanic slammed painfully to his knees beside the prone man. "Hey, O'Neill!" he cried and rolled him over, recoiling instantly from the sight of the Commander's features twisted by toxic reaction. He stared past Danziger's shoulder, eyes wide and unseeing—forever unseeing—and didn't blink when the mechanic cast his hand in front of them.

Danziger checked for heartbeat, then immediately ripped open O'Neill's shirt and began administering CPR with frantic efficiency. "Ohmigod, ohmigod . . ." His hands thrust at O'Neill's chest, pumping, pushing, praying for breath, just one breath. "C'mon, man, don't do this," he pleaded. Pump, pump, pump. Check. Pinch nose and breathe. Check. Pump, pump, pump. Over and over and over . . .

Movement across the way drew his eyes while his hands kept up their repetitious rhythm seemingly of their own volition. The critter, the cute little thing with the high-powered claws, was aping his movements, pumping away at the DuneRail seat with its paws cupped over each other,

178

puffing little critter breath into the fake leather of the seat cover.

In another place and time, a *better* place and time, Danziger would have laughed in appreciation. Now he only stared in mute horror as he worked, watching until the animal gave up the game and scampered into the distant brush to vanish with hardly a sound or a shift of vegetation to show where it had passed by. Still Danziger worked on, willing breath into O'Neill, willing life, willing things to be vastly, hugely different.

Chapter 14

• • • • • • • ●

Uly had never been to a funeral before. Sitting on his ATV with O'Neill's Indian nickel hidden like a secret against his palm, he craned his neck around as politely as he could without seeming to do it, in an attempt, with the morbid fascination of a child, to take in everything at once.

By the time Danziger returned to the campsite with Commander O'Neill's body, it had undergone subtle changes. Uly hadn't much chance to catch more than a fleeting glimpse of the corpse (Corpse! What a great word!) before his mother ruined everything by sweeping him out of sight, but that brief look was almost enough to satisfy his curiosity.

The whole thing was scary, but sort of neat, too. The adults' consternation and distress over the tragedy meant less to him than did his desire to get one really good look at the body, just to check it out well before they buried it. And maybe—if he *dared*—touch it.

He bit his lip, thinking. It was kind of strange how he didn't think of Commander O'Neill as himself anymore, but just as an "it."

The entire party gathered together on the crest of a hill above their campsite, clustered loosely around a six-foot rectangular hole some of the men had dug in the rich, dark earth. The morning sunlight was warm on their backs as the wind whistled gently in the tall grass, an earthly, musical counterpoint as Yale's deep, sonorous voice rolled gently over them.

"Forgive us, Lord, if this ceremony lacks grace. Burial is a tradition long lost to us over generations in space."

Devon's hand came to rest on Uly's shoulder. He cocked his head from its bent, prayerful position to glance up at her. She was white with shock and stress, her eyes darkly circled with fatigue and wet with tears. He felt an odd twinge of surprise. He knew his mother had liked O'Neill well enough and considered him something of a friend as well as a colleague in this venture, but he was startled to see her shed tears for the man. They hadn't exactly gotten along all the time or anything, and they weren't all that close. Her sadness was very confusing.

He shot a quick glance around the assemblage. True stood next to her father. Danziger (who Uly privately thought was a neat guy who deserved a much better kid than True, someone like *him* maybe) looked awful. He'd tried so hard to bring O'Neill back from death, but of course it hadn't worked. True kept casting anxious little looks up at him, one hand in his and the other stroking the curve of his bent knuckles in a soothing motion, as though she were the parent and he the child. Baines and the others from the ship were loosely ranged behind them. Julia stood to one side, in careful attendance of Alonzo on his stretcher. Both of their faces were white and pinched with emotion.

Yale had been talking all this while, and now Uly focused on the remainder of his words. "Bless our brother, Broderick O'Neill," the cyborg intoned, his head bent over the joined fingers of his hands. "Be gracious to him. Lift up your countenance upon him and grant him peace." He bent and took up a handful of dirt, then leaned forward to sprinkle it into the open grave. "Universe to universe, ashes to ashes, dust to dust." He paused, and Uly lifted his head, to be surprised that no one else had. No one but Yale, that is, who was watching him closely. He spared the boy a brief smile that was almost a benediction of some kind. It made him feel good all over at a time when he hadn't been feeling so great.

"And protect us, Lord," Yale went on. "Even as we might tread wearily into the unknown. And remember to your heart, our lost brethren, with whom we set forth on this mission. Protect them from evil, whether it be in life, or against our hope in death. Amen."

This last was echoed quietly by the others. They turned as almost one body to leave the hillside and descend to the makeshift camp pitched beside the cargo pod in the valley below. Two of the men stood nearby, waiting with shovels to fill in the hole, but they had their backs turned and were looking off into the distance, talking quietly between themselves. Uly lagged behind, certain his mother wouldn't notice in her grief and preoccupation. Besides, Danziger had already drawn her aside and was speaking to her quietly as they went down the hill together. That should buy him the few moments he needed. Carefully, trying to look as nonchalant as possible, he inched the ATV closer to the open grave. All he wanted was just one peek . . .

Movement on the other side of the narrow hole caught his

eye as True sidled forward, leaving her father to his discussion as she craned to peer over the lip of the grave. Evidently, she had the same interests as he. That thought put her in an entirely new light, and for once, he didn't begrudge her presence. There was something nice about having someone to share this with. They even managed to share a secret smile between them as they both reached the edge of the grave and leaned forward for a look at the shroud-wrapped corpse . . .

"Children," a ponderous voice intoned, seeming to come right out of the ground at their feet.

"Yow!"

"Eek!"

Both kids shrieked, clapping their hands over their mouths as they whipped around and discovered Yale standing a few feet away. "Sorry to have frightened you," he said, but Uly didn't think he sounded sorry at all.

"Didn't scare me," True declared, pulling herself up straight and staring defiantly into the elderly man's eyes.

"I don't scare," Uly reminded him.

"That's right. I'd forgotten." Yale knelt slowly, joints creaking, making his imposing height not quite so daunting to the children. He motioned for them to come closer. "You want to talk about what happened to Commander O'Neill?" he asked solemnly.

True shrugged. The expression on her face said it had all been sorted out. "He's dead." Her face screwed up. "Why're we putting him in the dirt?"

The old man toyed with the grass stems, flipping them this way and that with gentle sweeps of his hand. "Sometimes we need to return to where we think we came from," he explained. "Earth, even this new earth, is a place where life begins. And as life ends, it can be a place to rest."

"I didn't come from Earth," Uly said, wondering what was supposed to happen when he died. Was there going to be a place for him, or were they just going to leave him under a bush somewhere?

"Neither did I," True chimed in.

Uly reached down from the ATV and stopped the brush of the old man's hand, curling his young fingers around an index finger rough and lined with age. Their eyes met, Yale's dark brown and Uly's solemn blue. "Are we gonna all go in the dirt, Yale?" he asked seriously.

Zero was coming up the hill with a large piece of metal siding under one arm, with which to cover O'Neill's final resting place, and the men were turning to meet him with shovels ready to bite into the lumps of dark loam. His eyes never leaving Uly's face, Yale held up his other hand to forestall the closing of the grave for a minute and continue this small moment of privacy. "Not for a long, long time," he said, sounding like he meant it. "But we do have to be careful. We're in a new place. Everything is different. Commander O'Neill died because he forgot that. Because he forgot that even a little animal, cute as can be, can be deadly here."

Beside Uly, True shifted uncomfortably from foot to foot. He could hardly blame her. The Teacher's stare *was* pretty intense, even for him, and *he* was used to it.

"Now, I expect if either of you see anything like this, you'll stay far, far away." There was no question in his tone, and no careful speculation. This was an order. Yale very rarely gave orders and never without good reason.

For that reason, if nothing else, Uly nodded hard. "I will. I promise."

Yale squinted at True in consideration. She squinted back. "Uh-huh," she parroted. "Me, too. Far, *far* away."

."Good." He stood and, with a hand on each of their shoulders, turned them back down the hill. "Now, let's go join the others." A slight wave of his fingers was all the cue Zero and the men needed to begin filling and covering the grave behind them.

Bent at an odd angle, Danziger stood spread-legged atop the disassembled TransRover, standing practically on the engine mount itself as he worked to repair the antique land vehicle so they would have something to rely on besides the DuneRail (which now gave him the willies every time he looked at it, reminding him of that little critter pumping at the cushions) and Uly's ATV (which had become the boy's sole property anyway, as Danziger had somewhat planned and for which he didn't begrudge Uly in the least). Bits and pieces of machinery were spread all around him in a spray of ordered confusion, and he was in his element—except he kept finding it hard to keep his attention on his work due to Devon's presence in the makeshift work area nearby, where she was talking with Yale. He wasn't exactly certain just *why* Devon's presence should bother him so, but it did. And that bothered him even more.

"We dropped the communication dish here," he heard Yale say as he bent around to peer more closely at the TransRover's innards. "Cargo was due to land here, but— the other fifteen pods could be anywhere."

"And we are . . ." she coaxed, sounding daunted. The one quick glance Danziger gave her showed him a woman done in by stress and visibly shaken by the tragedy of O'Neill's death.

"Our e-vac pod jettisoned roughly here. With drift, I'd say we're in this area."

"So we *are* on the same landmass?" Devon sounded worried, as well she might.

Danziger glanced up again, ostensibly to wipe the sweat out of his eyes. Yale was projecting a magnified enhancement of the vast continent out of his arm. "New Pacifica's here, extending to this shoreline. And we are here . . . some five thousand four hundred and nine miles away, give or take."

There was part of the problem, Danziger thought, meaning the engine and not New Pacifica. Eyes and mind once more intent on his work, with his ears half-tuned elsewhere, Danziger stretched out a hand behind him. "Gimme a number nine anthro-sceptor."

Perched like a monkey farther back on the vehicle, True picked over the spread of tools and placed one into her father's hand.

"So, you know," Zero said from the ground, all but bouncing on his treads in his eagerness to help out, "I am equipped with a variety of sceptors and retractors."

"Not interested," True said bluntly.

Danziger shifted the tool around in his hands, then stared at it a second and handed it back with a black look. If she was going to be his helper, she was going to have to *listen* and *pay attention* and do it *right.* He'd told her that a thousand times before. "True, I said a nine."

"Sorry." She made the quick switch, and he gave her a smile to take some of the sting away from his tone. Okay, so her concentration was a little off. Whose wasn't? So what? Everybody makes mistakes, particularly in extenuating circumstances. And you couldn't get much more extenuating than being made castaway on an unexplored planet, with one of your leaders being killed by something that looked like a kid's particularly homely, oversized toy.

". . . then once we get the vehicles operational, we should head out." Devon's voice impinged once again on

Danziger's consciousness. He heard her sigh. "We wanted to be pioneers, Yale, and we've come this far . . ."

"Dad?" True's voice was tiny. He looked at her, meaning only to glance, but then found himself caught up by her eyes. She'd obviously been eavesdropping on the conversation, too, and her face looked small and wilted and frightened. "Are we ever gonna get to go home?" She bit her bottom lip.

That did it. Being distracted was one thing, but if his kid was scared and this woman was talking about what he *thought* she was talking about, then something had to be done. He tossed the wrench back at True with a lot more violence than he'd intended and ignored the look she gave him as he jumped down from the TransRover. He'd deal with her hurt feelings later. Right now, something else needed taking care of. Wiping his hands clean on his pants, he stalked toward Yale and Devon's little cubby beneath a billowing tarp.

"'Scuse me," he said with about all the brittle politeness he could muster at the moment. "I didn't mean to eavesdrop, but am I hearing this right? Are you planning a trip or something?"

Devon and Yale shared a look, and when Devon spoke, her voice was very carefully even. "We're charting our way to New Pacifica. Where we dropped our communications dish."

Danziger took this in with all the aplomb of something ingesting something else several times bigger than itself. Tension and irritation made his stomach do an uncomfortable little jig deep inside, but he restrained himself admirably as he turned toward Yale. "Why not give me a minute with your boss here." When the big man hesitated, Danziger managed to dredge up a smile that was hardly sincere.

"Don't worry. I'm a good guy." That earned him nothing more than a flick of Yale's eyes toward Devon. Only when she nodded did he move off to give them privacy.

Danziger took a half step closer and pitched his voice low. "You know something? You're crazier than I heard. You can't just drag this group across whatever the hell landmass this is. Half of us weren't supposed to set foot on this planet."

"And I'm sorry for that," she said sincerely. "But we didn't come this far to stop now." She glanced down at the table, her eyes tracking along the lines of a Mylar map.

Feeling summarily dismissed, Danziger lost it. He slapped his hand down hard onto the map, grabbing her attention as if he'd grabbed her and shook her, shutting up her Pollyanna platitudes if only for just a moment. "What're you—in shock, Adair? We *crashed* onto this planet." He said it with the careful enunciation usually reserved for small children who can't understand. "We *lost* most of our cargo. I watched a man get killed by a little lizard built like somebody's toddler. Maybe you haven't noticed, but your plans have changed. New Pacifica isn't a priority anymore."

She drew herself up, bristling. In another place and time, he might have admired her pluck. "It is for the two hundred forty-eight families on that Colony ship. Twenty-six months from now, they'll be here. I've promised them a fully operational outpost."

"That's *your* mission," he stressed, practically jabbing her in the chest with his forefinger. "The rest of us are trying to survive."

Devon leaned closer, quiet, intense. She unflinchingly met him eye-for-eye, looking straight up into his face. "You read the risk disclosure when you took this job. You were paid four times a standard cryo-sleep rate." She shoved a finger under his nose, and he thought fleetingly of biting it.

"And don't you dare invoke Broderick O'Neill's death here. The man was my friend."

Danziger bit off his words in brittle chunks. "This isn't about contracts or friendship. If you want to move on, put it to a vote." He let the challenge hang, knowing full well that if they all voted against her, she would probably grab her kid and Yale and head out without them. She looked to be that stubborn.

She stared at him, eyes blazing. He noticed her hand trembling faintly atop the map, but when she spoke, her voice was calm and level. "Thanks for your advice, Mr. . . ."

He saw the look of mortification. Caught in the middle of a heated argument, she picked now to forget his name. He could almost have found amusement in that, if he hadn't already been so angry. "Danziger," he unsmilingly reminded her.

She couldn't afford to do anything but let it slide. "But what I really need right now is a TransRover that's operational. Think you can handle that?"

Any momentary liking for the woman vanished like fog in the morning at the slightly acerbic tone of her voice. The retort that burned his tongue, begging for release, was never aired, as Julia, several yards away outside the circle of the camp, let out a loud shriek. "Oh, my God! On the hill!"

Danziger whirled around, Devon and their argument both forgotten as his eyes tracked first to Julia, then in the direction in which she pointed. When he saw what was there, fear came alive in his guts with the vengeance of long dormancy. If he thought he'd been frightened anytime before this, he'd only been fooling himself. This was the real thing.

Silhouetted against the bright backdrop of the sky stood

three tall, motionless figures—thick-waisted, broad-shouldered, each with something slender and spearlike in its hands. The neighbors—neighbors they hadn't even known were there—had come calling.

Chapter 15

Any argument Devon had with Danziger vanished from her mind as she whirled from the vision of the watchers on the hill, and searched about for some sign of her son and that blasted ATV. "Uly? Uly?" Panic rose within her in an engulfing wave. Where the hell was he? Had he gone into the woods? Why wasn't he here? Why— *"Uly!!"* she shrieked at the top of her lungs.

"I'm right here, Mom," he said quietly from behind her, and she spun around. Relief turned her knees to jelly, and she spared an instant to grab him, almost hauling him right off the ATV, and hugging him as hard as she could for an instant before pushing him away. "Get inside! Go! Hurry!"

He didn't need convincing, and he didn't need help backing and turning the vehicle, either. In a moment, the big wheeled conveyance was headed toward camp, trundling over the rough spots at its highest speed, with Uly bouncing along on top of it.

Devon watched him a moment longer to make sure of his safety, then turned to face the present danger with more bravado and challenge than she actually felt. Her eyes raked the hillside, and then the meadow where their pod had crashed. People streamed in from every direction, eyes wide in faces gone white and stark with dread. Did anyone else need help before she turned and fled with the others? Her feet danced in place, kinetic with the desire to flee, and she finally yielded.

True got the briefest glimpse of whatever (*who*ever?) was standing on the hill, and then her vision swam as her father grabbed her, scooping her up into his arms like she was just a little kid again and he was going to play "swirly" with her in the tub. He tossed her into the front cab of the TransRover like she didn't weigh anything at all. Instead of climbing in beside her as she expected, he slammed the door shut and issued a voice command. "Lock, secure—my order, voice print."

"What are you doing?!" True yelled, angry and frightened at one and the same time. "Daddy, get in here!"

His shout was muffled by the thick door and unbreakable windshield. "Stay in!" he ordered. His face wore the look she had learned, through painful trial and error, never to cross or attempt to bargain with. "Don't open it!" For an instant, his veneer cracked, and she saw how scared and worried he was, how very much he loved her, and that he would die to protect her. It didn't matter if that wasn't what *she* wanted. She knew full well just who she'd inherited her bullheaded stubbornness from.

As he turned away and jumped to the ground, bending to heft a piece of broken pipe in his hands before turning to face the newcomers, she swatted the glass between them in fury. How could he do this to her? She either wanted him locked in here with her, or her outside with him, facing whoever these . . . *things* were. Speaking of which— what *were* they, exactly?

She reached across the control panel and fiddled with the vid controls. The screen popped on immediately, flaring with light, panning and zooming under the whim of her fingers.

She was instantly sorry for her curiosity, as the camera focused sharply on the hillside figures and gave her a good, long look at a gape-mouthed face with leathery skin that looked like wax that had melted, run, and hardened again. The slight knob of nose was broad and flat, with wide, flaring nostrils—an animal's nose, and hardly there at all. The yellow eyes were all but hidden among folds of skin, but they locked on her as though the creatures knew they were being observed, how, and by whom.

Something primal took hold of her. Predator turned to prey and the True-that-was went away for a while as the True-that-was-now shrieked in fear for all she was worth.

Chaos reigned in the cargo pod camp, and there was nothing Yale could do about it. Uly and Devon were safe, for now, which was his prime concern, but he couldn't get any of the others to calm down for even an instant and hear him out no matter what he said or did. There was a lot of yelling and even more rushing about, but nothing constructive was being accomplished. It was really a case of too many cooks in the kitchen. Everyone had an opinion, everyone thought his or her opinion was the right one, and everyone wanted to be heard out, ignoring for the moment that there were at least some things they could do right now to protect themselves, and not all of them meant warfare against beings who, so far, had done nothing more than stare at them from a distance. Devon was arguing with the group, hands in the air, trying with all her might to coerce them away from their small cache of weapons. Shooting up the place (and the local population) wouldn't do them any sort of good, but it was hard to explain that in the face of blind panic.

Yale turned to go help her, to see if he could persuade the others to calm down and think rationally, and his eyes came to rest on Zero, just now putting Alonzo down near the open pod door. The Teacher's brow furrowed, watching the robot gently ease the injured pilot into a comfortable position. "Devon!" he called.

She turned immediately, her expression tense with strain, clearly not wanting to hear another single, solitary person call her name, but it gave her hope to see that it was he doing the calling.

He waved one hand to let her know it wasn't another request. "I have an idea . . ."

A few minutes later, Zero headed out of the cargo pod camp and up the hill, lumbering his way to meet the creatures, who remained unmoving on the crest. Back in camp, with Devon beside him and everyone else huddled silently at their backs, Yale spoke quietly into a hand-held mike. "We only want to make contact, Zero," he reminded the robot.

"Then contact it'll be," came the mechanical voice, tinny over the receiver's small speakers.

Devon leaned in toward the monitor, which showed Zero's point of view: blowing grass on the hillside and distant, tall figures, black against the backdrop of sky. Static crackled through the speakers and cleared. Zero was transmitting something back, something that sounded like . . . *music!*

Yale groaned. Devon shot him a look. "What *is* that?"

The old Teacher sighed and shook his head, closing his eyes and rubbing his temples with weary resignation. Life with the robot in attendance suddenly seemed interminably long. "The dolt's humming the 'Battle Hymn of the Republic,'" he replied.

The remark earned a sharp bark of near-hysterical laughter from Devon. Hand to mouth, she turned and stared up the hill at the robot's shambling form. Her hands slid into her hair, tangling it and pulling it tight, but her eyes never wavered from Zero's slowly progressing form as he advanced up the hill. Off to his right was the silent mound of rocks and dirt marking O'Neill's fresh grave. The quiet humming coming over the receiver struck a strange counterpoint to the tensely waiting crowd, hardly daring to breathe. Steadily Zero continued upward toward the creatures waiting as silent as statues only about a hundred yards above. His moving bulk slowly eclipsed them from view as he approached.

Yale's eyes shifted to the monitor, marking Zero's progress as though the robot's eyes were his own. The humming grew more pronounced with every step the robot took. Suddenly he began moving faster, his legs flashing in the longest strides he could manage. The song grew louder, like a bad soundtrack. Just as it reached a crescendo, the robot stopped dead, standing almost at the hill crest with his back to the cargo pod and its waiting occupants.

The cyborg had never understood the phrase "silence so thick you could cut it with a knife" until now. The weight of it bore down upon him from behind as he and the others crowded around the monitor to see what Zero saw.

Still slightly below the waiting figures, Zero was only thirty to forty yards away. This was close enough to get a good, hard look at their visitors. The mechanized sound of the robot focusing his internal optics came over the receiver.

"What are they?" someone asked from the back in a tiny, scared voice. Yale shushed them with a wave of his hand. He didn't want to miss any of this.

Just as the focus found its range, tantalizing those who watched with the first hint of sharp definition to the features of these beings, the creatures slowly moved their staffs together. As the tips touched, a blindingly luminescent glow filled the hillside, wiping everything else from sight. The monitor instantly went black, and the colonists moved like a single animal, turning to look and raising their hands to shield their sensitive eyes from a searing brightness.

It lasted only a moment and faded as quickly as it had come. Zero stood where he was, unmoving, the bulk of his mechanical body hiding any glimpse of the creatures. Someone made to move around Yale, to step away from the meager protection of the others and try to catch a glimpse for himself, but Yale's rigidly out-thrust arm held him back. No one was going anywhere until Yale found out what had just occurred.

"Zero?" Yale called into the transmitter, one eye still on the hillside. "You there?"

The robot's head pivoted to one side and then the other as he scanned the hilltop. "They're . . . nothing," came the simple reply. "I don't see them."

A rush of murmuring broke from the crowd at his words. Devon held up her hands for silence, demanding it and winning it with the simple gesture as she snatched the transmitter from Yale's hand. "They were just there! Where—"

"Hold it, hold it." Zero cut her off. "I've got movement." He strode to the crest of the hill and stopped.

"Zero!" Devon demanded. "What is it?" Yale fit a strong hand over her shoulder and squeezed.

Suddenly the monitor flared back to life, showing the rapid sweep of landscape as the robot scanned across the distant plain in a dizzying rush and pinpointed two tiny figures moving toward the camp. "They're definitely coming this way," he reported. "And . . ." Motors whirred as he flipped focus through a series of telescopic image enhancements. It was almost sickening to watch, but Yale couldn't have torn his eyes away if he tried. The image settled, going from fuzz to focus. The colonists held their breaths . . . and suddenly the cyborg recognized the incredibly weary forms of Morgan and Bess Martin, the woman in the lead walking with a tired, but easy, stride born of familiarity with that mode of travel. Her husband lagged behind at arm's length, his fingers entwined with hers, clearly huffing and wheezing, his skin and clothing slick with sweat.

Zero's voice, when it came again, had dropped to a whisper that sounded a lot like awe. "They're alive."

Devon stared at the mike. "What's that supposed to mean?" she asked no one in particular, not having even noticed that the monitor was now working.

Yale circled her shoulders with one arm while he removed the transmitter from her hand and placed it carefully on the makeshift table, then turned her to look at the screen. She gaped at it a minute in silence, then led the mass exodus out of the cargo pod and into the watery sunlight to watch the exhausted Martins struggle over the crest of the hill and down the other side toward the welcoming company of the crew.

Night had fallen, following the hectic afternoon with nary a tremor in the normal run of nature at her best. For a while, at least, the tall apparitions who had been (and then *not* been*) on the hillside were forgotten as Bess and Morgan were welcomed and congratulated for their strength and fortitude, and all the while Bess kept telling everyone how brave her husband was, how if it hadn't been for him they would almost certainly have died.

It was enough to make Danziger want to throw up.

He stood to one side, back at the edge of the crowd who were finishing the remainder of their meal, sitting circled around the roaring campfire. The dinner hadn't been much— food rations and an overabundance of well-preserved cheese, all found in the single intact cargo bay—but it had sure beaten the hell out of going hungry.

Morgan was holding court, delighted to be the center of attention. He hung onto that coveted role with the assurance of one completely confident that he deserved it. Considering the steady flow of food into his mouth, Danziger wondered how the little rodent found time to talk without choking to death.

"It was bedlam, wasn't it?" Morgan agreed in response to someone's comment from across the fire. "I mean, when that ship started going down, us in the clutches of gravity like that, my first thought was, y'know, we're going to be dead." He paused to chew and struggled to swallow the huge wad of food distending one cheek. He smiled and rubbed his belly. "Mm-mmmmm. Real food." Bess leaned forward, her hand gently touching her husband's knee in a gesture that spoke volumes of love and pride in the man. "I can't tell you the sick feeling I had, Morgan and I waiting and that wind shear just lopping us right off . . ."

Morgan cut into her narration, stealing back the attention which had begun to slip in her favor. "Ugh! The thought that we'd never see any of you again . . ." He shook his head sadly and dropped his eyes with all the professionalism of a seasoned performer. "*And* if someone had been trying to get in when that auto airlock snapped shut . . ." Another shake of the head.

It may have been the shift in the mechanic's silent, watchful stance as anger tensed his every muscle. It may have been merely a snake-like flick of his eyes caught in the fire's glow. It may have been the boiling venom of his thoughts blasting across to him. For whatever reason, Morgan picked that moment to look across the fireside picnic. For the first time since their arrival, he saw Danziger in the shadows, watching him.

He blanched, color fading from his sunburned cheeks as though he'd been suddenly sucked clean and dry by a vampire. They stared at each other for a long time. No one else seemed to notice the break in Morgan's narrative, since Bess had smoothly taken over. Danziger held the look stonily, silently daring Morgan to look away, silently challenging him to continue this charade, and silently condemning him for his cowardice.

Morgan shriveled under that glare. It took a lot of effort for him to break away from Danziger's dead-level gaze. When he did, it was to turn his eyes back toward the fire, sitting with his hands curled in his lap and his plate of food at least temporarily forgotten. "It was . . . y'know, it was . . . hell," he whispered simply, and Bess leaned over to slip a comforting, consoling arm around her husband's shoulders.

In the companionable, commiserating silence that followed, Julia spoke up, her voice quiet compared to Morgan's ebullience. All these hours later and she still sounded scared. Danziger didn't blame her. "Nobody wants to talk about what we saw today?"

The quiet hubbub of voices hushed completely. A few people shot her nasty looks, like she'd brought up something distasteful and rude.

Danziger shifted where he stood and stepped closer to the circle of light thrown by the fire. Let them fire their nasty looks at him. He wasn't feeling particularly charitable tonight anyway. "Thought everyone agreed they were animals."

"Animals don't carry staffs," one of the colonists said.

"No," Danziger agreed, then added pointedly, "none that we know of." When were these losers going to catch on to the fact that they were in unknown territory here? *Terra incognita,* wasn't that the phrase? They couldn't assume things were going to be the same here as they'd read about them being on Earth all those hundreds of years ago. Hadn't O'Neill's death proven anything?

"Maybe it was an illusion," another colonist put in with such false pertness Danziger wanted to slap her. "The tips of the rocks—"

"And the light?" Julia challenged, clearly wanting to understand just what had happened on the hillside. She waited for a response and got none. "Sun flares are not a reasonable answer."

Silence again. No ideas. Nothing forthcoming. No one wanting to fact this threat, if threat it was, head-on. Danziger silently wished them a sound sleep . . . if they could find it.

"Well, I don't know about lights," Morgan spoke up, his voice so authoritative the mechanic wanted to cram it back down his throat. True could have died because of him! "But we saw one of these things pretty close. It was like some sort of ape-thing." He bit into another block of cheese. "They're easily scared off," he added lazily, waving a hand laconically in the air as though that settled everything.

"Let's not make any assumptions." Devon set down her cup and laced her fingers together in front of her drawn-up knees. "There's a lot we don't know about this place . . ."

Danziger snorted in disgust. The more things changed, the more they stayed the same. "Fine time to realize that," he said sourly, catching her eyes with his before turning and walking away.

He came quietly into the silent camp and the company of those already asleep. Passing Alonzo, who twitched in his sleep as Danziger went by, he moved on to his own spot of staked-out ground and bent to check his daughter. True lay on her side, sound asleep and snoring gently into her bent elbow. The sight of her brought a smile to Danziger's face when nothing else could have. He studied her in the diffuse moonlight, then pulled the blanket up over her shoulder and tucked it under her chin before moving on into the night. He needed some time to himself, time to think, time to figure out what he was going to do for himself and for True. If need be, the rest could go hang. They weren't his responsibility.

More than half-asleep, True was still vaguely aware on some level of her father pulling the covers up and tucking her in. It brought a fleeting smile to her lips, though she wasn't completely conscious of it. It was nice knowing someone cared. Then again, her dad always cared. From the earliest moment she could remember, he had been the one always there for her no matter when, why, or how she needed him. In her own way, she tried to return the favor.

She was sliding back into pleasant dreams when something blew a puff of warm, gamey-smelling breath into her face. She started awake, wrinkling her nose at the odor, and blinked sleepily into focus the familiar face of the "kitty." Joy filled her for an instant, spreading into a wide grin that the animal aped—then she hesitated. After what had happened to Commander O'Neill . . .

She drew back suspiciously. The critter did the same and was so darned adorable about it that her heart just melted all over again. "You're dangerous," she told it, already lifting one edge of her blanket in response to its plaintive look. "I'm not supposed to . . ." Oh, what the heck. The animal happily crawled under with her, and she lay back, hugging it to her like a scaly teddy bear. It snuggled its nose against her neck, tickling her, and True giggled quietly. "Night, night," she whispered, then pulled the blanket up over both their heads and was soon asleep again.

The man who never dreamed . . . was dreaming again.

Alonzo stood atop a white mesa, dust blowing all around him. The area beyond was utterly featureless. His clothing fluttered in the wind, the breath of it warm and dry against his face, smelling of dirt. His legs were whole beneath him, strong and lean and supporting his weight without trouble or trauma or the need of anything remotely like splints or crutches.

A low, dull rumble sounded all around him, edging up on his hearing in a way that let him know it had probably been going on for quite some time before he noticed, starting low, where he couldn't perceive it as more than a vibration against some innate, sensitive nerve, and slowly growing into the audible ranges. He looked around in confusion as it grew louder and louder, increasing in urgency. The soles of his boots began to tremble. Suddenly he knew the sound was coming from the ground directly beneath him—and rising to the surface!

Some sixth sense warned him in time. He lunged out of the way as a massive creature erupted out of the ground right where he'd been standing a moment before. It pushed up out of the earth with the graceful, explosive force of a tree trunk thrusting itself skyward, showering him with small rocks and chunks of dark dirt that smelled like the wind. Alonzo shielded his head from the falling detritus and peered through the gloom to get a better look which he instantly regretted. A scream shredded his throat as the creature stared down at him from its imposing seven-foot height, out of a face like dried, seamed leather.

"What the hell—" Any tiny reserve of bravery within him shattered. Alonzo turned to run and managed one step before two more of the creatures burst from the ground directly in front of him, making him back-step fast. Hands out, they spoke to him, their speech a patchwork of broken birdlike notes and odd, echoey phrases.

"What're you—" Alonzo shook his head, not understanding. All he wanted was to get away from here! He clapped his hands to his ears in a useless effort to shut out the sounds. Almost in tears, he was unable to go forward and afraid to turn back. "What do you want?" he screamed.

Their broken tones were his only reply. He turned, spinning, desperately seeking escape, and suddenly found himself surrounded, as more of them erupted from the ground, materializing out of the earth with a silent, fluid facility that made his skin crawl with revulsion.

The string of broken notes and echoed calls went on, intensifying, lapping over one another and convoluting like mating snakes. Among the piping notes and unearthly trills, Alonzo thought he caught a snatch of familiar words. Or were his ears just playing tricks?

". . . the hell . . ."

His eyes darted in the direction of the words, steering clear of the leathery faces and slitted eyes staring down at him. "What was that? Who said that?"

Behind him came another voice, or was it the same voice? ". . . What the hell . . ."

Completely bewildered, he spun again, searching faces he'd rather never have seen. Another of the creatures spoke, and then another. (Not *creatures*, came the knowledge from somewhere, springing unbidden into his mind. That was a word for animals, for the koba and their ilk. *Terrian* was the word he wanted, the ancient word for these people, the unfamiliar word to mean them all. The word popped into existence and took up permanent, solid residence in his skull.)

". . . What are you . . ."

". . . What do you want . . . ?"

Alonzo turned and turned, dizzy with movement and exhausted with fear, searching, chasing what he thought were English words, *human* words, coming out of inhuman throats. The Terrians drew closer, moving in on him without any sense of movement, shifting like the sand, their eyes implacable.

"What is this place?" Alonzo cried, the question a searing moan. He crumbled to his knees. "Please stop! Who are you . . . ?" He bent forward and wrapped his arms around his head. *"No!"* he screamed, desperate to block out the sound of their voices, even if it was with his voice alone. *"Please! Leave me . . ."*

Something touched him. It was a light caress, a hand . . . but a human hand, not one of the Terrian's crusty, leathery appendages. Alonzo reached for it frantically, grabbed it as if it were a final lifeline and let it draw him back, away from the Terrians, and out into the real world.

He was on the ground beneath his hammock, curled into a fetal position and crying for all he was worth. His legs hammered with pain from the fall he had taken, but he welcomed it like a long-lost lover. It let him know he was still here . . . *here* in the camp with the others. Alive. Pain made it easier to escape from the dream, to put it at bay and cut off its cloying, reaching arms, arms like the Terrians . . .

Julia knelt beside him, stroking the hair back from his sweaty forehead and murmuring soothing, nonsense words. He glanced at her, still shaking with fear, and she bent to gather him into her arms. He let her, needing the feel of another human being as he had never needed it before, needing the warmth of arms around him, the soothing motion of rocking, and the sound of her quiet voice in his ear.

It took him a few moments to register the distant fire, with the others gathered around, the moons overhead, the huddled shapes of the other sleepers. Wisps of dream images shuddered through his memory, shambling like walking corpses.

"I don't have dreams," he murmured softly, the statement a plaintive cry of deceit. "I don't have dreams . . ."

But that clearly wasn't the case anymore. Carved-in-stone truth had ceased to exist, and Alonzo Solace didn't know what to believe anymore.

Chapter 16

Uly lay awake in the night and stared at the sky. It was a shroud of darkness punctuated by the glow of the moons and the glitter of starry constellations familiar to him only from Yale's tutoring. Here there was no Dipper, no Big or Little Bear, no Orion. Scattered clouds moved across the heavens, blocking out the view here and there, passing like the stately, silent ghosts of Earth's long-dead buffalo. Hidden in the leafy bowers of the trees and bushes, birds not yet named or cataloged by the colonists twittered and shifted in their sleep, not quite ready to begin rehearsal of their wake-up songs, in preparation for a full-throated reveille. The only other sounds were the faint murmur of Zero's voice, cadence-marching himself around the camp's perimeter as he stood watch, and Uly's own breath rasping through the respirator.

God, but he hated this thing! He'd been tempted more than once in his young life to snatch the breathing tube from his mouth and take his chances with the real world. He never did it, of course, partly out of fear of the consequences and partly because of a desire not to hurt his mother and Yale if something *did* go wrong. He didn't want to die. He wanted to live! But the option of a shortened life tied to a respirator sometimes made him consider the odds, even if he was only eight years old.

But his mother had fought a hard battle and won him a second chance at life free of the physical handicaps brought on by The Syndrome. If the planet would cooperate, he'd give everything he had to keep up his end of the bargain.

He stretched in all directions, careful not to disturb his mother sleeping at his side, or Yale snoring gently beyond her. Though he sensed that the night was little more than half over, he felt pleasantly rested after yesterday's ordeal, and curious about the sudden appearance of what was apparently a native population on this planet. He believed his mother when she said she'd never known there was sentient, humanoid life here. So where had they hid themselves, that all those surveys never found even a hint of their existence?

And, if Mr. and Mrs. Martin's story could be believed (he liked Bess but had his doubts about Morgan), there was a second life-form as well, or an offshoot of the same. Morgan's description sure hadn't sounded like what the rest of them had seen.

God, but he was itching to get out there into the world—*his* world!—and find things out for himself! Being tied to the respirator might just kill him out of sheer frustration!

Subtle movement off to one side caught his breath in his throat and sent his heart hammering against his lungs. Were those creatures back, come to check out the colonists more closely or kill them while they slept, despite the vigilance of Zero and whoever else was on the lookout with him?

He was about to rouse his mother and Yale with his concerns when the movement came again, but closer this time, and he saw by the moons' light that it was True and not one of the ugly creatures they'd seen yesterday. (Though, if asked, he couldn't have told you which was worse. Given a choice, he just might have taken the natives over her any day.)

She was clearly taking special care not to be heard as she tiptoed around her father's sleeping form and slipped carefully among the other sprawled sleepers. She kept looking around, casting furtive glances over her shoulder, fearful of being observed. Uly held himself very still, keeping his breathing slow and steady and his eyes slitted to cracks as she passed by and slowly disappeared beyond the grassy crest of a hill. Her arms were crossed in an odd manner across her stomach and Uly wondered if maybe she was sick. But if that were the case, why didn't she wake her father or Julia to help her? And why look so nervous about it, if she were sick? What the heck was she up to?

Curiosity may have killed the cat, but it had never done Ulysses Adair more harm than to get him in trouble with Devon and Yale, so he was more than willing to risk it again by following True. She was up to something, and he felt it was his job, as son of the team leader (well, the team leader now that Commander O'Neill was dead), to hold up his end of things and keep an eye on her. Besides, he was nosy and hoped whatever it was would get her in deep trouble.

He slowly sat up and paused, watching for any sign from his mother or Yale that he'd been heard. Neither shifted in sleep, and the steady sound of their breathing never wavered. Convinced they were dead asleep, he rose as quietly as he could and tiptoed to the ATV, freezing every time one of his leg braces clanked. One hand on the vehicle's controls and the other on the seat's thick padding, he slowly pushed the ATV toward the hill. It wasn't particularly heavy, but it was more strenuous work than Uly was used to. A sweat broke out all over his body, drenching the interior of the immuno-suit and beading the fine hairs covering his top lip. Despite the effort, he persevered, fighting against tiredness and loss of breath, shoving the vehicle along until it crested the top of the hill and began a slow roll down the other side. Only then did he jump on with a huge sigh of relief and cut in the engine, keeping it at a low, barely audible throb as he set out slowly after True.

She wasn't hard to follow in the open territory leading down to the edge of a dense forest. She moved across the rocky terrain, picking her way carefully in the moons' light. He wondered if she would enter the thick covering of trees. Despair clutched at him at that possibility. He'd never be able to follow her in there with the ATV, and he was certainly too weak to attempt it on foot. The thought that his secretive adventure might be over so soon rankled him.

He was grateful when she stopped right at the forest's edge and knelt down on the hard-packed soil. Uly cut the engine back even lower, coasting slowly toward her as she opened her shirt and pulled out . . . What the heck was this? She held the tiny creature in her hands for a moment, shadowed by her body, and stared down at it with an expression he could not see clearly. Sighing heavily, she set it on the ground and pulled her hands away.

Uly gasped wordlessly. The thing standing in front of True on stocky hind legs looked exactly like what Danziger described as having killed Commander O'Neill! Was it the same one? Did Danziger know about this? Had he known all along? Did this make True a murderer? A thousand questions cascaded through his brain as he watched True say good-bye to her pet.

"You can't stay with us anymore," she whispered sadly. "They say you're too dangerous." She stood and waved farewell. The tiny animal waved back, its face pulled down in an expression of sadness to rival the girl's. True snuffled, the tears finally starting, and the beast scrambled toward her, grabbing the trailing end of her shirt and clambering into her arms again. True buried her face against it as the animal cuddled in close to her neck, its little arms slung around her like a baby's. Her laughter sounded weak and watery as she patted its bottom. The critter rubbed its nose against her hair, pausing to raise its head and blink wide eyes as it noticed Uly for the first time. It made a half-curious, half-surprised squeaking sound, and True spun around.

Her eyes went from huge to dangerously narrow when she saw who it was. "What're you doing here?" she demanded, her voice a cracking whisper.

For a change, he wasn't put off by that tone. He was too frightened of the thing in her arms to pay much attention to how she was speaking to him. He might not have seen all of what it did to Commander O'Neill, but he'd heard enough details, being in the envious position of the quiet little kid (with an active brain and ears as big as the whole outdoors) adults often forget is close by. He knew precisely what that little animal could do.

"Is that one of those things that killed the Commander?" he asked, knowing it had to be, but hoping she would tell him he was wrong.

"Just go back to camp," she hissed. "You're not s'posed to be out here—"

"Yeah?" he asked, tooling the ATV a little closer and keeping an eye on the animal clinging to her shirt, in case it

213

tried to attack either of them. "Well, neither are you. And those things are evil. Yale told us to keep away from them."

"It's not evil!" True declared with righteous vehemence, hugging the little animal close against her. "*You're* evil! It's your fault you got sick and we came here in the first place!"

"So?" Uly retorted, meeting her snottiness note for note. "You're gonna get us *all* killed by those things, and I'm gonna tell." He hauled on the controls and began turning the ATV in a tight, lumbering circle, ready to gun it back toward camp.

"No, you're not." True went ballistic. With the little lizard still clutching to her shirt, she threw herself at him, scrambling up onto the ATV with all the agility of an ape, to beat at him with her fists.

Uly flung up his hands to protect his head and fought back, trying to push her off rather than slug her. His hand came in brief contact with the animal swinging from the loose tail of her shirt, and he shied away in fear, falling backward and inadvertently triggering the throttle to maximum. With a high whine, the ATV hurtled into the forest at high speed with Uly caught backward in his seat as True pressed her assault.

She hit like a second prizefighter. Every single blow landed, and every one of them hurt like hell. Pushing her had no positive effect whatsoever. She just bounced back swinging even harder, finally forcing Uly to resort to punches of his own. He landed a few, one that nearly knocked her right out of the ATV, but still she clung on tenaciously, determined to beat the living daylights out of him.

"Let go of me, you idiot!" he yelled as the vehicle swerved and swayed, dipping and yawing with the force of their fight. Trees whizzed by on both sides, blurred with dizzying speed, and Uly wondered fleetingly why they hadn't already crashed into one of them and exploded.

"It's your fault!" True shrieked furiously. "The whole thing is your fault—you and your Syndrome—!"

"Lemme go!" He wrestled free of her grip, prying back her clutching fingers far enough to make her yelp, then stepped back for balance and shoved her hard. That finally put an end to it. The ATV swerved and bounced, slicing through a thick stand of bushes, sending foliage flying in every direction, and Uly suddenly found himself airborne.

In retrospect, the moment lasted forever. In reality, he hit the dirt fast, landing hard on his butt and jarring the length of his spine until his head rang. His jaw snapped together hard, rattling his teeth. True, the critter, and the ATV continued on, disappearing into the dense overgrowth of the deep forest. The last thing Uly saw, before the vegetation closed behind them, was the moonlike disk of True's surprised face looking back at him.

"Hey!!" he called and lifted an arm in supplication. *"Hey!!!"* But she was gone . . . and he was suddenly all alone in a place he did not know or understand, lost in the depths of a forest on a world with which he was utterly unfamiliar.

He sat there a moment, trying to ignore the fear and loneliness and yet get used to them at the same time. Alone. He had often dreamed of being alone, but that was always on the stipulation of his being sound, hale, healthy, and able to fend for himself. Nothing in his list of dreams said anything about being on his own in a strange place, with nothing between him and danger but the faint and fallacious protection of an immuno-suit.

He looked around. As far as the eye could see (and that wasn't very far among the dense, drooping, leaf-heavy limbs of the trees and bushes) everything was still. This deep into the forest, even the birds did not sing, or they had been struck dumb by the ATV's passage. All he heard was the sound of his breathing, and that seemed uncommonly loud.

A twig snapped nearby. Uly's head jerked toward the sound, seeking the cause and praying it was True and not something else. There was nothing to see among the gently moving fronds and no other sound . . .

. . . except, perhaps, a faint whisper.

"Hello?" Uly ventured timidly, his voice hardly audible. "Is someone there?" No answer. He lay where he'd fallen, tired and hurting in every bone and muscle, and wished desperately for his mother, for Yale, for someone, *anyone,* even True, to find him. He was too young to be out here by himself. Self-pity and fear mingled and swirled within him, making his throat tighten with unshed tears.

Recriminations rose with the tears. This was no way for the son of the group leader to act, and it was certainly no way for him to act if he ever hoped to be whole and on his own. Danziger and his mother both had told him he'd have to work at getting well, so what was he going to do—sit here until someone happened to come along and find him? Or was he going to take steps to insure his safety and find his own way back to the camp?

The former was the easier route, and attractive because of it. The latter was by far the more difficult way to go, but it was the one he chose. Aching everywhere, he slowly stood and turned in a circle, studying the forest around him. Which way out? Well, that part was fairly easy. The ATV had cut a discernible swath through the forest undergrowth, bending and breaking branches and shredding leaves in its erratic passage. It shouldn't be all that difficult to backtrack his way out, as long as he took his time, studied his trail, and didn't overexert himself.

He had begun moving out onto the trail, taking the first step on his path of independence, when another twig cracked sharply. He froze where he stood. Another one cracked. And a third, and more, as something made its way toward him through the forest.

Fear prickled his skin, raising the hair on his scalp and trickling uncomfortably under his flesh as if he were a skin sack filled with bugs. Another twig cracked, this time even closer! It was too much for Uly. He broke and ran, shambling and uncoordinated from lack of experience. The braces he used for walking were never meant to let him run. He staggered, bouncing from tree to tree catching himself against their trunks, scoring his hands and snagging his suit on the rough bark. The crackling footsteps followed him no matter where he went or which way he turned, keeping pace and accelerating to catch up. Whatever was out there was bent on overtaking him, and it would, because he was weak—weak and sick!

Terror hitched in his chest, catching around a sob. There was nowhere to go, no way to escape! Hobbling in panic, he lost direction among the trees, and now there was no telling which way led to the ATV's broken trail. The footsteps gained on him, drawing closer, and he craned his head back over his shoulder in an attempt to catch sight of his pursuer.

Without his eyes to guide them, his feet caught and fouled under the unexpected edge of a fallen log. He pitched forward and landed hard, sprawling facedown in wet, mucky, swampy soil. Mud flew in all directions, splattering the leaves and caking him from head to toe with impenetrable muck. Still the steps came on, more quickly now, charging. Blinded by the mud, Uly wiped frantically at his eyes, fighting to clear away the gunk before the thing was on him.

As he blinked at the mud-smeared world, the thing broke

217

clear of the trees and came at him, launching itself the last several feet. Uly shrieked piercingly, his heart in his throat. The animal stopped practically in midair, thumped to the ground, and shrieked back at him. Uly blinked with stunned surprise as the little lizard thing—True's little lizard thing, no doubt—gave him a thoroughly scrutinizing look that told him it thought he was nuts, and then bounded forward, eager to play.

A breath the size of the planet rushed out of him, leaving him feeling weak and washed out. Blood thundered in his ears so loudly that he could hardly hear, and he was too exhausted by fear and exertion to be afraid of the little animal any longer. Its posturing and wrinkle-faced expressions were so cute that, against his better judgment, he laughed. The aftermath of extreme fear has a tendency to work that way, and soon Uly was sprawled on his back, clutching his stomach with both hands and howling with laughter. The animal, delighted by the boy's antics as much as Uly was by its own, rolled around on its butt, arms crossed on its stomach and mouth wide in a gape-faced grin of pure enjoyment.

Danger be damned. Uly reached to pet the creature and dissolved into more laughter as it returned the favor, stroking his hair and the fabric of his suit with a paw that was soft and gentle despite the impression of its claws. Now he could understand what True found so endearing and intriguing about this little animal. He had heard every word of Danziger's report and Yale's warning, but now, petting the beast, he found it hard to imagine something this cute actually hurting anybody, let alone killing someone. Maybe Mr. Danziger was wrong. Then again, considering what Commander O'Neill tried to do to the animal, maybe the notion of retaliation shouldn't be such a surprise after all.

There was nothing to bother them, nothing to break this

idyllic moment, until the lizard suddenly screamed with terror. It thumped its hind legs several times on the ground, then bolted out of the comforting circle of Uly's arms and streaked into the forest to hide itself away. Uly sat up fast, looking around in confusion and concern at absolutely nothing that should have frightened the animal.

. . . except some faint rumbling noise . . .

Without warning, two massive arms thrust themselves through the earth on either side of him, grabbing him and twining around his waist like choking vines. For an instant, he was pinned to the ground in stark, screaming terror, then his fear broke all bounds and careened off into emotions for which the child had no name, as he was dragged, kicking and shrieking for all he was worth, into the ground!

The last sight he had of the upper world was True coming back, riding the ATV with a facility and daring recklessness he'd yet to master, clearly drawn by his cries. She slammed the vehicle to a halt and vaulted to the ground at a run, but it was already too late. Dirt filled his eyes and nose. He couldn't see! He couldn't breathe! The last thing he heard, before gritty earth and sand filled his ears and he vanished completely underground, was the sound of True screaming his name.

Chapter 17

Somewhere nearby his child was crying. For the first time in True's life, Danziger had to turn her a deaf ear, though his heart was torn by her hysterical sobbing. Dirt stained the knees of his pants, clogged in black crescents under his fingernails, and flew in all directions as he knelt in the forest loam beside Devon, both of them digging furiously at the soft, turned earth with their bare hands, working as hard and as fast as they could while she frantically tried to reach her son over their connecting headgear.

"Uly! Answer me! Where are you?!" She shook her head in frustration, hearing nothing in reply, and dug all the harder, thrusting the loosened earth back between her legs like a dog hunting for a favorite bone.

"I don't know!" True gasped in answer to someone's question. Glancing over his shoulder to check on her,

Danziger saw Yale crouched beside the frantic girl with one comforting arm around her shoulders. He winged the cyborg a silent, slightly jealous word of thanks for giving her some kind of support. "We were goofing, and I . . . I . . . these *arms,* they just came up and . . . and it was so *fast,* and then he was just under . . ." Her huge eyes filled with tears again, and she buried her face in her hands.

"Uly?" Devon called stridently, her face bloodless with panic. Her arms were caked with dirt to the elbows. "Uly? Can you hear me?" Her frantic eyes sought Danziger's face for a moment before veering away to concentrate on the widening hole beneath their hands. "Where is he?! Please . . ." It was a prayer, but whether to God or him or to them both, Danziger wasn't certain.

The sound of an engine announced the DuneRail's arrival, with Julia, Baines, and another of the crew aboard. The doctor vaulted to the ground and immediately began prepping the medical supplies she had brought.

"Dammit, Zero!" Danziger huffed, breathing hard and flinging dirt aside with huge sweeps of his arms. "How much further?!"

The robot stood near the deepening hole, monitoring the signal from Uly's suit on his internal system. "You're, you're directly over him," he replied promptly. "Twenty-four more inches."

"Thank God," Devon gasped and kept digging.

"Why aren't you having *him* dig?" the crewman wanted to know, shooting a glance at Zero. "He's made for this kind of work."

Devon ignored him, so it was Danziger who answered. "He's made for heavy-duty work. He's too mechanical for something this delicate!" he snapped. "He could inadvertently hurt the kid!" He grabbed a shovel lying nearby and attacked the hard edges of the hole with a vengeance, taking out a foot of dirt with two quick passes. Caught by the work light, his shadow bobbed and danced like a gigantic demon out of some fairy story. Casting the shovel aside, he dropped to his knees and pulled loose soil away as fast as he could. "I see him," he grunted, scrabbling with his fingers in the dirt, thrusting them down through the soil as he sought the missing child. "I think we got him." His fingers sifted, burrowed, caught on something, grabbed it and pulled.

And came up with a piece of Uly's immuno-suit.

A wave of horror engulfed the group, silencing all but True's sniffling. Devon snatched the gear from Danziger's hands with palsied fingers and pressed it to her face, sagging onto her heels, deflated with pain and loss, her head bowed in misery. Her shoulders shook hard once, twice, a dozen times, and she pressed the cast-off immuno-suit harder against her face.

Danziger stared at the lying hole. "We're going at this wrong," he murmured, not quite certain yet of what he meant, but with the inkling growing even as he spoke. "There's a way in . . ." He stood and straightened, easing his aching back and meeting True's horrified, tearful gaze across the clearing. Their eyes locked only for a second before she launched herself at her father, throwing her arms around his waist and burying her face in his chest. He hugged her tightly, unable to offer any words of comfort right now, and jerked his head at Julia. "We need everyone out of here," he said quietly. "If those creatures are still around, we don't need all of us being captured. I'll stay with Zero and that's it. Everyone else goes back to camp."

"Dad—" True started to protest, but she clamped her lips tight when he shook his head.

"*Everyone,*" he stressed in that no-argument tone he knew she hated.

Julia nodded wordlessly at his orders, glancing once at

223

the miserable huddle that was Devon Adair. Danziger followed the look and found those piercing, tearful Adair eyes locked on him. There was no mistaking the message they sent. This lady was going nowhere.

"No," he said firmly and shook his head. "It's too dangerous. I'll get your kid. Somehow." A hand on her arm stilled Julia as she bent to pack her things. "Leave the supplies. I know how to respirate."

She blinked at him in surprise, and he thought she would either question how he knew (which was none of her business) or argue the point in her favor. After a moment, she did neither, but merely nodded and left things where they were, stepping back and shoving her hands into her pockets.

Devon stood, her chin high and her son's equipment clutched to her chest. "I'm staying here till we find him," she said, the words simple and very, very firm in their adamance. She sniffed once and blinked away tears, wiping a grubby hand across her eyes and leaving behind a smear of dirt.

Danziger had learned a long time ago when it was better just to give in rather than continue a pointless argument he had no hope of winning. Besides, arguing wasted precious time, and really, who could blame her? If True were down that hole, did he honestly think anyone could keep him away? It wasn't likely. Not without the use of several pneumatic sledges.

He nodded sharply in agreement. "Julia, we're going to stay in contact over gear. If you lose us, if you hear anything happen to us, pull up stakes and get the hell away from here as fast as you can. I don't know where you'll go, but go you will. You got that?"

Oh, she got it, but she didn't like it one bit. Other people had been in charge up until now, and here was Danziger putting her in charge of getting the others moving in the likely event he and Devon met their maker sometime soon. He didn't know if she was right for the job. Hell, he half-expected she *wasn't*, but he'd seen her exert her authority over Alonzo's stubbornness. She was just going to have to learn to do it on a larger scale.

Julia glanced quickly at Devon, looking for confirmation of his orders and finding it in the other woman's blazing eyes and brief nod. Still looking as if she'd rather take on almost any other task, she turned away and began herding the others toward the DuneRail and the TransRover Danziger had used to get here.

Only when the others were moving did Danziger loosen True's grip on him and kneel down to look into her streaming eyes. "Listen to your dad, kid. You finish what we started on that TransRover." He broke off as her tears increased. Her hands scrubbed at her face, hiding her eyes. "True." He never raised his voice, but his firmer tone got her attention. She blinked at him over the balled contours of her fists. "You're a good mechanic. I'm counting on you."

She blinked rapidly, willing back more tears, and took a deep, shaky breath before nodding decisively. "Okay, Dad," she said, her voice wavering. "I'm on it." She hugged him tightly, then walked toward one of the vehicles without once looking back.

"You're good with her."

Danziger glanced at Devon as True slung her lanky frame into the driver's seat, before some adult beat her to it, and started the engine. He was surprised and a little embarrassed by the praise. He'd never much thought about it. He and True just *were*, together. "Thanks. You're not such a bad parent yourself." Clutching her son's immuno-suit, she didn't look as if she much believed him. "C'mon. Let's get to work and get Uly out of there."

"John."

He jerked, startled to hear someone use his first name. He hadn't even been aware anyone in the group *knew* his first name. He turned around, and Yale gestured with a long stick toward the roots of an old, moss-covered, overturned tree. "There's something here I think you should see."

"I thought I said *everyone* was supposed to leave except Devon, Zero, and me?" Danziger challenged.

The cyborg shrugged. "In a lot of ways," he said quietly, "Uly is *my* son, too. At least I think of him that way. So I'm not going anywhere. Besides, I'm bigger and meaner than both of you put together." He smiled fleetingly. "Now, come take a look at what I've found."

Back in the pod camp, a gentle breeze rippled the silken weight of the tarpaulins strung from poles and handy branches to serve as sun shelters during the day and protected sleep areas by night, for those who didn't feel like sleeping directly under the stars. For his part, Alonzo was beginning to like it. Nighttime at least reminded him of what it was like to be in space . . .

Flat on his back in his hammock, Alonzo was free to do little but look and listen and think. Thinking brought on thoughts and images he didn't care to explore too closely, so he spent as much time as possible in the diversion of watching and listening to the others in camp.

Most of the group had broken up into sullen huddles as they waited for word on Uly from Devon and Danziger. Children had never been a big a deal to the pilot. He was sort of ambivalent on the subject, never having fathered any he knew of, but he sincerely hoped nothing awful had happened to the Adair kid and that he would be found soon and safely. Apart from his being so sick, he didn't appear to be a bad kid, just the usual run-of-the-mill imaginative, ornery child. In some respects, Uly reminded Alonzo of himself, more years ago than he cared to contemplate.

"Things that large don't just swim out of the ground," Morgan said from beneath the next shelter, where he sat alone with Bess. Alonzo couldn't figure how the woman stood being in his company. Oh, sure, she was married to him so it was practically required, but still . . .

"We're buying into some kid's imagination." He shot a glance across the camp at True sitting hunched under a work light atop the TransRover, with a tool in each hand, working nervously to get the vehicle up and running.

Bess wrapped her arms around her drawn-up legs. "What about that thing that ripped the door off our pod, honey? I mean, how do you explain *that*?"

Morgan rolled his eyes and gave his wife a look that quite eloquently said he was trying to make a point and would she butt out of the conversation, please? "I don't know. Maybe there *are* reasons why this thing was never authorized. Maybe if our esteemed leader had stopped playing God for one moment in her life, we wouldn't be in this mess."

Bess watched him silently for a moment, her brows drawn together. Alonzo couldn't tell if she was upset, angry, or both, but one foot jiggled with suppressed emotion of some kind. When she finally spoke, her voice was tight and controlled. "You know, Morgan," she said icily, "her child is missing right now."

He spread his hands, open, politic, and so very, very smooth. "Hey, *I* care about the boy as much as anyone. It just doesn't make any sense, that's all. Creatures erupting out of the earth? Physics can't work that way."

You don't know everything, pal, Alonzo thought. Could he have prevented this if he'd only told someone about his dreams? The thought terrified Alonzo. Even with crisis and, possibly, tragedy at hand, that information remained locked

227

behind his tongue, fixed to the roof of his mouth as though with glue. How could the man with no dreams talk about what he had seen in the not-so-quiet realm of his own head?

He turned away, shifting over onto his side, and ignored the rest of their conversation. There wasn't any more he needed to hear. He already knew more than he'd ever wanted to know.

The length of filament rope slid smoothly through Danziger's fingers, looping in tangle-free swirls at his feet as he pulled Zero's head up out of the narrow hole Yale had discovered at the base of the tree's dried-out root system. Flecks of dirt sprinkled the robot's head like decorations on a dessert. "Looks like some sort of tunnel," he reported.

"Will a man fit down there?" Danziger asked, staring down into the yawning blackness that didn't look too threatening from up here, but most certainly would from the other side.

"Yes." The robot's body drew itself up while its head remained tethered to the rope, swinging like a pendulum in the mechanic's hands. "But as a Zero unit, I come with a variety of excavation accessories."

Danziger pursed his lips and nodded, just to let the robot know he was listening. It was a nice offer, but— He unhooked the robot's head from the tether and tossed it to Yale so he could reattach it to the body unit.

"Course," Zero continued blithely, "they were all stolen, but—"

Devon stepped forward, standing close to Danziger. "I'm going down," she said firmly.

Danziger saw the look that crossed Yale's face. The expression told him he wasn't going to win this one without some sort of battle. "With all due respect," he began politely. "Like hell."

"That's my son down there!"

"I appreciate that, Devon, more than you know," he replied gently, but firmly, wishing he had Morgan's way with words and knowing all he could rely on was his habitual slash-and-burn-through-the-bullshit manner. Blatant, bald-faced honesty had gotten him in trouble more than once, but Danziger couldn't seem to give up the habit. "But we've already lost one of our leaders to a stupid mistake that killed him. We don't need the other one trying to do the same, when there *are* alternatives. I'm not keen on going down this hole *or* getting myself killed, but there are a lot more people involved in this than just Uly. People who are counting on you."

It was a low blow, but it hit her where she lived. Like it or not, she was fairy godmother to the whole kit and caboodle of them. He bent and rooted for a headgear set in the supply pile, then fixed it over his head with an ease of long experience, and attached the end of the cable to his belt. "I'll keep you on gear the whole time, let you know everything I see," he assured her gently.

He could tell the argument infuriated her, that she hated his being right and there being nothing she could do about it. He looked at Zero as he double-checked the knot. "Pal, if you hear me scream with terror, take that as your cue to start yanking me out."

"Gotcha."

Danziger nodded once, adrenaline already making his heart race as he tried not to think about what might be waiting for him down there in the dark. Without another look at the others, he stepped to the rim of the hole and dropped himself over the edge.

Legs dangling in midair as the rope was slowly lowered, Danziger flashed his hand light around on the cavern's dirt walls and the floor far, far below. "Zero," he spoke into his headset. "Can your gear track me down here?"

"Sir," came back the reply, "I have excellent tracking abilities."

Good, Danziger thought. *Let's just hope they weren't stolen, too.* Reaching the bottom, he steadied himself, beaming his light in all directions, and then slowly un-hooked the cable from his belt, setting himself free in unknown territory. The smell of dirt filled his nose as he set off down the arm of a nearby tunnel.

True stared at the torn-apart engine of the TransRover without really seeing it, her tool forgotten in her hand. It wasn't difficulty in the repairs that made her stop, but an overwhelming wave of sadness and guilt. If Uly died, it would be her fault because she'd had no business having anything to do with the kitty, particularly after Commander O'Neill was killed. Assuredly, if she'd minded her own business and kept her distance from the creature, she and Uly would never have had the fight and he would never have been knocked off the ATV and grabbed by . . . by . . . Tears filled her eyes again, for the umpteenth time that night, and she furiously brushed them away with the back of her hand.

"How's it going there, little girl?"

True turned self-consciously, wanting to see who had snuck up on her unawares and had the effrontery to call her such a stupid name. *Little girl?!* First O'Neill and now— Bess Morgan's friendly face regarded her from a few feet away.

She couldn't face the openness of the woman's expres-sion, inviting something she didn't care to give. "I'm fixing the TransRover," she said pointedly, almost sullenly, and hunched back over her work, hoping Bess would take the hint.

The woman was either an idiot or as stubborn as True was. She didn't go away. "Anything I can do to help?" she offered. When True didn't reply, she leaned on the Trans-Rover and held out her right hand for a shake. "I'm Bess. We haven't actually met. What's your name?"

Reluctantly, not wanting to be completely rude, because her father had taught her better, True stopped working and raised her eyes, though she didn't take the offered hand. "True Danziger. And *no,* there's nothing you can do to help."

Dammit! Still the woman would not go away! Bess stepped around for a better look at the vehicle's engine. "I don't know," she murmured. "We used to have a mine tractor back home that I used to tinker with out behind my parents' house." She flicked a glance at the girl and smiled sweetly.

True blinked like a snake. "I'm not impressed," she said flatly and went back to work with a firm and devout decision not to look up again no matter what the woman said next. If she was smart, she wouldn't say anything and would just go away.

She wasn't that smart. She actually had the unmitigated *gall* to put her hand atop True's, stilling her busy fingers. True froze under the touch, rivetting her eyes on the metal beneath her hands, rather than stare at their fingers, which were almost, but not quite, entwined.

"It's not your fault, True," Bess said quietly. "We'll find Uly. We're all in this together."

Something in True wanted to rail at Bess's platitudes, but couldn't. The words were frozen in her lungs, icy, burning lumps in her throat that would not break free. She barely remembered her mother. Certainly, she did not remember any parental touch other than her dad's. And now here was this woman, this stranger, offering her a sort of comfort she could not remember ever having had . . . though once upon a time she had wanted it.

She waited, willing Bess to leave. After a moment, she did so, sliding her hand away and moving away toward her husband. True listened to her retreating footsteps swishing gently through the grass and grinding faintly on the gravel. Only when they were faint did she hazard a look over her shoulder at Bess's back, studying it questioningly, wonderingly . . .

Something else caught her eye, some slight movement on the ridge overlooking the camp. Three lone figures, backlit and bright-edged by the stars, stark and pale beneath the light of the moons. "Oh, no," she moaned, wanting her father desperately. Her quiet voice drew the attention of everyone nearby. "They're back."

Chapter 18

Something cold and fearful sprang to life in Julia's chest as she watched the three creatures on the hill ridge be joined by two more . . . then one . . . and another two. Now they were eight, standing motionless, stark and spare, highlighted by the faint glow of the camp's fires, black silhouettes against the jewl-like glory of the night sky. A gentle wind, belying the intensity of the moment, lifted her hair and blew it across her eyes. When she cleared it, blinking, another figure had joined its eight companions. Another. Still another. And now two more . . .

A strangled sound from Alonzo made her look his way. His face was stark white and tight with anxiety as he struggled to sit up in the weaving hammock. She watched him a moment, strangely feeling no inclination to help him, then her attention was inexorably drawn back to the hill crest as two more figures rose into view. The creatures were appearing at the rate of one or two every few seconds now, rising with an apparent effortlessness over the ridge and standing there, as still as trees, doing nothing but watching the group below.

And being watched in turn, especially by Morgan, who had found a telescanner somewhere and now held it to his eyes, peering through it and working the controls to zero in on whoever it was who had come calling. "Oh. . . ." His quiet moan was a long, drawn-out sigh of air. "Lord . . ."

Bess clutched his sleeve, her eyes riveted on the brow of the hill as more and more of the creatures appeared. "Those aren't like the thing we saw, Morgan."

"I can see that, Bess," he snapped, but she didn't pay him any mind.

Now there were sixteen of them, and more coming. The entire camp remained motionless, transfixed by the eerie, silent regard coming from the top of the hill. This was worse than just being attacked outright . . .

Suddenly, Morgan dropped the scanner and scrambled for a weapon left unattended on a nearby table. "What're we waiting for?" he demanded, brandishing the gun. "Them to kill *us*?!"

"Morgan, be careful!" Bess warned and grabbed for his wrist, trying to keep the gun from flailing around. "Don't—!"

"Morgan!" Julia cried shrilly. "No!" She stepped toward him without a single clear idea of what she intended to do, but it was already too late.

Swinging the rifle up to his shoulder, he sighted down the barrel and sent an aggressive blast into the hillside just below where the creatures stood. They shifted slightly, as though moved by the breeze and nothing more, then were still again, staring silently. Swearing in amazement, Morgan brought the weapon up for another shot. Before he could squeeze the trigger, the creatures vanished as effortlessly as they had first appeared, dropping down below the ridge line in one solid mass. There was a faint, hardly discernible, rumble and then nothing but the sound of the wind through the leaves.

A prideful grin split Morgan's face, and he propped the rifle on his shoulder as if he were some sort of conquering hero. "See? Everyone understands the universal language of power. We'll show these things who's boss on this planet."

Julia hardly heard him, her attention still fixed on the brow of the hill, replaying in her mind's eye how the creatures had smoothly appeared and vanished, and remembering the subtle rumble, like the sound of falling earth, and what True had told them when she raced, sobbing, back to camp without Uly.

She sprang past Morgan, jabbing him with one elbow to brush him out of her path. "You idiot," she called back.

"Hey!" He staggered and caught himself against Bess. "Where're you going?"

Unmindful of the danger, unmindful of Danziger's orders that put her in charge, and not giving a rat's ass what Morgan or anyone else might think, Julia raced up the hillside, sprinting as fast as she could up the steep, gravelly embankment. She stopped short at the crest, stumbling and catching herself breathlessly before she pitched over and tumbled down the other side. Panting, her lungs heaving painfully, she hunted the terrain as far as her eyes could penetrate in the moon-shot gloom, and found nothing—no creatures, not even any sign that such creatures had ever been here. Nothing except—

She looked down, and the hard-won breath abruptly stalled in her lungs. Right there, right in plain sight for anyone with the brains to see, was everything she needed to know. Here at the crest of the hill, where each creature had stood, was a little mound of softened, disturbed dirt, humped up from the ground in a small hillock, just like the ground where Uly had vanished.

Trembling, Julia bent and gently sifted the loosened soil through her fingers, staring at the dirt as it trickled across her hand in fine rivulets as soft as a lost child's cheek.

"Uly? Can you hear me, Uly?"

Moving at a slow pace almost painful to maintain, Danziger moved along the maze of narrow, dim tunnels carved beneath the planet's surface. Scattered points of light filtered in from unseen areas as though phosphorescent fungus or something like it grew there to provide scant illumination. He didn't take the time to explore further and find out if that was the case. He might discover that the stuff was planted there on purpose, and that brought up a bunch of possibilities he didn't like to consider just yet. There was quite enough on his plate at the moment already, thank you very much.

His hand light projected a weak beam, guiding him with faint fingers of illumination that did little good, but were reassuring to have in any case. Hearing something faint down one of the off-shooting passages, he stopped and listened hard for a few moments before continuing on. It was nothing more than the hollow sough of wind eddying through these tunnels, bringing fresh air so far underground. Some sort of engineering feat had mastered that impossibility. That these tunnels had been dug by hand could not be questioned. The floor was worn smooth with the passage of years and many feet, and the walls bore an odd sort of symmetry.

Danziger spoke quietly into his headgear. "It's like an underground river down here, or an abandoned mine." He ducked his head under a particularly low passage and continued on.

Devon's voice came to him over the link, made tinny and small. "Any sign?" she asked, though she must have known full well she'd be the first to know if he did. "Footprints? Signs of struggle?"

Her voice was filled with pain. Their brave leader was as scared as she'd ever been in her life and trying damned hard not to show it. He hated having nothing to give her to ease that fear. "Nothing. It's like it's been empty forever."

And how long *was* forever around here? he wondered. Something had lived here once. The unsubstantiated certainty of that burned in his guts. Something might yet, but the place certainly *looked* vacant and up for rent.

He came to an intersection of two wide, dark tunnels. Their sheer size marked them as main thoroughfares for whatever had once dwelled here. He stood at the crossroads and peered uselessly in each direction. "Uly? Uly!" His voice reverberated off the cold tunnel walls and gave back nothing but echoes. Sighing, Danziger chose a direction and pressed onward.

Julia wondered if everyone who ever dealt with Morgan Martin came to the decision to kill him at the earliest possible opportunity. How the hell did Bess, who seemed like a nice, normal, level-headed sort of person, put up with him? Now he was arguing with her (though he *called* it nothing more than a "conference," as if they were still on the station), taking the vanguard of a group of people who were so stressed that they could be swayed in whichever direction the wind happened to be blowing. Danziger had put her in charge and she had her backers, but it was clear Morgan wanted to be running things his way, even if his way meant shooting up the place. Dammit! Hadn't he learned anything from the news of O'Neill's death?

"Julia!" someone called stridently. "Julia!" Hands clutched hard at her shirttail, almost pulling her over backward. She rounded fast, ready to blast whoever it was, and startled a white-faced, gasping True.

She grabbed the girl's shoulders. "What is it, honey? What's the matter?" *Now what?*

"It's . . ." The child gasped and coughed hard. "It's Alonzo. He keeps calling for you."

Well, that was a change of pace. True dragged at her arm, and Julia let herself be pulled along in the girl's wake, quite aware that some of the others came along for the ride, edgy, but still curious to see what was happening now— especially if it was happening to someone other than themselves. The human race never seemed to change.

The pilot looked like hell, whey-faced and staring blankly into the distance. Julia warned the others back with her eyes, then knelt and touched him gently on the shoulder. "Alonzo? You all right?"

His eyes were practically glazed, so fixed were they on the horizon. His lips moved slightly, mumbling, but she couldn't make out the words.

"What did you say?" she asked, leaning closer.

His tongue flicked nervously over his lips, wetting them. "They're . . . Terrians," he whispered.

She blinked at him, utterly confused. What the hell did that mean? "What? What'd you say, Alonzo? *What* are Terrians?"

His eyes stayed trained on the distant horizon, running back and forth across it as though searching for something, or on the lookout for it. That thought brought a profound chill to Julia's body. "They are," he replied, as though it should be perfectly obvious. "The creatures. The ones who swim up from the earth."

She ignored the rising wave of murmurs behind her. "Alonzo, are you with us? Alonzo?" She snapped her fingers in front of his eyes.

He hardly reacted, just turned mildly to face her. In her professional, clinical, dispassionate opinion, he suddenly seemed normal given their extreme situation. He was shaken by all that had happened, but who wouldn't be? Everyone was on edge. One wouldn't expect otherwise. Still . . . there was something else going on behind his eyes. Julia was certain of it and hated like hell that she had to pursue it. "Alonzo, how do you know what they're called?"

He blinked at her, though she wasn't certain he actually saw her. Behind her, someone mumbled something about heat stroke and it made her angry. She'd worked damned hard to make sure he didn't suffer from that. Hadn't he already enough to bear?

She closed her ears on the remark, holding Alonzo's eyes with hers and trying to send him all the encouragement she could through that link. Finally, he licked his lips again and she leaned forward, straining to hear the faint whisper of his voice when it came.

"I . . . I talked to them," he said, his voice pinched and tiny, as frightened as a child's. He sounded like he was going to cry at any moment.

Still meeting his eyes, Julia sat back on her heels in wonder. "You what?" she asked, as the full import of what he said tumbled into place in her head, couched in an idea of utterly fantastic proportions.

Never in her life had Devon felt so drained, so weary. Not when she was fighting her way up the ranks of station designers to become number one. Not when she discovered Uly had The Syndrome. Not even in all the years it took to bring her dream of a new home for him to fruition. Her son's disappearance had taken all the strength she had right out of her. Listlessly she watched Zero track Danziger's movements underground.

Yale shifted beside her on the fallen tree they used as an impromptu bench. She knew he must be tired, too, and just as worried and discouraged as she. "Devon, go back to the camp and get some rest. I'll stay."

He must have known she'd refuse, so she didn't even bother shaking her head to let him know she'd heard. "Twenty-two light-years. For this." Her hands flapped uselessly.

"I haven't given up," the Teacher said simply, as though this matter of faith was of no more import or effort than scratching a bug bite on his ankle. He looked down at her. "And I know you haven't, either. We *will* find him."

She wanted to believe that more than anything in the world, but it was hard, oh so hard, and she hated herself for her doubts. "What was I thinking?" she asked, looking up at him, seeking an answer to what she saw as her own stupidity. "Why did I bring all these people . . . ?"

"You didn't *bring* them, Devon," Yale said calmly. "They *followed* you. Two-hundred-fifty families still out in space will tell you that in person when they reach this planet. I thought that was obvious."

The quiet force of those words, and the profound faith behind them, left Devon feeling shaken. For a moment, she didn't know what to say or do, as the reality of her responsibility loomed ever larger. "I don't know. Maybe we had no right, Yale," she said quietly, around the painful knot lodged deep inside her. "Maybe we're not supposed to go to the end of the universe to save ourselves."

Yale reached out and gently tilted her chin up until she was forced to meet his eyes. He held her gaze for a long moment. "Maybe we just haven't gotten there yet," he said firmly.

She sighed, uncertain, not knowing what to say to that. Suddenly her gear flashed and Julia's voice filtered through. "Devon? Devon, you there?" She sounded excited as hell. God, what else had happened?

Glancing at Yale, Devon flipped down the optic feeders and began speaking before the doctor's image became clear. "I'm on. What—"

Julia cut her off, eyes shining. "I think we've got a way—"

"What are you talking about?" Devon demanded, beating back the bubble, the wave, of hope that had immediately risen in her at the words. Not yet, not just yet . . .

Julia shot a significant look off-screen at someone. "Uly," she said, as though that were explanation enough. "I think we know who or what has him. We might be able to reach him."

"What?!" Devon blinked at her, utterly lost. As the doctor continued speaking, explaining what she knew, Devon tried to digest what sounded like nonsense . . . and felt the rose of hope bloom anew deep inside her with a burst of vitality no number of winters would ever quell.

Chapter 19

· · · • • • ● ●

The twin moons hung over the forest at the plains' edge, illuminating the night with their glow. The four of them had sat here for hours, with Zero continuing his monitoring of Danziger's progress, but Julia still wasn't certain Devon and Yale completely understood or accepted what she was telling them. Still, she had to try, and she would continue trying until she convinced them, though she wasn't even certain Devon was paying much attention. She seemed to be, but most of the time her eyes were far away as she listened in on the headset for any sound from Danziger slowly making his way through the Terrians' labyrinthine tunnels.

"I'm not saying I'm sure it'll work," Julia persisted. "But I think it makes the most sense. The soil was disrupted on the ridge just like it was here." She sought Devon's eyes,

could not gain them, and settled for Yale's steady, contemplative gaze. "Alonzo's dreams *might* have been their
attempt to approach us."

Devon surprised Julia by actually looking at her. "And
you think they'll try to reach us again."

"You're at the eight-hundred-foot mark," Zero calmly
reported to Danziger.

Julia's eyes flicked toward Yale and away. "I don't know.
All we can do is send Alonzo to sleep and try." She looked
at the pilot, seated stiffly on the ground beside her.

Her shifted uncomfortably, looking haggard with his
haunted, shadowed, sleepless eyes. He licked his lips and
shrugged. "Hey, all I said is I saw them in a dream."

"Uly was not taken in a dream," Yale said firmly, his eyes
hard.

"Guys?" Danziger's voice over the link was a hard fierce
whisper that cut the conversation in two. "Guys, you up
there?"

Devon snapped her optic feeders into place so she could
see Danziger up close and personal. "What?" she demanded. "What is it?"

"I . . . I'm onto something here."

Julia leaned sideways to look over Devon's shoulder and
catch a glimpse of what the other woman saw. Alonzo
shifted, wanting to see, too, but unable to move into a better
position. He was white with strain and fear. After a
moment's hesitation, Julia took his hand, squeezing it in
comfort and lacing her fingers with his.

"Hang on a second," Danziger said. He shifted his
headset, reversing the optic feeders in an attempt to give
them a clear look at what he was seeing. His hand light
barely illuminated the vast area, exposing in front of him the
vague, looming contours of a well-designed recessed arch-
way carved between the gently in-sloping walls. "Can you

guys make this out?" he questioned. He stared at the structure in wonder. "Whatever lives down here, I don't think it's animals."

The doctor knew she was being stared at before she turned to meet Devon's steady, stubborn, rock-hard gaze. "So what're we gonna do?" Julia asked quietly.

Devon stood. "*I'm* going after him," she said adamantly. "I'll take the sedi-derm."

"Devon, it's too—" Yale began.

"Don't you think Alonzo is better—" Julia tried, knowing any argument was truly futile when Devon slipped the derm-app sedation device out of her grip as handily as would a pickpocket working a crowd, and applied it to her neck before Julia could react.

"Whatever happens, don't pull me out," Devon ordered, demanding compliance with her eyes. At this juncture, what else could they give her? In a matter of moments, Devon's features went slack. Her head dropped back and she started to fall, but Yale caught her with gentle efficiency and settled her to the ground with her head in his lap and her arms folded limply across her abdomen.

Julia waited several minutes, then leaned over to check Devon's vitals. She was filled with unease. "No REM," she said, pointing at the woman's closed eyes and motionless lids. "This isn't right, Alonzo. You're the one they approached. You've got to go with her."

A swirl of undefinable emotion crossed the pilot's handsome face, leaving him looking as pliable and unfixed as a lump of clay. "I . . ." He stared at her, past her to Devon's face, flaccid in dreamless sleep, and abruptly sagged in acceptance of his fate. Without a word, he stretched out on the ground beside Devon and waited silently while Julia applied the sedi-derm to his neck. He was asleep in moments.

Hands moving with swift confidence, Julia hooked them both to a small device which would electronically monitor their heart rates and other vital signs. Devon's heart was already racing, the pace increasing as they watched, her eyes active with REM. God knows what she was seeing, doing, feeling. Alonzo's heart rate continued its normal pattern. Julia sighed and looked away, running her hands through her hair in frustration.

"Julia . . . ," Yale warned.

Her head snapped back around. Alonzo's eyelids were wild with REM activity. She spun back toward the monitor in time to see his heart rate skyrocket, matching Devon's in a maddened cadence of incredible speed that continued to climb in a way no human's heart was meant to do.

Danziger stopped, holding his breath amid the dark webwork of the tunnels so he could hear better. Had it just been the wind again or had he actually heard a voice?

The cry came again, too far away to be decipherable, but clearly the voice of a woman calling, crying out in despair, her voice echoing and distorting down the winding paths of the tunnels. One of those creatures . . . or someone else? Someone who didn't give a fig about the danger? Someone amazingly stubborn and determined to have her own way when it came to anything having to do with her child?

He knew of only one woman who fit that bill so perfectly. Swearing under his breath with all the facility of twenty years or more of being a mechanic, Danziger moved quickly in the direction of the cry, drawing closer, running through dark tunnels and around blind corners he knew he had no business traversing at such speed, struggling to follow the sound of a voice that had suddenly—if his ears weren't fooling him—become more than one!

• • •

Devon opened her eyes to find herself lying on the cool floor of a cavern. The smooth, worn dirt beneath her head smelled pleasantly of life and things growing. The walls of the chamber were simply detailed, with little of anything that could be termed decoration, other than several narrow arches carved into the dirt and rock walls.

"Uly?" she called quietly, and slowly got to her feet. "Uly?" She turned, yelling, though there seemed nowhere, precisely, to yell *to*. "*Uly!*"

No answer. Nothing but the mocking sound of her own voice being swallowed by the earth. Moving carefully, she circled the chamber, searching the walls. There was nothing except the arches, shallow-cut and leading nowhere. She could find no exit. The only light was a translucent glow beaming dimly from different areas in the walls and ceiling. Provided by what, she didn't know.

She passed an arch, trailing her fingers over the slight indentation, and suddenly felt as if she were being watched. She swung around fast, but nothing was there except the blank dirt wall. Still, she could have sworn . . .

Suddenly someone was behind her, holding her, strong arms crossed over her own! She fought hard, hitting and screaming, then all at once her brain reacted to the touch and the murmur of the voice in her ear, and she realized there was no hostility behind the action. She stopped struggling in the gentle, firm embrace and leaned her head back against Alonzo's chest.

"I'm here, Devon," he said quietly and released her. "I'm here. You're not alone."

She stepped away and turned to look up at him, relieved and indescribably grateful to find him there. He was standing (*standing!*) on his own, looking as he had the first time she saw him, all full of life. This, if nothing else, gave her assurance that she had, indeed, passed over into the Terrian dreamworld and was not captive inside some dream-making of her own. She didn't think her practical mind could have come up with something this fantastic.

She swallowed hard and was trying to speak, trying to tell him how glad she was to see him, when a rumble sounded through the chamber and stilled the words in her throat. It built, drowning out even her thoughts, rising to a crescendo as a Terrian slowly erupted through the chamber floor, moving with the slow upthrust of a seeking root. Devon recoiled, backing as far away from it as possible, and a second appeared out of one of the blank-walled archways. She and Alonzo spun, and a third Terrian appeared behind them, effectively hemming them in with no hope of escape, if there'd ever been one to make.

Devon glared at them, heart beating with furious fear. "My son!" she demanded, not knowing if they understood her words, but feeling certain they must understand her intent. "Where is he?! What have you done with him?!"

They said nothing, but their pointed gazes, drawn from Devon's face to the ground at their feet, gave eloquence to the small hand, the familiar child's hand, valiantly pushing its way up through the floor, fighting and straining against all the laws of physics to break through the earth and into the air beyond!

"*Uly!*" Devon wailed and then lunged, throwing herself across the ten feet that separated her from her son . . . and found herself on the floor in the cold-sleep area of the Advance ship. No one else was around, or so she thought until movement from above caught her eye and she looked up.

"I assume you know the risks a child like Uly faces, going into cold sleep . . . ," Julia said, *resaid,* as she had before, twenty-two light-years in the past. Only this time she was standing on the catwalk high above, hands in her pockets, facing an image of Devon herself, looking grave and concerned and angry and maternal.

"I'm aware of the risks," the Devon-thing replied, her voice a dim, watery-sounding echo of Devon's own. "We don't have much choice, do we?" The image turned then, and stared directly into the real Devon's eyes.

She might have stayed there forever, trapped in the impossible gaze of her own eyes, had a sound not drawn her attention away. Behind her lay a row of cold-sleep capsules. Another Devon-self was putting Uly to bed in one of them, holding his hand as she had done, reaching to push back his hair and earn the half-irritated, half-tolerant look she knew so well. Devon's heart ached with loss as the boy-image smiled up at his mother. "I love you, Mom," he said sleepily to this other woman-thing.

It was so real Devon couldn't stop herself from walking toward them, one arm stretched out in hopeful supplication. "Uly . . . ?"

And now she was somewhere else in the ship, a vacant corridor that might have been anywhere aboard the big vessel. Silence except for a single sound beyond the beat of her heart. Turning fast, she spied Uly's empty wheelchair heading down the corridor away from her under its own power. It took a corner on one wheel and vanished around the bend. Swearing, Devon broke into a run, following it, almost falling as she skidded around the corner to find blinding white light that cooked her vision. In the center of it, buoyed up in the way that people used to ride an ocean's waves, stood Uly—healthy, pink-cheeked, and bright-eyed. It was a vision of her child which Devon had only dreamed before, but it was the dream that drove her entire life.

"Mom . . . ?" he called confusedly, staring down at his new body, flexing his arms and legs in growing wonder.

249

Squinting hard against the light, Devon ran toward him, bent on rescuing her son, on holding him in her arms, on taking him out of here. She sprinted, throwing herself across the last few feet that separated them . . . and found herself standing ankle-deep in sand on a mesa. White dust blew everywhere, coating everything with a layer of chalky grit. It was hot here, the sun beating down unmercifully, and if she had thought the light was bright before, it was nothing compared to this. Her eyes felt as if they were going to parboil in their sockets.

"They fear us."

Devon spun, dizzied by it all and angry at being played with. It was Alonzo who spoke, standing quietly behind her, his clothing fluttering in the harsh gusts of wind, his hair and eyelashes frosted with white dust. "They're confused by us," he continued. His eyes had a funny glazed look to them, though he was clearly looking right at her and seeing her.

"Why?" Devon asked. "Why are they doing this?"

In answer, Alonzo's gaze shifted beyond her right shoulder and he lifted his chin in indication. Beyond them, on a sand dune, stood the silent row of Terrians. The sand roiled at their feet, moving with a life of its own, foaming and forming into an image of Uly in relief.

Devon sprang for it, certain she would find herself elsewhere in an instant, but this time she didn't. Thumping to her knees in the sand, she grabbed for an earthen hand only to have it recede at her touch, disintegrating into nothing but a handful of white earth.

Her heart breaking, Devon lurched to her feet, staggering against the buffet of a rising wind. "*Uly!*" she wailed. Light flared around her in a blinding nimbus, washing out Alonzo, washing out the Terrians and the vanishing form at their feet, and she found herself back in the subterranean chamber, standing and staring fixedly at her hand while white earth slipped between her fingers. The Terrians were there, and Alonzo, but there was no Uly, and that came as no surprise now. She felt beaten, defeated. There wasn't a thing she could do here, in this dreamworld, that the Terrians couldn't better manipulate. It was their world, after all, just like the other world, the real world, the world Earth called G889, and which she had foolishly assumed she could make hers just on her own say-so.

The Terrians all began speaking at the same time, their voices rising and falling. Their whispering, fluting language—nothing more than a series of broken notes to her ears—made Devon want to scream in frustration. Hands to her head, she whirled around, seeking some way to communicate, and found Alonzo standing still with his head cocked to one side, his expression one of confusion, but listening. Actually *listening*! And, more amazingly still, *understanding*.

"They . . . they claim we've been here before. To this planet."

"What are they talking about?" Devon demanded. She shook her head hard, wanting them to understand her and hoping their sign for no was the same as hers. "No! We've never been here. Never!"

Piping, whispery sounds filled the air, fluttering into a series of harsher notes as the Terrians spoke to Alonzo. Devon's eyes widened as Alonzo responded in a series of notes as fluid as those uttered by the Terrians, questioning them in their own language!

"They say we have," he repeated after a moment. She could tell he believed the Terrians, or at least believed *they* believed it. "And they fear us. They fear we're evil. We left our mark on the planet already."

Devon shook her head again, adamantly opposed to the tale they spun. "No! We came for life. For a chance to live!

251

We—" Her voice died in her throat as an image formed on the chamber floor at their feet, a design emerging out of the hard-packed earth. For a moment it was confusing, like a swirl of graffiti, but then it became chillingly clear: "E2." Completely confounded, she stared in amazement as dirt poured away from the design, leaving it clean and precise against the background.

Devon finally pulled her gaze away and looked up directly into the faces of the three Terrians, trying not to recoil at something so different, trying hard to find something common between them and her.

A single Terrian voice trilled, and Alonzo licked his lips, looking unhappy. "Uly's return is not a gift," he said slowly. "It would have . . . a price."

"What is it?" Devon asked immediately, the question directed toward Alonzo, but her eyes hard on the three Terrians. "Tell us what it is!"

"Devon," the pilot warned. "You might not want—"

"We'll do anything," she stressed, trying to hide her eagerness. Any price was worth paying, if it got Uly back.

"*Devon,*" Alonzo said more firmly and lay a hand on her arm, which she immediately shook off. "It's not our fight."

"I don't care! I *will* do *anything*." She raised her chin and stared straight into the Terrians' strangely hooded eyes. "Take *my* life for my son's," she offered.

Alonzo's eyes bugged as the Terrians continued staring in their infuriatingly silent way, studying her as though memorizing this strange creature in their midst. "Devon, they . . ." He was struggling, trying to find a way to express something that had come to him in trembling notes. ". . . doubt us," he finally said. "Our purity, our will, our life. It's different for them." His eyes gave hint to the fathoms of difference.

The Terrians moved, shifting slightly as though touched

252

by a breeze unfelt by the others, and slowly backed against the dirt wall behind them, *into* the wall, merging with it as smoothly as if their skins and the earth were one element. The last hesitated before vanishing completely, the outlines of his face and body vague among the textures of soil, root, and rock. He held out his hand in mute invitation for Devon to join them.

She clutched Alonzo's sleeve. "What're they doing? Tell them to stop—my son—*please!*" Frantically she watched the last Terrian recede from sight, disappearing until only his hand was left, stuck out of the wall like some bizarre decoration. Even that began to fade away, the wrist slipping beyond the confines of the room, the palm, the fingers . . .

It was too much for Devon. Better to fail in the trying than never to make the attempt at all. In one smooth movement, she stepped away from Alonzo and seized the hand just as it was about to vanish from sight. "Uly?" she asked tentatively.

Strong fingers tightened suddenly around hers, trapping her hand against skin that was dry and coarse, drawing her through the wall, pulling steadily, inexorably. Devon dug in her heels, suddenly frightened, and the tug increased. "Alonzo!" she cried, panicking, and snapped her head around, searching frantically for him. But the pilot was gone, vanished as though he'd never been, just as she was vanishing.

She watched with horrified fascination as her hand and wrist disappeared, then her arm up to her elbow. The dirt wall crept up her arm like a disease, swallowing her without disturbing so much as a single grain of soil. It reached her chest, hovering just a few inches in front of her nose, and she shut her eyes as the cool of earth touched her face.

• • •

Danziger heard Devon's sharp cry and stopped to get his bearings. His hand rested gingerly on the dirt wall to his left, cool and granular against his fingertips and smelling like nothing he'd ever encountered anywhere but in his dreams. It sounded as if she were just on the other side of this barrier, as though the wall were nothing more than a few inches thick, but when he dug in his finger, exploring, it was clear that it was thicker than that. Was she really there, a chamber away, or had it been a trick of acoustics? He admired her pluck, even as he was damning her to hell. Didn't he have enough to do, searching for a sick kid eight hundred feet underground, without having to worry about rescuing his mother as well? They'd had one handlight among them. Was she really roaming around down here in the dark without any light at all? If so, he didn't know whether to give her points for sheer reckless bravery or label her a complete ass.

Trotting, one hand brushing the wall as an occasional guide so as not to miss any corridor junctures, Danziger moved on. His ears strained for any sound, and his eyes scanned ahead, moving from side to side across the wide corridor with an almost metronomic precision. He pressed on, moving faster than he should have with his way lit only by the tiny beam of the handlight. He rounded a corner into an open area, another one of the impromptu Terrian "rooms," and staggered to a stop, catching himself before he fell. Collapsed in a loose-limbed bundle in the center of the space was Uly, arms and legs sprawled, head tilted to one side, looking for all the world like a broken marionette.

Please don't let him be dead, Danziger prayed silently. He didn't know how he'd break the news to Devon if Uly were dead. How could he? How could anyone? He rushed to

254

the boy's side and knelt, touching him gently, brushing the hair back away from his closed eyes. "Uly—"

No response. He was covered from head to foot in a white dust Danziger had never seen before. It looked like the stuff of deserts, blown sand kicked up by the unending wind, but if so, how had Uly come to be covered with it this far underground?

Danziger's hand sought the base of Uly's neck, pressing against the carotid artery. The strong pulse throbbing beneath his fingers made him grin with shaky relief. The kid was breathing! That's all that mattered. He picked up Uly, remembering the slightness of the eight-year-old's weight, and was surprised to find him heavier, maybe even slightly bulkier than before. That *had* to be his imagination.

Standing carefully, he continued through the room and up the passage he'd been following. For a brief instant Danziger felt as if he were being watched. Then the sensation receded. He shook his shoulders to rid himself of the last of it and continued on.

Several minutes later, he topped a gradual slope in the floor to meet the first ambient light of dawn piercing the gray light of the cave from a nearby entrance to the surface. For a moment, he just stopped, resting with the boy in his arms and staring with relief at the growing light of day, paling from gray to faint yellow as he watched.

Movement at the cave mouth put him on guard. A lone Terrian stood there, stepping away from the wall not so much as if it had been standing against it, but as if it had been standing *in* it. It stared at Danziger, and the mechanic stared back, getting an eyeful in his first close-up of a native. They weren't the prettiest race Danziger had ever seen, but he could think of a few space sailors he knew who looked worse—and not just after a bar brawl.

Contemplation was getting him nowhere. Suddenly he

was as tired as he had ever been, as he'd ever thought he *could* be. He'd spent all night underground searching for this child. He had what he came for, unless Devon was somewhere down there, too, in which case he'd have to go back. But that was later. As for now, it was time to take Uly home.

He took the first step up the incline toward the light and the Terrian faded from view—vanishing, merging—Danziger didn't know which and didn't much care. He'd had enough of being underground, maybe for the rest of his life.

Shifting the child in his arms into a more comfortable position, with Uly's head lolling against his shoulder, Danziger stepped forward into the morning.

Devon's eyes drifted open with the heaviness of deep slumber and focused blearily on Julia's face bent over her. She frowned, muddled and trying to remember, then suddenly *did* remember it all and sat up fast. Too fast, as it turned out. The head rush almost made her pass out. She wavered sideways and caught herself against the doctor's shoulder as her vision faded from gray to black and then came back again.

"Are you all right, Devon?" Julia asked worriedly. "What happened?"

"I . . . I'm not sure." She looked around, trying to orient herself to the real world after where she'd been. Alonzo lay beside her, out cold, but sleeping peacefully, with a faint smile on his lips. A warm flow of affection flooded her. He had braved so much in coming with her.

"Devon!" Beyond Julia, Yale was on his feet, looking not at her, but off toward the horizon beyond a thin copse of trees, his exhausted face filled with an eager glow she had never seen before.

Anticipation gripped her, feeding in fear and anxiety as she jumped to her feet, slapping aside Julia's helping hands. Devon strained her eyes through the trees toward a rapidly approaching speck in the distance.

Make that two specks. Even from here she saw it was Uly who crested the distant hill first and started toward her with a laughing (*laughing?!*) Danziger no more than a few yards behind. The boy ran hard, his arms and legs pumping rhythmically in a way they had never been able to do before, moving without the use or support of an immuno-suit and braces, breathing without a respirator, laughing the high, full-throated laughter of a happy, unencumbered child.

"Dear God," she, Julia, and Yale all murmured at once. Devon started running, tearing through the trees, racing to meet her son, racing to welcome him back to the life he should have had all along, the life she had fought so hard to win him.

They collided in the middle of the field, almost knocking each other over in the fierce crush of their emotions and their need for each other. Devon hugged her son tightly, then held him back from her at arm's length to take a good, long, *wondering* look. Healthy, dirty, his face scratched and smudged with soil, his clothing filthy with dust, his eyes bright with joy—yes, it was all real. It had happened. Somehow, some way, the Terrians had done what no one else had ever been able to achieve, what *she* had never been able to achieve. She didn't know what price she would have to pay, or what would be the final cost, but neither did she care. It was all worth it, just for this moment. She pulled Uly to her and held him tightly as he flung his arms around her and squeezed for all he was worth.

"I'm here," he whispered into her shoulder, consoling her, consoling them both. "I'm here, Mom."

The tears would not be held at bay any longer, so Devon

let them flow, blinking wetly at Danziger as he finally arrived, breathless and hanging back out of a wish not to intrude on this moment. She let him have his space for an instant, then she and Uly drew him into a group hug, the three of them embracing fiercely as Yale, Zero, and Julia ran to join them.

Chapter 20

. . . . ●

The sun shone directly into Devon's face as she spoke to the assembled group back at the cargo pod camp, and she let them think that was the reason for her need to constantly wipe her eyes. Uly stood at her side, strong and whole and healthy, a tangible miracle. Though she knew the others were listening to her, she couldn't blame them for staring at her son in wonder. She found herself doing it, too, about every half minute or so.

"If we can average twelve miles a day, we'll make it to New Pacifica in nine months. Then we'll still have a year to prep for our colonists." She paused to wipe her eyes again and caught Danziger giving her a slight smile from where he sat atop the TransRover with his arms wrapped tightly around True, who sat between his knees. "It won't be easy. And I don't understand this new world better than any of you. But I know New Pacifica is here. And I know somehow we'll be all right there." She glanced at Uly, then couldn't help herself from putting an arm around him and squeezing him against her, astonishment running through her for the umpteenth time since he'd first come running over the hill. She smiled down at him and then brought her gaze back to the others. "I think we've all seen something here to help us believe that."

"So that's it?" Morgan chimed in, his usual obstinate self. Several people in the back of the crowd groaned lightly, and Devon couldn't blame them. Why did he always have to put in his two cents' worth? For her part, Bess looked mortified. "You just think we should take off? Just like that?"

"No," Devon replied simply and honestly. She sought Danziger's eyes over the crowd and gave him a look full of meaning. "I think we should take a vote."

A stoic grin graced the mechanic's features, and he winked with solemn approval.

"I vote we go." Julia raised her hand high above her head where the others could see it. Beside her, Alonzo did likewise. The pilot had been quietly contemplative since their return from the Terrian dreamworld, and Devon wondered what thoughts were going through his mind.

Beyond them, Yale raised his meaty hand. Then another went up. And another. Smiling brightly, Bess Martin raised her hand and, when Morgan gave her a dirty look, raised his as well and leaned over to kiss him sweetly on the cheek. Devon suppressed a smile. Maybe Bess knew what she was doing after all, when it came to being married to Morgan Martin.

She looked for Danziger again. True had her hand in the air, waving it wildly about in confirmation of her vote, but he had yet to raise his. Trepidation filled Devon for a

moment as she studied him, he returning the steady regard a thousandfold. Then he slowly raised his hand.

She breathed a silent sigh of relief, staring at the outstretched arms and waving hands. They might have come to this planet as strangers, and they might be heading out on this journey still as strangers, but they were united in this goal, and for now, that was plenty for her.

They were lined up and ready to go, a ragtag line made up of a few mechanized vehicles, a robot, a cyborg, and a group of people bursting with optimism. Only days ago, with her heart in her throat and Broderick O'Neill dead, Devon would not have thought it possible, but here they were, on their way at last.

She stood on the crest of the hill, telescanner to her eyes, hunting the horizon. The ground vibrated slightly under her feet, but this was no Terrian attack, just the approach of the TransRover, loaded down with people and the remaining supplies from the ransacked cargo pod. She lowered the scanner and looked up at Danziger, perched in the driver's seat as comfortably as if he'd been born to it. They traded friendly nods and he started the vehicle slowly down the slope. Behind him, True drove the DuneRail at a sedate pace, with Uly, wide-eyed and serious, walking along beside and listening closely as she described how the machine worked.

Devon let it pass, knowing there was no way of stopping it now and immensely grateful for that, and raised the scanner to her eyes again. Nothing to worry about so far. No figures painted against the horizon, though she'd be stupid to think the Terrians weren't completely aware of their every move. A race that can blend with the earth of their world must know almost everything that happens on it.

"Four days ago, aliens landed on a distant planet. And we are them."

She looked up at Yale questioningly. She'd never thought of herself as an alien before. It took some getting used to. "And?" she prompted.

"And now we light out across an unknown planet, an uncharted world, hoping against hope there's merit to that late-twentieth-century axiom 'Getting there is half the fun.'" He smiled at her laughter. "And looking all the while for that moment when we must fulfill our promise to the Terrians, wondering only what will stand in our way."

She nodded, made suddenly solemn by his words. The unexpected sound of Zero singing from somewhere in the wagon train made her laugh again. "It might be wondering whether we can survive traveling with Zero without killing him."

"Deactivating a voice module isn't the same thing as murder," Yale replied loftily and moved off to follow the train.

The sound of an engine announced Alonzo's arrival aboard the ATV, which Uly had been only too glad to bequeath to the pilot after carefully instructing the seasoned, immensely patient spacer on how to use it.

Devon looked over at him and smiled. "What's up, Alonzo?"

He shook his head, looking worried. "I don't know, Devon. I don't know what kind of promise we made. What price we're going to have to pay."

She knew he didn't regret their visit with the Terrians, but he needed reassurance. Devon wasn't certain she had any to give him. She glanced ahead at Uly, walking healthy and strong beside the DuneRail, occasionally darting ahead to examine something that struck his fancy. She took a deep breath. "I don't know either." She gave him a significant look. "But I'd do it again," she said, a firm declaration, and turned her face toward the future.

The little lizard, True's "kitty," called a *koba* by the Terrians, snuffled around in the deserted campsite, poking at tracks, and watched the wagon train dwindle in the distance. It had enjoyed the company of the strange creature who fed and cuddled it. While it didn't precisely *miss* True, somewhere its brain registered and signified her absence with a certain amount of animal regret and a desire to, maybe, follow her.

There was the sharp sound of metal scraping on rock. The koba sat bolt upright, pointed ears at attention and widening to catch the noise again. Grinning toothily, it gamboled up a rocky hilltop, then crept closer to hide among the rocks and peer over the side. Maybe everyone wasn't gone after all!

When it saw what made the noise, it hunched down further, not liking the squat humanoid sitting several yards below. The Grendler sat splay-footed beside a slab of metal, its butt close to the ground as it worked methodically with a handheld tool to dig aside the cairn of rocks and hard earth the strange creatures had used to cover their koba-killed dead. The koba wrinkled its nose in distaste. Grendlers would eat almost anything.

Footsteps made the little animal crouch lower in its hiding place as a strange creature, one it had never seen before, one who wasn't part of the group now leaving the area, stepped into view from behind a large boulder. He was tall and full-bodied, deep-chested and foreboding. His tattered robes fluttered in the wind. The koba thought about visiting him, shimmying up his leg to see if he had any food or a good cuddle, but then it glimpsed the strange one's eyes and hissed to itself, wishing it had better cover.

"Gaal." The Grendler spoke gutturally, the word unfamiliar on a tongue not used to speech. The strange creature turned and reached out to accept something long and narrow the Grendler handed it from the grave. Lean, strong fingers caressed the length of O'Neill's rifle before the strange one swung it up by the strap to hang from his shoulder. Stepping around the Grendler, he turned to watch the last of the wagon train disappear over the hillside. What began as a smirk bloomed into a full smile, an unfriendly smile full of bad intent as the stranger raised his hand and rubbed softly at the small symbol—the same stylized "E2" which had appeared to Devon in the dirt of the Terrian caves—tattooed onto his neck.